Beautiful Chaos

Amber Rodriguez

Contents

Beautiful Chaos

Amber Rodriguez

Other Works by Amber Rodriguez

Trigger Warnings

Not all readers may find this book suitable, as it contains mentions of sexual assault, attempt of sexual assault, Death, Grief, Kidnapping, and Violence. Readers Discretion is Advised.

Dedications Page

This goes out to middle school me, who knew all she wanted to do was write books for the rest of her life, even if she didn't know how.

You did it.

Beautiful Chaos

Written by Amber Rodriguez

Enjoy!

1. Prologue

I wonder where happiness begins and ends in our life. Does everyone come across it? How do you know it is real, or is it just a deception of the mind? Only existing for that lucky few. Maybe it's meant for none of us.

Sitting against the tree in our front yard, I write in my red notebook of the thoughts that consume me. My best friend, Jackie approaches me. She calls my name, "Melina." Emotions of pain wash over me as she reaches out her hand towards me, "They're leaving."

I finally look up at her as her long brown wavy hair lay on her shoulder in a braid. Her baby hairs dance in the cool autumn air. Her brown skin matches her eyes as she stares down at me, her face full of sorrow.

Today is a sad day. It's the anniversary of my mother's death. Every year I'm reminded of how this day will always be my fault. Jackie gives me a sympathetic smile as we wave my grandparents goodbye, knowing they're going to visit my mother's grave. "How come you never go with them?" Jackie says as we walk back into the house. I sigh. She asks this question every year.

We make our way to my soon-to-be old bedroom. Jackie says, "Well, Happy Birthday, Melina." I sigh, "Thanks." I follow her down the hall as she says, "So we move in a few days. My dad's got most of the house ready, now we're just waiting on a couple of things." Jackie looks over my almost empty bedroom, "I so can't wait to get you out of this depressing house." I laugh lightly, "It's not depressing; I just live with old people."

2. The Start of an End

The atmosphere is much lighter today, so instead of being in my room, I set my laptop up in the kitchen as my grandmother dances to music while making lunch. I sit down quickly, opening up my laptop. Immediately though, I get a call from Jackie, and I answer, "Hey, what's up?"

"So, you know the beach close to campus," she says while sounding like she's shuffling some stuff around in the background.

"Okay, which beach?" I reply.

"Huntsman Beach."

"What about it?" I ask, still hearing papers shuffling.

"There's going to be a party later," She pauses momentarily, and the shuffling stops, "I can't believe it's all almost over." I can hear the nervousness in her voice as we both think about our last semester as college students. She continues, "But there's no backing out now. If I give up now, my dad will never let me do anything on my own again."

"That and we've been working our butts off since sophomore year for this moment. Plus, I don't think I can bear to be in this house any longer," I say, whispering the last part.

Jackie sighs, "I know, I know." She changes the subject, "Anyway, the beach. So, there's going to be a little party. It's later tonight. Want to go?"

"Is Jackie Green actually asking me this time?" I say sarcastically.

"Pick you up at seven."

I just know she's rolling her eyes. "I'm taking my notebook," I reply. When she hangs up, I sigh, "The college festivities never end."

***

The beach is beautiful as always and clean, and the party is in full swing. There's music in the background and set-up beer-pong tables, and a fire where some people are roasting marshmallows.

It's sentimental knowing this is one of our last few nights as undergrads. We reach the end of the sand, and Jackie looks me up and down, saying, "I still think you should have worn a dress." She shakes her head and continues, "It would have complimented your curves beautifully."

I look down at my dark blue high-waist jeans and black graphic t-shirt. I made sure to style my black shoulder length curls in a low pony tail. Allowing two strands to hang near my eyes.

Jackie knows I don't like to draw attention to myself; being a darkskin plus-size girl does that enough for me. But to Jackie, anything fashion-related can always be better. Regardless of whatever I wear, when you put that next to Jackie Green, who wears anything expensive and short, I'll always look less appealing.

I hold my notebook close as we walk onto the sandy beach. The closer we get, the louder the music becomes. Some guys are yelling and chest bumping at the beer pong tables. I follow Jackie while trying to dodge red cups and unwanted attention as she leads us to the beer source.

I shouldn't be surprised to see Troy with a football in one arm and a beer in the other. "Jackie!" He says with a smirk on his face. Jackie grabs two cups, holds them up, and sarcastically asks him to fill them. He doesn't hesitate to ask, "So are you going to give me another chance, babe?" She tries to hide a smile as she responds, "We'll see after I've had a few drinks." She hands me a cup and diverts all her attention to him. I roll my eyes. Here we go again. Jackie and Troy have been off and on since our high school years. They're a hot mess.

As they begin talking, I slowly drift away. Well, she's occupied. I pour out the liquid in the cup and replace it with a water bottle I find in a nearby cooler, wishing it was coffee instead.

I walk around, drinking the water. Some familiar and unfamiliar faces pass by me as I make myself comfortable sitting in the sand by the fire. Why do I always come to these things knowing I never enjoy them? I sigh, looking over at Jackie. Well, at least she's having fun, and the fire's warm. I set the bottle down and begin drawing mindlessly.

After a while, Jackie finds me with Troy right behind her. She yells, "Melina, there you are! Come and dance with me! Here, drink this!" She tugs at my wrist and shoves another red cup in my hand before I can protest. We join all the others crowding around each other, dancing. Jackie smiles at me while she dances. She's clearly enjoying herself.

I take a sip of the bitter liquid as I nod my head to the music. "Loosen up, Melina!" she yells, turning to see Troy seductively watching her. She wraps her arms around him and into their little bubble they go. I wonder what that feels like.

I instantly get the urge to pee, so I leave them once again, heading to the beach bathroom stalls. The dimly lit area is quiet as I approach the door. I swing it open quickly stepping inside and I gasp.

I see a guy pinning a girl into the wall. He's covering her mouth as she moans while he pumps into her. He's panting, and neither of them seems to acknowledge my presence. I stand there watching like an idiot. He uncovers her mouth, and she moans louder, finally opening her eyes. "What the fuck!" she yells. This snaps me out of my trance, and I reach for the door. "I am so sorry," I say, rushing out.

I run back to the car while embarrassment heats my face. Why did I sit there like a dummy? I'm so thankful for the darkness; I hope to God they couldn't see my face. Moving to sit on the hood, I clutch my notebook to my chest as the adrenaline settles. I begin to watch people dancing and enjoying themselves.

I sigh, looking around the parking lot. There are couples here, but no one is too close to me. Content, I draw mindlessly in my notebook. After a while, I hear a couple walking over to the car on the left side of me. A female voice whines, "But why not Mat? We're supposed to be together anyway." She is complaining, but her voice is cute. He replies, "I told you why."

She taps him, annoyed, "Oh Mateo, you're so stubborn."

"Now you know better not to call me that." The harshness in his voice gives me chills as I eavesdrop.

She doesn't respond, and I look over at them. He's leaning against the car facing towards me. He looks attractive. He stands over her by a few inches, although she is the height of a model. His arms wrap around her as she looks up at him, she's wearing a jean skirt and a pink top with a little handbag that matches.

They pay no attention to me while I stare; his wavy black hair rests on his shoulders, with a few strands of hair hanging beside his eyes. His gaze finally meets mine, and I rush to look away, hurrying to lay down on the hood of the car and face the stars.

I hear his voice again, "Natalie, go get us a few drinks. I'm feeling a little *parched*."

Heat runs to my cheeks as I first hear the girl's heels click off into the distance. Then I panic as I hear his footsteps getting closer. Oh god, no, please don't walk over here. His voice cuts off my mind rambling, "Did you enjoy the show?" I sit up slowly, embarrassment clear in my voice, "I am so sorry, I just had to use the bathroom, and the door was unlocked."

He laughs, "Relax." Now standing in front of me, he continues, "It's what you should expect when you fuck in public places." He speaks casually, like it's no big deal. "Yeah..." I say awkwardly.

"What's your name?" I ask, unsure of what else to say, considering he hasn't walked away yet. "It's Mateo Crow. But my friends call me Mat," He smiles lightly and puts out his hand. I look down at his hand and up at his face before gently placing my hand in his. "Uh, I'm Melina, Sky," I say, adding my last name since he told me his. He shakes my hand but isn't quick to pull away as I look into his honey-brown eyes.

But then I hear a familiar voice that makes me jump, removing my hand from his touch. "Jackie said you'd be up here," His deep voice always catches me off guard. "Hey, Elijah," I say. Elijah is the same height as me. He is wearing swim shorts and a loose tank top. His loose curls lay messily on the top of his head. His complexion was lighter than mine but still caramel-looking. He turns his gaze to Mateo, "Who's this?"

I awkwardly introduce him, "Um, this is Mateo." He chimes in, "Call me Mat."

Elijah doesn't seem pleased as he turns his attention to me, "Jackie sent me. Can I sit?"

"Yeah," I move over as he sits on my right side.

We see the girl coming back, and Mateo dismisses himself, "It's nice meeting you, Melina. I hope to see you around." He flashes a beautiful smile before turning and walking away. I watch him until Elijah catches my attention, "So what's Up, Melina?"

"Nothing really, just ready to go home," I reply.

"So, Jackie dragged you out once again?" He asks smiling.

"You bet."

"Well, at least I'm here now," he says playfully.

"Yeah, you've totally saved the day," I respond amused. I glance back at Mateo, "So do you know what's the deal with them?" Following my gaze, he replies, "I don't know about the guy, but the girl's name is Natalie. She just transferred this semester."

"Hmm," is all I say. "She's hot, though," Elijah adds, making me playfully roll my eyes. He is such a horny college boy.

I check the time, and it's almost midnight. The security will roll around to kick people out soon. "It's getting late. I should probably go find Jackie so we can go home," I say sliding off the hood to call Jackie's cell. "Have a good night, Melina," Elijah waves as I walk to the other end of the car. "Night," I reply before Jackie answers the other line.

***

It's the beginning of spring, and it is cold out as I argue with Jackie about having the heater on in the car. Jackie yells in frustration, "But it's already warm!"

"Leave it on!" I lightly pop her hand. She whines and turns to her phone. We're going to see the last-minute things we'd need for our apartment today. I say, "Classes start tomorrow at 8:30 a.m. so we have to leave around seven."

"Are we stopping to get breakfast?" she asks as I slow at a stop sign.

"We can if I make it to your dad's house exactly at seven."

"Okay. What do your grandparents have planned for your last night at home?" She asks as we pull forward.

"We'll probably go out for dinner like all the other families," I lie. We turn onto the street of our new house and I ask, "What do you think your dad has planned for you?"

She shrugs in response, and soon we park in front of our new home. I grab a bag out of the back seat, and we walk up to the front door. She has to put a pin on the lock that's on the doorknob to get the keys. "Here's yours," she says, handing me a silver key. We walk inside the already-furnished house.

It's a small modern two-bedroom house. There isn't much of a kitchen, but the living room is big enough. "Okay, I think we just need to buy our bed sets," Jackie says, walking towards her bedroom as I follow. Most of everything is already here, even our clothes in the closet.

I walk into my bedroom across from hers and head over to my dresser. I open the bag and pull out my sketchbook and some new art supplies, setting them neatly on the top of the dresser. Lastly, I almost reluctantly set down the only picture I allow myself to keep of my mother, "There."

We left the house to go pick out our bed sets and now find ourselves wandering the aisles. "So, did you and Troy have sex? Are you guys a thing again?" I ask as I can't find anything that appeals to me. She sighs dramatically while walking in front of the basket saying, "Ugh, don't remind me about him."

"What happened?" I question.

"It was going fine at first. I was standing my ground, but you know how Troy is with his persuasive looks. Then one thing led to another, and so yeah, I think we're a thing again." She pauses before speaking again, "Speaking of guys, Elijah told me you guys met someone named Mat, so how was that? What do you think about him? Elijah said he wants to stir up some plan to get the new girl away from him so that he can shoot his shot." She laughs, using air quotations for the last part.

"Well, I'm glad you and Troy are talking again," I avoid answering her question about Mateo, knowing I haven't told her about walking in on them. I examine the gray and white bed set before tossing it to Jackie to look at it. "It's plain, but it's you, and come on, Tell me something juicy about him. Elijah told me how you were eyeing him last night," she says before handing it back to me.

"I like it. It's simple," I examine it once more before tossing it into the basket and pushing it forward. Sighing I reply, "Mateo's okay, but it doesn't matter."

She moves in front of the basket to stop me, "Are you telling me he didn't interest you one tiny bit? You're telling me you were totally unbothered by his presence."

"Of course he's attractive, but he wasn't alone," I roll my eyes. I try to move the basket saying, "The new girl was with him, you know, and her name's Natalie. Besides, she seems like a nice girl, and I'm not like that; plus, we're supposed to be focusing on graduating."

She totally ignores my statement about him not being alone and says, "You can't keep using graduation as an excuse."

I sigh, not budging, even though Mateo's face flashes across my mind, "Jackie, can we talk about something else."

"Fine, this conversation isn't over."

I shrug in response.

I take Jackie back to her dad's house before heading home. It's a typical scene for my grandparent's house. Grandpa's sitting in the living room clutching a beer while watching the world burn itself to ashes and my grandma cooking up something delicious. I walk into the kitchen, "Hey, Grandma."

"Evening, sweetheart. How was your day?"

"It was okay. I got a bed set for my room. Can I help with anything?" I turn the little radio box down a bit. She loves loud music. "That's good dear. If you want to start on dessert, that'll be great," she turns it back up. We dance and cook in rhythm, enjoying each other's company. I set the table as she puts dinner and dessert in the middle of it. When my grandfather walks in, I awkwardly smile at him. "Afternoon," he says as he sits at the table. We cut the music to a low and join him in a quiet meal.

After dinner, I dismiss myself from the table and head to my room. I try to ignore the memories stained in my mind from this room as I lock my door and get ready for bed. Just one more night, I say as I force myself to sleep.

*You did it! This is your fault! His voice starts as whispers, and I can feel his indent on the edge of the bed. She's gone because of you! In a flash, I'm suddenly in a dark hallway, struggling to stay hidden. I hear a familiar voice try to defend me, "You can't blame her!" I want to run, to get away, but I can't move my legs. I try to speak, to apologize, to say something, and I suddenly feel his cold, rough hands brushing the side of my face, and I squirm, trying to get away. His voice makes me shiver, "This is your fault; don't you dare move!" And I scream. *

I wake, sitting upright as I try to catch my breath. It takes a minute before I remember where I am and rest my head in my hands. I clutch my chest as if that'll soothe the pain. After calming down, I sigh getting out of bed. Checking my phone, it's only 4:15 a.m. so I head into the kitchen and quietly make a cup of coffee. I decide to sit on the porch to enjoy the cool air until it's time to get dressed.

I make it to Jackie's dad's house at 6:50 a.m. so we get breakfast before hitting the freeway. "Just the egg and cheese, no sausage in my breakfast sandwich, please," Jackie says over me to the person taking our order. "Sure thing," they reply while pressing buttons.

We make it to the campus, and it's overflowing with cars and students. Students pack the driveway, the curb, and parking spots. "We're never going to find a parking spot," Jackie yells after checking the time. "Perfect," I reply apathetically. Slowly but surely, we find a spot a block away from the school.

We rush, making it through the main auditorium. Then, we stop at the office to get our new schedules for this semester. We look for where our last classes would be, and I feel a sense of satisfaction as freshmen scramble around campus, looking for their classes or dorms. "Why is your schedule so different from mine?" Jackie whines as we walk across campus. "Because They know we cause too much trouble when we're together," I say jokingly.

After, we stop at the coffee shop near campus, I'll soon be working at for lunch. Since I'll be closer to campus this semester, I chose to transfer to a closer location. Halfway through our food, Jackie's phone rings. When she looks at the caller ID, she rolls her eyes and puts her phone on silent. She never puts her phone on silent.

"Okay, who was that?" I ask, taking a sip of my drink. "Troy," she says the name sourly.

"Of course."

"I don't know what to do with him," she sighs, taking a sip of her iced tea.

I laugh, "Oh, so you guys are really doing this again."

"And now I suffer the consequences," she sighs.

***

It's past sunset when I make it home, so it's a surprise to see my grandmother still awake. I greet her as I walk to my soon-to-be old bedroom. I sigh, the reality of it all settling in. This is really the last night I'll spend in the home that raised me, and I couldn't be happier.

I decide to take a shower which helps ease the excitement for tomorrow. After getting out, I stare at myself in the mirror. Sad brown eyes stare back at me. I sigh twisting my wet curls into two French braids that rest just above my shoulders. My dark brown skin glistens from the water as I finish getting ready for bed.

I head back to my bedroom and I see my grandmother's sitting on the bed waiting for me with a little box in her lap.

"Hi," I say, walking to put my towel and other necessities back in my suitcase. "Come sit, sweetie," she smiles, patting the spot beside her on the bed. I feel like a child getting in trouble, and I'm sure she can see the confusion on my face.

I slowly move to sit beside her, she places a little box in my hand, "I never knew when the right time would be, but I think this is the perfect time." She smiles, and her warmth radiates off of her like the sun.

I slowly open the box and gasp at what it reveals. It's a golden necklace; the pendant is a small, red ruby wrapped in a gold lining. She waits a few seconds more as I examine it before saying, "This was my great-grandmother's wedding gift. My great-grandfather wanted her to know no matter what, she'd always have his heart."

She smiles looking at me briefly before looking back at the box, "After he passed, it became a symbol of love, honor, and faith in our family. We have passed it down in every single generation for years. Our only family heirloom." She carefully pulls it out of the box, "My mother gave it to me, I gave it to your mom, and now I'm giving it to you." She put it around my neck.

"It's beautiful," I say, "My mother wore this?" The only thing I had of my mother was the picture. "I can't take this," I try to unfasten it, but she immediately grabs my hands and pulls them down to hold in hers. She always gives me little gifts, but this is more than a gift.

"Yes sweetie, you can," she replies softly. Gently squeezing my hands she continues, "I gave it to your mother, and I remember her wearing it the day you were born." She takes a deep breath, "She never took it off." Her eyes become watery, and she looks away, not wanting to seem weak. Even in the purest of moments, she had to be strong. I hugged her tightly, "Thank you."

She leaves my room, and I lock the door behind her. I move to the bed and run my fingertips over the ruby as I can feel the cold from it on my collarbone before drifting off to sleep.

I wake in cold sweats and hurry to take a shower, letting the heat wash away the last of my nightmare. When I'm ready to go, the smell of coffee fills the kitchen air as my grandparents sit in conversation, waiting to see me off. I speak softly, "Today's the day." Slowly, my grandfather stands saying, "Good Luck kid." I nod in response.

Grandma hands me my favorite coffee cup before hugging me, "Are you sure you can't finish the rest of the semester here at home?" I laughed half-heartedly, "and leave that entire house for Jackie to maintain by herself. She wouldn't last a week. Besides, I'll still visit." *Maybe.*

She sighs, "Be safe, my dear."

"I will."

The sun is rising as I leave, so when my phone rings, I take a few seconds to answer, "Hello."

"Hey! Where are you at right now?" Jackie's voice booms through the phone.

"I'm on the freeway."

"Okay, do we have time to meet up?"

If I went just a little faster, I'm sure I would have enough time, "I'll try. Call you if I can't."

We have around thirty minutes or less, and Jackie clearly doesn't acknowledge that. We're walking down the hall of dorm rooms as I say, "Jackie, so help me if you don't tell me where we're going-"

"We're here," she cuts me off. Pointing to the brown door she continues, "This is Troy's Dorm." There's a large man in a black suit standing across from the dorm room. It weirdly dawns on me that I never actually knew where Troy was staying during the years. We stop in front of His door, and Jackie knocks lightly, "Ignore that guy. Elijah said he's here with Mateo."

I scrunch my nose in confusion, "Why would Elijah invite Mateo over?" She laughs, "He didn't. He invited Natalie over, and she brought Mateo." Shortly, the door opens to reveal Natalie from the beach party. She smiles, and I awkwardly smile as she opens the door to let us in.

We see Elijah, Troy, and Mateo sitting around the room. Natalie says nothing as she takes a seat between Elijah and Mateo. Another guy is sitting in the room, but he doesn't bother introducing himself. Mateo looks strangely out of place. He sits with good posture, wearing black pants with a cream-colored shirt. He almost looks annoyed to be here, but when he sees me, he smiles.

Everyone has a drink in their hand except Mateo. "You guys are drinking right before class? Really?" I say as Jackie surprisingly moves to stand next to Troy. "Of course," Elijah replies, downing the rest of his beer. I roll my eyes as Elijah just turned 21, so of course he's drinking.

"We came over, so what's up?" Jackie speaks in general as Troy wraps his arm around her. Wasn't she just mad at him? "I need a couple of shots of the guys for a project I'm working on. Your buddy Elijah didn't want to go unless I invited you," The unintroduced guy says, pointing at Elijah and then nodding off at me. I look at the time. If I speed, I can still make it to class, "sounds fun, but we have class today, so we have to go." Elijah responds, "So, skip it."

"Skip it? No thanks," I look at Jackie as she makes no move to leave.

"Okay, we'll go later, and I can pick you up," Elijah says.

"I have something going on later-" Natalie injects. I cut her off, "I'm pretty busy the rest of the day, anyway. Maybe next time."

Elijah pouts. I look at Mateo, and he's staring at me with an expression I can't read. It makes my face heat up. When Natalie notices, she moves closer to him. Okay, time to leave.

3. Where Being Bold Will Get You

I almost bump into someone while trying not to trip over my feet on the way to class. This is my History Arts class. It is surprisingly full, but luckily, I find a spot in the front, and quickly settle in. "Morning, class," The professor walks around an abnormally large desk at the front of the room with a cup in hand. He's tall with short hair and glasses that enhance his attractiveness. It's like a choir when all the girls eagerly respond in sync.

Ugh, this is going to be a long semester. He begins, "I need to review a few personal rules; first and foremost, I will only answer questions about this class. No outside conversations whatsoever. Second, if you violate my first rule, I will kick you out for the rest of the day."

He takes a sip of his drink, and I can see a ring on his left finger, "Lastly, try to have fun. Now all of you will need to acquire a notebook of any kind. Every day starting tomorrow, everyone will be taking daily notes." Oh boy, this is going to be fun.

As soon as I leave class, I surprisingly see Elijah waiting by the door. "Hey," he says. "Hi," I respond. Confused, I ask, "What are you doing here?"

"I was waiting for you."

"Oh, okay." Seeing the confusion on my face, he continues, "I know you said you were busy, but I'm hoping that's a lie. So, you wouldn't have to come, knowing you're not exactly a social butterfly and all."

"Well, it wasn't a lie, but I don't need to be at work for another hour. Since you're here, you might as well come to the store with me."

"Okay," He smiles.

When we get to the store, he walks directly behind me as I search the shelves. I can feel his stare piercing me, making me uncomfortable. "So, what are you looking for?" he picks up a nearby ball and starts tossing it. "Hopefully, a notebook," I reply. "For what?" he questions. I continue to look through the shelves, "For class."

He scoffs playfully, "I should have known."

"Considering you knew where it was, yes, you should have known," I say, examining a book that I think is suitable. "Speaking of, which elective did you choose this semester?" I stop to look at him, as he's already looking at me. "Mechanics," he says after a moment. "Weren't you going to take chemistry?" I ask, scanning the books one more time. He replies happily, "Yeah, but I took your advice and actually picked something I wanted." I smile, saying, "That's great. I'm proud of you."

"I think I like this one," I say, picking up the same one I put back twice. "And I think I like your smile," he says. I look away, then back at him again, "Elijah, we've been through this." I've known Elijah since Elementary, but that doesn't mean I view him that way, even after all I've been through; plus, he's a total whore. He looks embarrassed as he scratches the back of his head, "Okay, sorry."

We quickly make it to the coffee shop. "Catch you later Elijah," I say, adjusting my small crossbody bag. He nods and leaves, "See you later." I enter the shop noticing it's busy, and walk over to the counter. "Hello!" A cheerful girl says to me.

"Hi, my name is Melina. I'm here for orientation," I say. She nods knowingly, "Come with me this way." I follow her behind the counter and into the back, where there is a well-hidden break room. We stop in front of a door, she knocks before walking in, and I follow her.

I spent the entire time shadowing and taking notes. I already know how to do most of the work she's shown me, so I was more than relieved when I could go home. As I walk out the door with all my orientation papers, keys, and notes, I accidentally bump into someone, and my papers immediately fall from my hands.

I apologize as I bend down to collect the documents, "I'm so sorry." I stop, surprised to see Mateo. He's bending down to help me, "Don't apologize, it was my fault." he grabs a few papers he was holding and some of mine.

We stand as he hands some back to me. Now that the sun is out, I can see just how attractive he is. His honey-brown eyes glow against his tan sun-kissed skin, and his hair is actually a blackish brown in the sun. I take a step back, feeling too close. "Hi," I say shyly.

"Hi, Melina," He smiles down at me, and the way he says my name sends butterflies to my core. "Uh, what are you doing here?" I ask, curious.

"Natalie wanted to stop for coffee and drop off some papers to the manager," he points back at a black BMW that has a clean shine. Hmm, that's a pretty expensive car. "Oh, that's nice. Is she applying here?" I try to hide my annoyance at this thought.

He laughs a little, "She doesn't need to, although doing so would give her some well-needed real-world experience." My face scrunches, reacting to his smugness, "You guys are new here, right? Why'd you transfer during your last semester?"

"Natalie transferred. She wants to finish college in person instead of online. Her family thinks it's a load of shit, but I make sure she doesn't get in trouble. Call it babysitting, if you will. Me, on the other hand, I've already graduated," he explains.

"So, if you're not a student, what are you then, besides a babysitter, I mean?" I ask. "A businessman," He replies. Forgive me for being stereotypical; he does not look like a businessman. "Hmm, when did you graduate?"

"Three years ago, I preferred online schooling."

"Oh," I continue to eye him, noticing how well he dresses. He's wearing a nicely ironed basic black shirt with rolled short sleeves and khaki pants. He compliments his outfit with a simple gold chain on his wrist. I wonder if he's an athlete considering the slightly visible veins in his arm. He has taste. This makes me wonder about his seemingly luxurious lifestyle.

"Nice car," I motion back to the vehicle. "Thanks, it was a gift," He smiles as he stands there confidently, and I nervously sway my weight from one foot to another. A car as a gift, I could only imagine.

Looking at him and the car, he definitely comes from wealth. This somehow makes me dislike him. "I've got to go, I hope Natalie adjusts well," I say, leaving, but not before catching a glimpse of Natalie staring from the passenger seat of his car.

He's okay, I guess. I walk to my car as he waves and continues into the store. My phone rings, notifying me of a text. I quickly pull it out.

Jackie: Hey beautiful, I know you probably have work to do but don't be mad; I invited Troy over; see you when you get here!!

Me: You and Troy are giving me whiplash!

Makin it home, I announce, "I'm home!" I open the door closing it behind me loudly. She responds from the couch, "Hey babes, how was orientation?" Jackie sits lazily on the couch with the remote in her hand as Troy has his arm around her shoulder. "It was okay, my manager seems nice."

She replies, "That's good." I smirk at them before heading to the kitchen to get water from the fridge before walking back into the living room. I tease, "So I'm assuming a little make-up session happened between the lines?"

She and Troy are clearly on good terms again. She doesn't respond, but Troy moves to kiss her with a smile. I wonder if the night at the beach was better than Jackie was leading on. I move, standing directly in front of Jackie, "Troy, can I steal her for just a moment? I promise you can have her back."

"Sure," He responds simply. Jackie looks at me and rolls her eyes as she allows me to drag her to the room.

She closes my bedroom door behind her as I set my papers down and undress to redress into more comfortable clothes. Jackie plops on my bed and waits for me to speak. "I ran into Mateo today," I stand sorting through the papers like I'm forgetting something.

"You did!" She sits up, and her entire demeanor changes.

"Well yeah, I mean kind of," I reply and suddenly I'm thankful for my melanin skin, for I'd be blushing bright red if otherwise.

"So what happened? Did you get his number?" Jackie says, crossing her legs. I begin, "Well, no. I bumped into him and dropped my orientation papers." She shakes her head but allows me to continue, "I think he comes from a wealthy family. I think they both do." I move towards the door. She squeals, "Oh my gosh, yes! Okay, you've got to be bold, this is how it starts! By the way, I've ordered a vegan pizza, so can I go back to Troy now?"

"Yeah," I'm not sure getting involved with anyone is what I want right now, and she conveniently keeps forgetting about Natalie, the girl I didn't tell her I saw him fucking in the bathroom. "You guys are being all affectionate," I blurt out, changing the subject.

"Yes, that's legal here you know," She moves off the bed like an eager toddler.

"You're a smiling mess, you know that right," I lean against the door, blocking her from leaving just yet.

"Well, he makes me smile," she says as she lights up.

"Yes, and the last time we talked about him, you said you were suffering consequences," I finally move from the door.

"Misinterpretation," she shrugs as she walks past me back into the living room, shutting the door behind her.

***

My classes were short today, thankfully. As I'm approaching my car, my phone rings and I answer. "Hey dear," my grandmother's voice purrs through the phone.

"Hey, Grandma."

"Hi, sweetheart, how are you?"

"I'm doing okay," I say as I unlock my car door. She replies, "That's good dear. Well, how are your friends? How's the new house?" I sit inside, tossing my books in the backseat of my car, "They're okay, and so far, it's good." I couldn't be happier that I'm no longer living under that roof.

"That's wonderful dear. Well, I just called to tell you I miss you, and so does your grandfather." I sigh feeling a little guilty, "I miss you too." I fiddle with my keys, not rushing to put them in the ignition. "So, have you met any boys yet? How are your classes going? You still have that pepper spray I gave you, right, sweetie?" She sounds off her questions.

I ignore most of them as I reply, "Yes I do, look, grandma, I have to go now, okay…I love you too, bye." I toss my phone in the center console and lean against the steering wheel. Even though things are going well, I can't help but feel like it's going badly.

I take a deep breath, badly wanting a hot cup of coffee. I touch the necklace on my neck and jump when I hear a tap on the passenger side window. I look up, and Mateo is standing there, waving. Taking a deep breath, I unlock the door, and he gets inside the car. "Hey," I say in the small space next to him.

"Hi Melina, I found this with my papers last night. I'm sure you want it back," He hands me some orientation papers I didn't realize were missing. "Oh, thank you," I reply.

"No problem," He replies and seconds of silence pass. Remember what Jackie said, be bold. "Do you…do you want to come over?" I offer, not knowing what else to say. He pulls out his phone, types something then says, "Okay, honey, ready when you are." I blink twice, "What?"

"Your name; it means honey," he seems to be amused by this. I refrain from talking about the compliment thing with him because, well, was that even a compliment? I don't know. I shake it off.

"So Mateo thinks I'm sweet," I say, trying to match his energy, but just like that, his smile disappears. "I'd rather you not call me that," he says, all playfulness gone. Well, crap. "Okay, well, in what language?" I ask, trying to save the mood. He shrugs his shoulders, "In Greece." I sigh and start up the car.

After some time passes, the silence is unbearable, "You can play something if you'd like or turn on the radio." He shakes his head, "I think the silence is nice." Okay, no music, then. What kind of rich guy doesn't like music? I listen to my unbalanced breathing as I try to concentrate on driving. "You don't like the silence?" He asks. "Silence isn't really a good sign in my house," I say honestly.

When we arrive, Jackie sits in the living room with two text-books, a designer mannequin, and a few loose fabrics. "Hey, Melina," she says without looking away from her work. "Hey Jackie," I say. Mateo walks in behind me and she finally looks up in surprise, "*And* Mat," she gives me an approving nod. I roll my eyes ignoring her gesture.

"Homework already?" I ask as I shut the front door behind Mateo. "Yeah, but don't mind me. I was just going back to my room," She arches an eyebrow. I eye her suspiciously as she leaves her things and hurries away. "Nice place," Mateo says as he sits down on the couch, "too modern, though."

I nod, "I agree it's very...cold." I sit cautiously next to him. "Cold?" He looks me in the eye, and I can't bear to hold his gaze. I stand, saying, "You can still have simplicity or nice things without being dull or boring, so to speak." I point to the kitchen, "Would you like some coffee?" He nods and follows me. He leans against the counter as he watches me, "So, are you a book and coffee kind of girl?"

"Books? Not really," I fiddle with the coffeepot turning it on. Then I move to grab two coffee cups; Jackie's pink one and the matte green one my grandmother bought me for Christmas. "But I do like poetry and art. So I guess that counts, right?" I say placing the cups in front of the coffee pot and turn to face a smiling contagious Mateo.

He moves to stand closer in front of me, and butterflies erupt in my stomach, and I spin around to hide it. I've felt butterflies before, but not the good kind. When the coffee's ready, I fill the small cups. Taking a deep breath, I slowly turn back around to hand him the matte green one. As he takes it, his fingers brush over mine. "So earlier, in the car, you didn't want the music on; is there a story behind that?" I question. "One, I don't want to tell," he nods, taking a sip of his coffee without taking his eyes off me.

"Okay then," I head back into the living room and resume my spot on the couch as he follows. Briefly glancing at Jackie's mannequin, I pick up the remote and ask, "Is the TV an exception?" He nods in response. I turn the TV on and lower the volume. We sit in comfortable silence, until the sunlight from the sunset shines through the window upon our faces.

After a while, he says, "The sun brings color to your eyes, Melina, they're beautiful." I unwillingly smile. The way he says my name seems to do something to me. I look down at the semi-empty cup in my hands saying, "Thank you." He smiles in response, taking the last sip of his coffee, and asks to take the cups back to the kitchen sink. I feel a bubbly feeling in my stomach as I watch him walk away, so I pull out my cell phone and scroll through social media until he returns.

"You said you like art. How come I don't see any paintings?" Mateo says as he re-enters the room. I laugh, "Because they're all in my bedroom."

"Well, may I have a tour?" he smiles, and his charm is contagious. I almost say no, but no one's ever seen my paintings. So I turn off the TV and lead him to my bedroom. I glance at Jackie's door, which is cracked open. I roll my eyes, but I am a little relieved she's eavesdropping.

Mateo walks into my room as I quietly stand by the door. My bedroom walls are crystal white; beside my bed stands a dark wooden nightstand and a dresser that matches. In the corner, a dark wooden easel stands with a blank canvas on it, and beside it, upon the wall, hangs two of my very own abstract paintings. He steps in front of one of my oldest ones and stares momentarily before asking, "What's this one?"

"I keep trying to figure that out myself," I reply, moving to sit on my bed. Feeling a little more comfortable in his presence, I continue, "The day I painted it was... a difficult one." My heart speeds up, recounting the memory, "But that's the outcome." He continues to study them, and it makes me anxious. Does he like them? He probably thinks they're stupid. They probably are stupid. He probably thinks they're ugly and doesn't know how to say it.

"These are beautiful, Melina," he says after what feels like an eternity. He thinks they're beautiful, really? I'm doing a happy dance in my mind as I say, "thank you." He walks around my room. His phone goes off, and he stops to look at it. Something bad must be on the screen because his smile disappears, and anger floods his face. He sighs, "I should get going."

"Okay, well, let me walk you out," I scramble to my feet as he walks to my bedroom door. He waits for me to open it before following behind me as we walk to the front door. I can feel his gaze on me, and it's giving me...butterflies. I open the door for him, "Thanks for spending the day with me." His contagious smile returns briefly. "Anytime," he says, lingering.

He slowly moves to touch my face, and I allow him to, "I want to see you again." His voice isn't harsh, but it definitely doesn't seem like he's asking. "Okay," I respond, and he smiles approvingly. He looks at me a moment more before walking out the door. I notice he gets into the back of a black SUV instead of the BMW i first saw him in.

I shut the door smiling and began processing the events of today. Mateo seems just as closed off as I am, but he seems happy to have spent the day with me. He likes my paintings. Caught up in my thoughts, I unintentionally ignore Jackie while walking back to my bedroom. "Umm, hello," she says as I plop on my bed.

"Oh, sorry, I was just in my head."

She hurries to sit on the end of my bed. Her voice is laced with anticipation, "Tell me all about it. He spent the *entire* afternoon here, and you guys were in the bedroom."

"Well, we didn't do what you were thinking, you naughty spirit."

She laughs and pushes me playfully. I continue, "But I find him...attractive."

"So you like him," She sits with her arms crossed with that I told you face. "I find him interesting," I try not to smile. "I'm glad you find him interesting," she playfully mocks me. "Don't second guess it, okay? You deserve just as much happiness as anybody else," she says. Then she gives me a reassuring hug before standing, "Well, I won't keep you up any later. Get some sleep." I roll my eyes, "Okay." Sleep is the last thing I want to endure.

It's early in the morning as I make a cup of coffee with the cup Mateo drank out of. "I've got to get to class a bit early today, and I made a grocery list. Can you stop at the store when you get the chance? The fridge is a little empty. See you later," Jackie says a mouthful while brushing her hair down the hall. Laughing, I head into the living room to finish my coffee, reminiscing about the previous day.

I put my cup in the sink, then return to my room to prepare for class. Quickly, I put on yoga pants and a thin gray t-shirt. Then attempt to tame my curls in a slick back bun, but my hair has a mind of its own today, so I settle with a low ponytail and two curls hanging from my sideburns. The drive to campus is short, giving me time to snack on a bagel and use the bathroom.

As I'm washing my hands, Natalie and two other girls walk into the bathroom, but they fall silent as they see me. Natalie snickers, "That's her." She makes friends fast. Here we go, just keep washing your hands and-

"Hey!" She yells. I stop mid-scrub. Crap. I don't turn around, but they face me anyway. Natalie begins, "I don't know if you haven't heard, but Mat is mine. May I remind you; he came to the school with me. I remember you. You're the creep who was watching us in the bathroom on the beach. You better know your place, bitch." They linger a moment more before turning to leave. I don't reply as I stare at them through the mirror. All three of them eye me up and down before leaving out the door. Just great.

4. Interrogation

Class was a bit frustrating today, but I'm thankful it's over. I couldn't shake the feeling of being watched all day, which only made me more stressed. Setting my belongings on my bed, I think to myself. I know I *saw* them together, but Mateo hasn't technically said they were together.

Feeling the tension in my body, I try to take a calming breath, which I fail miserably. She is right, though. It's not like I'm *not* responsive to Mateo's presence. Grabbing my red notebook, I quickly make a cup of coffee before plopping down on the couch and trying to distract myself.

After a while, I sigh and begin fiddling with my necklace. I still have some of the day left, so I snag the grocery list and head to the store.

Placing a box of cereal in the basket and some milk, I decide to get ice cream and a few candy bars too. I find myself thinking of Mateo unwillingly and smiling, reminiscing on his reaction to my paintings. I still don't believe that he actually likes them. I suddenly feel that chill of being watched again as I head to the checkout and brush it off.

After quickly making it home, I walk through the door. "Well, there you are," Jackie says, sitting in the living room. "Hey," I say, sighing. I head into the kitchen to put some of the groceries up. Then I grab the ice cream tub along with a spoon, and join her on the couch, asking, "How were your classes?"

"Today was slow, I had to sit through a thirty-minute presentation on the evolution of fashion, it's horrible how much damage fast fashion is doing to the economy," She sighs dramatically. I nod, "Well, at least you're obtaining knowledge." A few seconds later, she pulls out her phone and giggles at her screen. She asks, "You wouldn't mind Troy coming over, would you?" she reaches for my spoon and takes a small scoop of ice cream.

"Only if you promise not to be so loud," I reply wiggling my eyebrows.

***

I can't tell what's more distracting; my teacher or the girl's constantly eyeing him. He speaks, "I will collect your notebooks at the end of class in three minutes, so make it interesting." I sigh, writing a brief summary for my sketch of a sign with multiple arrows pointing in different directions; Showing me direction but not leading the way. This is life's confusions. Telling you to go right but not when to turn left. Afraid to move forward, but not wanting to go back.

The Professor signals the class dismissed, and everyone quickly packs up to leave. He yells, "Set your notebooks on my desk on your way out."

Today is Friday. The poetry club is throwing their annual meet and greet at a local karaoke bar, and every year Jackie makes me go to get me to join, knowing damn well I'd never. I wonder if Mateo will be there, though. I text Jackie as I walk out of the building to my car, replying to her telling me when to get ready and when we'll leave.

When I make it to our house, Jackie and Troy are sitting on the couch. "Hey guys," I wave, closing the door and head to my room. I have about three hours to spare, so I decide to confront the blank canvas that's been staring at me all this week.

Time flies by, and suddenly Jackie comes in, "Are we still going, Melina?" I have paint on my fingers and a bit on my clothes, "Yeah, how much time do I have?" I quickly look at my painting, totally unsatisfied. "About thirty minutes, and oh, apparently, There's a new dress code this year. They want us to dress formally," She says while closing my door.

I quickly wash up, throwing on some jeans and a plain shirt, and then I change. Formal. Think, formal clothes. I struggle to look through my closet and settle on a high-waist long black skirt with an off-the-shoulder long-sleeve off white top and some soft black flats. I wet my hair, letting my curls hang loose, add some moose so they'll stay tamed, and spray some perfume. "Ready?" I ask, entering the living room, and Troy and Jackie are waiting by the door. He opens it, and we leave.

First arriving, you can't even tell there's a party. It's so peaceful outside I feel nervous. The building is very discreet but welcoming. It's dimly lit on the inside, but the party is in full swing, with school flags hanging by the front door.

You can see a group of people dancing by the DJ, and towards the front of the building sit a few tables and chairs. Music is playing but low enough so you can still hear. We decide to sit at a table near the front. After a few minutes more people start crowing in. There's definitely more people than just the poetry club here.

As we sit in a small discussion, Jackie quietly whispers to me, "I should have gone with the red dress." She's wearing a short black single-strap dress that looks beautiful to me. I say truthfully, "You look breathtaking, Jackie."

After a while, the club president yells to quiet everyone down. He stands where they've deemed the center of the room. There's a table with a hook-up microphone. "Welcome everyone to our Seventh Annual PC PARTY!" He speaks.

Everyone claps, and he continues, "Newcomers, please enjoy yourself. There's plenty of beer to go around, and don't forget to stop at the bar for those famous onion lotus flowers. They taste amazing! Feel free to move around and meet club members. They're the ones wearing name tags." I find myself searching the room but afraid to get up.

"Okay, well, while you sit here, I'm going to the bar," Jackie finally says, snagging Troy with her. It literally never fails. I always end up alone somewhere, regretting the decision to come.

A few minutes pass and the vice president is now talking into the microphone to get everyone's attention, "Alright, people, time for tradition. All of our newest members, please make your way up front. Now don't be alarmed. This isn't a satanic ritual or anything." The crowd laughs.

"This year, we're having our newcomers read a poem of any kind to signify their membership."

Well, that wasn't in the party description. The first guy up looks like he's ready to vomit; he wipes the sweat on the back of his arm when it's his turn. I can't even hear what he is saying as Jackie is suddenly yanking me out of my seat and pulling me up toward them.

"You should get up there, girl!" she says, and I panic. When did she get back? "Absolutely not!" I whisper yell, but it is no use. She is already dragging me to the foot of the crowd. I take a deep breath, terrified. I bet this was a setup. Jackie, count your days.

I close my eyes and breathe again. The crowd claps after the guy finishes, and my eyes shoot open. This is going to be bad. I can hear my heart thumping in my ears as Jackie gives me one last push. I turn to see her giving me a thumbs up before I reluctantly step to the microphone.

I take a deep breath again, and then I see him. Standing there in black dress pants that fit him better than they should, along with a cream-colored dress shirt. He's smiling at me and it sends warmth through my blood, a sense of calmness and safety.

The words simply fall from my lips. "If nihilistic thoughts arise, could you still see the beauty in my eyes? If fear grew close, and pain became difficult to ease. Would you like me then or succumb to leave?"

Although I see his posture change, his smile shooting me with intensity, pure curiosity. I continue, "Would you still be interested or think my smile is as bright if you saw the demons I deal with throughout the night." My voice trails off as I can't think of anything else to say.

The crowd applauds, and I make my way through the crowd and back to my seat. "That's what you write in your book all day!" Jackie says in shock. She smiles continuing, "I'm so proud of you!"

"Thanks" I say briefly rubbing my arm. "Melina," I hear his voice and feel warmth in my stomach. He's standing right behind me. "Mateo," I say turning to face him. He smiles smugly at his name but doesn't call me out on it.

He moves to sit beside me, and I look over at Jackie, who's smiling like a proud momma. But she doesn't interrupt. "I didn't think you'd be here," I shift towards him, unconsciously wanting to be close to him. He replies, "Yeah, and I'm glad I am. I got a peep inside your mind."

"Well, you're very closed off yourself, you know."

He gives me a look that doesn't say I'm wrong. He stands, asking, "Would you like to go somewhere else?" I nod, and he reaches out his hand. I hesitate, and he says, "You can trust me." I pause for a second longer before setting my hand in his. He doesn't let go as he guides me through the exit. "Where are we going?" I ask as we walk calmly. "Anywhere from here," He replies.

As we reach his car, he lets go of my hand, and moves to open the passenger door. "After you," he says, his voice feeling like silk around my body and I smile. That new car smell floods my nose as I wait for him to take the driver seat.

As he starts the car, I say, "You didn't like the party?" I look out the window as the car begins to reverse. He glimpses at me, "Where I'm from, parties are a pretty frequent thing. They're repetitive, but to be fair, this one was quite different." I don't reply and fiddle with my fingers as we leave the area.

"Are you hungry?" He asks making a turn onto a busy street.

I'm unsure if I can stomach food at the moment, but I nod anyway. Soon we're pulling into a quiet diner. We quickly find a seat near the window, and the waiter starts us off with water. "Do you like poetry?" I ask as he looks at the menu. He just nods his head. I look out the window, not knowing what else to say.

When I glance back at him, he's already staring at me. "What are you thinking?" he asks, placing the menu back on the table. I rub my forearm, looking at my cup of coffee, saying, "I could ask you the same." He sighs and leans back, "Clearly, we're not going to get anywhere like this." I watch him as he runs his fingers through his hair, and I suddenly want to do the same. "What do you want to know?" he says, just as the waiter walks back over to us. He orders us a coffee as the waiter sets down a pitcher of water and two cups.

"Why don't you like your name?" I say the first thing that pops into my head. He sighs and runs his fingers through his hair again, "Because it was my grandfather's name, and he wasn't the nicest person." I move to stuff my hands between my thighs. "But I like your name," I say more to myself.

I think it surprises him because he pauses for a second, then quickly takes a sip of his water. "I like being around you," I continue, feeling the warmth from my thighs spread to my fingers. I quickly glance at him, and he's smirking, "As I, you."

The waiter brings us coffee and asks if we're ready to order. Mateo nods, "What would you like?" I haven't had a chance to browse the menu, "I'll take what you're having." He lightly smiles before turning to the waiter, "We'll take your Special BLT with fries." The waiter smiles before collecting the menus, then leaves.

Mateo turns his attention back to me, and I feel all fidgety. "Your turn," he says, pouring sugar and creamer into his coffee, then into mine. "What would you like to know?" I reply, grabbing a spoon to mix my cup. "Elijah told me you don't like compliments?" I sigh. What, he and Elijah are suddenly the best of friends? But of course he did, "I don't feel deserving of them." I take a sip and hum as the hot liquid slides down my throat.

"Well, I believe there are people in this world who don't deserve them, but you are definitely not one of those people."

"You know, you're very kind for a spoiled little rich boy," I say. Our food arrives, and he playfully responds, "Spoiled little rich boy?" He thanks the waiter before setting my plate in front of me.

"That's just how I was raised, and for the record. I come from wealth, but I am not spoiled," he says, taking a few bites of his food. I find his lips distracting as I try to focus on the plate in front of me.

Taking a brief sip of my coffee, I say, "That's something a spoiled little rich boy would say." Then nibble on my fries. He asks, "How old are you?" He takes a few more bits, and I respond, "I'm twenty-two. What about you?"

He pops a fry into his mouth. "Twenty-four," he says. *Twenty-four?* This immediately makes me wonder how old Natalie is, but I just nod in acknowledgment. He eats another fry as he continues, "So you're living on your own. Why not the dorms?" I finish the rest of my coffee before responding, "Well, Jackie and I didn't want to risk being roommates with anyone else. Her father travels a lot for work, and she got tired of being alone, so we made an agreement with my grandparents and her dad, and now we're living together." I take a small bite of my food.

"That must be fun," he finishes his coffee before moving to take a bite of his BLT. He looks like he's contemplating something as he chews. "What about you? I mean, I know you said you already graduated, so are you living with Natalie or?" I ask curiously reaching for a french fry.

"For now, I'm staying at one of my father's properties here in town."

Properties? As in plural? What the hell does his family do for a living? I ask, "Oh, right. So you're a businessman?" He replies, "Yes, though not in the traditional way."

"So why business?" I ask. He laughs, "Well I'm good at it, but mostly because it's the family's business." A family business, hmm. "Because you're good at it," I repeat, my voice laced with sarcasm and amusement. I continue, "You know that's a spoiled little rich boy response." He laughs, "Maybe."

I decide to ask the important question no longer interested in the food Infront of me, "And what about Natalie? Are you guys a thing?" He sighs, "You may have complicated that situation." He leans back a little.

"So you guys *are* dating?" I ask, a little confused. "I fuck her from time to time," He says all to bluntly. My eyes widen at his response but that doesn't really answer my question, so I don't respond. He takes a deep breath, "Let's just say our families have an agreement. One I'm not particularly fond of, but it's been established."

After our very informative dinner, he pays for our food. I receive a text from Jackie:

Hey love, I know you're okay and all, but just making sure. Call me.

I laugh as I call her phone, "Hey Jackie." Mateo watches me as I continue, "Yes, I'm okay, and he is still here." He smiles while watching me, and it's contagious. "Okay. Okay, bye," I hang up the phone. Mateo leads us out of the diner, "Shall we."

After he parks the car on the curb of my house, I actually feel a little sad that I have to go. He's been keeping me company, and it feels nice. He walks me to the door, but I don't rush inside. "Thank you for dinner," I say, looking up at him. "It's my pleasure," He responds, standing only a foot away. I wish I could say more, but I guess I don't really know what to say. So I settle for goodbye, "Goodnight Mateo." He gives a dashing smile, "Night, Melina." God, he really is handsome. I linger a moment more before turning to go inside. He doesn't move to leave until I completely close the door.

"Melina!" Jackie screams before I've had the chance to process today. "Hey, Jackie," I turn to walk straight to my bedroom. She yells, "So where did he take you? What did you guys do?"

"We went out to a diner, and we talked," I say, taking off my shoes. She looks more than surprised as she crosses her arms, "He took you...not to his house?" she questions, "Melina, that's not normal. Did you at least kiss?" I rub my face and say, "Jackie, you explicit human. He took me out to eat. That is normal."

"Okay, so you went on a date," She sits on my bed and continues, "Tell me all the details" After getting comfy, I sit on the bed with her, "Well, he certainly is sweet, but I don't think it was a date, more like an interrogation." I smile, "It was nice."

She awes and tells me about her day with Troy before she finally leaves to call him. It's 11:03 p.m. and I don't want to go to bed, so I decide to do a little doodling until I unwillingly fall asleep.

***

"Melina, can you please wear a dress today? Dad wants to take us out for dinner, and I'd like you to look presentable."

Ouch, Jackie. I roll my eyes as I dig through my closet for something to her standards of appropriateness. I don't own a dress. A few minutes later, she comes in, "Here, wear this. I picked it out on the way home. You wear a 1x, right?" She tosses a simple black slim dress on the bed, and I wince. She just wants my stomach to peek out. She adds, "And shave those legs, or I'll do it for you." She leaves my room, and I have to remind myself she was born high-handed, being the only child and all. I am going for her support.

I quickly shave my legs before getting dressed, and we're out the door at 8:45 a.m. We get into her car, and she types in the place we're meeting him into her GPS before starting up the vehicle. I scroll through my phone while unconsciously thinking of my night at the diner with Mateo.

Quickly arriving, I try not to be so self-conscious as her dad greets her with a bear hug. He respects my space as he smiles and waves to me. We follow her dad into an establishment I've never been to before.

Chandeliers and angel baby paintings cover the ceilings. Bronze trim and white walls set the mood as a clean, and high-profile restaurant. We join him at a small table near the corner of the restaurant. A waiter immediately brings us menus and water as her dad begins conversation, "So, how's school going? Any professors available?"

He wiggles his eyebrows, and Jackie playfully punches him ignoring his question. "How's mom?" Jackie asks as the waiter takes our orders. "She's doing good, I'm sure. You know kid, you should ask her yourself," He replies and Jackie rolls her eyes. We all know Jackie's the one who caught her mom cheating and she literally hasn't spoken to her since. Jackie huffs, "Just because I ask how she is doesn't mean I want to talk to her."

"She's still your mom, kid," Is all her dad responds. He changes the subject. "How do you girls like the house? Nothing's caved in yet, has it?" Jackie's mood has changed and I can tells she's irritated so I smile, "Well, we've still got our limbs, and the roofs still intact. I think it's good." He laughs as Jackie pulls out her phone to reply to Troy.

The food arrives shortly; her dad ordered himself a steak, I went with southern fried chicken, and Jackie ordered veggie pasta.

After we finish eating, her father pops the question we know he is dying to ask, "So, any boy business?" He eyes us both, and I give nothing away, drinking the rest of my water. "Dad, do you really want to know the answer to that?" Jackie questions while wiping her mouth with the cloth napkin. He takes a moment before responding, "Not really, no." After a while, he waves down the waiter for the check.

The sun is setting as we stand out front of the establishment, saying our goodbyes. "Well, I guess I'll let your mother know you said hi," he says. They hug, and Jackie replies, "Yeah, and I'll tell Miss Hansen she has a secret admirer." They both laugh, and He waves goodbye to us as we get in her car and leave.

***

I am exhausted as my classes finally come to an end. "Hey, Melina," I'm surprised to see Elijah waiting outside my classroom again. "Oh, hey Elijah, what's up?" I begin walking. He follows, asking, "I was wondering if you want to go to the skate park? My roommate wants to shoot some more pictures, and I figured since you didn't go last time, you might want to go this time." I don't really have anything planned today.

I wonder what Jackie's up to? "Sure. Who's all going to be there?" I ask pulling out my phone to text Jackie about it, and of course, she says yes. "Well Troy and I for sure, but you know, a bunch of people should be there," he finishes as we reach my car. I agree, "Okay, well, let me stop at the house and-"

"You could give me your number again, and I can pick you up if you want," he rushes out his words cutting me off. Oh, Elijah, "The last time I did, you blew up my phone."

"That's because you don't respond," he says, hurrying to pull his phone out, and I reluctantly put my number in it. After, he waves, "See you in a bit." I get inside my car, watching him smile like a little schoolboy as I drive off. I sigh. I really hope that wasn't a bad idea.

I make it home shortly, quickly getting out of the car and through the front door. "Jackie, you here?" I yell as soon as I walk into the house. Elijah sends me a text. I ignore it. "I'm in the bathroom. I have to pick Troy up, so I'll catch you there, okay," Jackie calls from the hall. I head towards my room, "Okay, I'm going to put some stuff away and change really fast."

5. Nobody's Second Choice

I sit on the passenger side of Elijah's car as he seems excited for me to be here. "So, how's work been?" he asks. "It's been okay, not too harsh," I say simply. "That's good. I know how hard it is to be a full-time student while also trying to be a full-time employee. Shits stressful," he says sympathetically.

I nod in agreement, knowing we both could only dream of graduating college debt-free. The drive wasn't very long, and Elijah, thankfully, wasn't too talkative. As soon as he parks, we get out of the car.

The skate park is small; the lot is mostly flower fields besides the parking lot. There are more guys here than girls. After a while, Jackie arrives with Troy. They walk over towards me. Then he kisses her in a way not meant for the public before he leaves to go find Elijah.

"Public affection," I hum to Jackie, and she rolls her eyes. Watching people skate is interesting; after a while, you can kind of identify the showoffs, the real daredevils, and those who are just here because it's cool. But I know I'm not just watching people.

I see Elijah heading towards me. "Hey Melina, can I tell you something in private?" he gestures to me to follow him, so I unwillingly get up from my seat. I walk behind him as we approach his car. He begins to pull out his phone to show me something, but I look up, and my heart drops.

I don't remember seeing his car when we got here, but there it is. There he is, leaning against his trunk, hugging up and talking with Natalie. "What?" I whisper to myself. "I thought..." I wrap my arms around my body, suddenly feeling cold as pain erupts in my chest.

"What?" Elijah takes his view from his phone, and I turn away before he can see my face. I knew it. I freaking knew it. I should have known. He was hers. I try to fight the tears and disappointment as I quickly approach Jackie. "Can we go home," I whisper in fear of my voice giving me away.

As soon as she looks at me, her smile fades and she stands as I head towards her car. She looks for Troy before following behind me. After getting into her car, I can't fight it any longer, and the tears silently roll down my face.

Jackie doesn't question me as she gets in and starts the car. We pass by Mateo towards the exit. He doesn't even flinch as he sees me, and my chest hurts more. This is why, exactly why, I don't put myself out there. Nobody wants a traumatized, plus-size, black girl. God, I don't even have a right to be so upset. It's not like he said he liked me or wanted me at that.

I don't remember getting out of the car or walking through the house, but I find myself in my bed, curling up into a ball so desperately, trying to soothe the hurt in my chest. A few moments later, Jackie comes in, but I don't look up. I feel her lay beside me and rub my shoulder, "I'm sorry, Melina." That's the only thing I remember before falling asleep.

***

I know I am awake, but I didn't want to be. Even if the dreams are worse than reality. I'm not ready for the world again, but I get up anyway. I feel so exhausted, I put a little more coffee in the pot than usual. I have a few messages from Elijah, but I don't care and don't bother checking the time. I know by the place of the sun I am late for class.

I did this to myself. All I said was that I liked being around him. He technically didn't deny being in a relationship with Natalie, so it's my fault for thinking things are what they aren't. I take a white cup of coffee and slug to my room. I told you not to do this, and you did it anyway. I attempt to silence my mind with a cold shower.

After I get out, Jackie is sitting in my bedroom. "How are you feeling?" She asks. I don't respond for a moment, really trying to understand my emotions, "disappointed, I guess." I move to my dresser, and she gets up to leave the room, saying, "Well, we have a fresh pint of ice cream, and I cleared my schedule. I'm all yours today." This makes me smile. I love her so much. She smiles, "See; I knew you'd smile. I'll be in the living room."

Jackie sits on the couch with two blankets and a dozen romance movies, "I've already popped one in." She moves to get up as I sit down, "Let me go get the ice cream." I wait for her to return with two spoons and the ice cream before I press play. "You're literally the best thing that has ever happened to me," I say as we get comfortable.

Hours go by as we devour the ice cream and watch a few of the movies. I feel a little better now and insist Jackie to invite Troy over. "Yes, Jackie, it's fine for the millionth time. I'll just take a trip to visit my grandparents. It's not too late in the day yet," I reassure her.

"Are you sure you feel okay enough to drive?" She holds her phone to her chest. Not one hundred percent sure, but I nod in response, "Jackie I'm heartbroken not drunk, it's okay I swear."

She finally agrees and quickly calls Troy. I slip my shoes on, not bothered by my appearance, and head to my car. After leaving the block, I decide to call and let her know I'm coming, "Hey, Grandma."

"Hey sweetie," Her voice flows in excitement.

"How's your evening going?"

"It's peaceful, my dear; we're just about to go out for dinner."

Dang it. "Oh, really," I reply. Instead of turning onto the ramp of the freeway, I go straight. She asks, "Was there something you wanted, dear?"

"Oh no, I'm just checking in. I miss you; I have to come to see you soon," I lie. She coos, "We miss you too, sweetie."

"Well, have a nice dinner, I love you, bye." I sigh while hanging up the phone. I can hear the change of the wheels on the ground as I go from the cement to the rocks and pebbles of the beach parking lot. It's almost empty, and I park close to the exit. Turning off the car, I lay my head on the steering wheel. "Damn you, Melina." I get out and walk to the sand.

Sitting by the shore, I remove my shoes and rest my feet in the cold water. I dove headfirst. Again. Jackie makes it seem so easy. I take a deep breath. Don't get all worked up over one guy. I try to counsel myself as the coldness of the water becomes unbearable. I remove my feet and lay beside it instead. I don't know how much time has passed, but my cell phone rings; it's Jackie. "Hello?" I answer, sitting up.

"Did you make it there? You didn't call or anything. I was getting worried," The surrounding silence makes her voice seem louder through the phone.

"No, I didn't. They went out for dinner, so I came to the beach instead," I say. "Oh, Melina, it's dark out. Come back to the house, please." She begs. I thought I was the motherly figure, "Okay." I stand, "I'll be on my way." I hang up and quickly head back to the car to go home.

I'm right around the block when Jackie calls again, "Hey, Elijah is here. He said you've been ignoring his texts." I sigh, "Okay," and hang up.

When I enter the house, Elijah sits alone in the living room but stands when I walk in. "Hey," he says, looking at the ground. "Hi," I reply sleepily.

"Are you okay? Did I do something?"

I sigh. "No, Elijah, you didn't; I'm fine." I sound apathetic, but I don't care. I walk to my room, "I'll be right back." I enter my room and close the door, locking it out of habit. I slip off my shoes and set the keys down. I'm not really in the mood to entertain right now, but oh well. I walk back into the living room.

"Would you like some coffee?" I offer while walking towards the kitchen. "Oh, no thanks, I don't like coffee," He doesn't follow me, and I'm thankful for it. "More for me then," I quickly make myself a cup and grab a water bottle from the fridge. "Water, okay?" I hand it to him. "Thanks," He replies. I sit and take a sip of my coffee, closing my eyes to savor the flavor, "Mmm."

"Melina," he calls, and I look over at him. He continues, "I don't know what happened, but I'm sorry." I feel like his words don't reach his eyes, so I take another sip of my coffee. "What are you doing here, Elijah?"

"I came to see you."

"Why?"

"Because I like you, Melina," he says. I sigh, stating, "Elijah, we've been over this." His persistence annoys me, and I set my cup on the coffee table. "Why not?" he says, standing in frustration, which makes me a little nervous. He speaks frustratedly, "You're not seeing anyone, you're not dating anyone, so why not?"

"Elijah, please," I sigh and put my head in my hands. After I don't respond, he sits back down. He speaks again, his voice calmer now, "Fine, Melina. I'll wait, I'll be patient, but I won't stop trying." He waits a moment for me to say something, but I don't.

I should like him; I should want to try with him. We've known each other practically our whole lives, and I know his family, but I don't feel for him the way he does for me. Plus, he's a horny college boy. I don't want that kind of drama in my life.

He sighs after a while of silence. Sounding defeated, he says, "I know you're tired. I'll let you get some sleep." He gets up to leave, and when I hear the door close, I stand to take my cup back to the kitchen as frustration rolls off of me.

A few days have passed, and although I feel better, I still want nothing to do with the world, but college won't pay for itself. I make it through the day without seeing *him,* which makes it a little easier to focus. I walk to my last class, unbothered by all the googly eyes at our art teacher. He begins, "Alright, class, today's lesson: What is art? Can someone answer that for me?"

A student raises her hand, and he points at her, "Art is a masterpiece created and approved by the world." She smiles at him. He nods, "True, sometimes." He continues, "But mostly art is creativity. Art is Passion, you create it from the heart, and it tells a story. It is emotion; fear, pain, happiness. Art is Expression. How you feel, what you don't feel. Now you're lucky if the world approves of it, but art is an extension of you."

After class, I hurry home, satisfied that I didn't see him at all, although I feel like I've been seen. I decide to take a shower. When I'm finished, Jackie and Troy are in the living room watching TV. I make my way to the kitchen, trying not to disturb them. I feel exhausted, so I pour a small cup of coffee and lean against the counter.

I can hear them talking and her giggles. I sigh, heading back to my room. The canvas is the first thing that's looking at me, but I move to my drawer to pull out my sketchbook instead. Opening it, I see the plastic bracelet made with red hearts and flowers that Jackie gave me when we were younger. I lightly smile at the memory;

*"Hey, wait up," I hear someone call after me, "Melina!" I stop and turn around. "Hi," I say when she reaches me out of breath. It's a girl from my class; she always leaves stickers for me at lunch. "You're Jackie, right?" I ask. It's that or Jaclyn. "Yeah, it's Jackie," she says, breathing normally again. I check my mini mouse watch for the time; My grandma says I have to be home no later than an hour from when I get out of school.

"I wanted to give you something," she says, taking off her purple backpack and setting it on the ground. I look around and fiddle with my fingers, then she hands me a box, "I think you're pretty, and you're really nice, so will you be my girlfriend?" I take the box. "Girlfriend? You mean like girlfriend and girlfriend?"" I ask, I didn't know we could do that.

She just nods in response, and I open the box, which reveals a pretty bracelet, the one I saw her making in class on Valentine's Day.

"Okay, and if that doesn't work out, we can be best friends. Deal?" I say, touching the bracelet. She nods her head happily, "Deal. Here, let me put it on for you." Jackie takes it out of the box and slides it on my wrist. It's a little too big, but it's so pretty. *

I haven't worn it in a long time because we were in elementary school, and it no longer fits my wrist. I set my cup down and take out my sketchbook, a pencil, and my keys. I decide to head to the park to sit and draw the trees. That should be harmless, right? I sit against a tree trunk and pick the one that sticks out to me the most. I remove myself from reality as I focus on the trunk and the details between.

The sunset distracts me, and I realize hours have passed; I had three missed calls from Jackie and a text from Elijah. I sigh. You can only escape for so long.

As I head back to the house, I get a call while driving, "Melina, hey, it's Jackie. I just want to give you a heads-up. Elijah's here."

I roll my eyes. "Jackie, really, I don't think-"

"I think you should. Maybe it'll lift your spirits. It's been a few days now, and you're still moping; I would say vibe one out, but I know you don't own a vibrator."

"Goodness Jackie, really, vibe one out," I repeat.

"What? Sometimes it helps," she responds in a matter-of-fact voice. "I'll be home soon," I say before hanging up the phone. I know she cares and wants me to be happy. I take the long way home, trying to come up with a reason for Elijah to leave. When I finally make it there, I put the car in park. Elijah is sitting on the doorstep. I get out of my car and walk towards him.

He stands, "Before you say anything, I know I've already said what I had to say before. I don't know what you're sad about, and I know I probably won't help very much, but still, let me be here for you. After all, we are still friends."

What I was prepared to say would seem so rude now. "Okay," I reply letting out a deep breath, and He follows me into the house. I set my keys on the table as I move to sit facing him on the opposite end of the couch. He begins, "You know my dad asks about you."

"How has he been?" I ask.

"He's doing good; he wishes you'd visit again soon," he says. "Yeah right," I said while messing with my fingers, "and deal with your mother's piercing eyes."

"She doesn't hate you, you know," He quickly defends. I don't speak, knowing it's easy to rile him, and he continues, "Plus, Dad encourages her not to get upset, so it doesn't affect the baby." This is news. I look at him, surprised, "She's pregnant?"

"Yes," he says, slightly annoyed, "I thought I'd be the only one, but I guess not." He takes out his phone and begins to show me the text between his father and him, "This is what I was trying to tell you about before."

"That's exciting!" I say happy for them, "Now I really do have to come to visit and give my congrats."

"Let me know when and I'll tell Dad to fire up the," Elijah is cut off by knocking on the door. Elijah doesn't move to answer it, and neither do I. I check the time, which shows 9:05 p.m. "Are you going to get that?" Elijah asks when the knocking comes again. I set my phone down and move to answer the door. Elijah follows a few steps behind me. I open the door, and there he stands. My heart flutters, and it makes me mad.

I barely even know the guy, and I'm reacting like this. "Mateo," I say, forcing myself to sound cold. "Melina," he says, noticing Elijah standing behind me. "What do you want?" I ask and it dawns on me that he remembers my address, but why is he here? "I want to talk to you," his eyes move back to mine, which ignites more butterflies. I huff, "I don't think we have much to talk about."

"Melina," he says my name sternly, and it shuts me up. I turn to look at Elijah, His fist are balled, and his eyebrows are knitted together. I step out onto the porch, closing the door behind me, folding my arms while keeping a distance, even though I feel com-pletely at ease in his presence. He speaks, "I told you, Natalie, and I had an agreement." So he came over to tell me he chose her. Ouch.

He continues, "And I know I have to honor that. I promised to honor that."

"So do it," I cut him off, not wanting to hear him talk about her anymore. "What?" he responds. "If you have to make a choice, choose her. I may not know a whole lot about anything, but I do know I don't want to be somebody's second choice," I speak coldly, knowing I want him to tell me I'm wrong. To tell me he came here for me. I wait for him to speak, but he seems lost in his head. He begins to say something as Elijah opens the door behind me. "Everything okay out here?" He asks. If looks could kill. Elijah is clearly upset at Mateo's presence.

"Everything's fine," I say, trying to pull back the door. I turn to look back at Mateo, but he is already walking away. So that's it, then. He chose her. "Are you coming back inside?" Elijah asks, opening the door more now that I am alone on the porch. "Sure," I reply, walking inside, feeling defeated.

6. You Can't Have Your Cake and Eat It To

I walk into work, still bothered by the other night. Cynthia greets me at the counter, and I immediately turn my happy switch on. "Hey," I say with a smile. "Are you ready to make the locals happy!" She asks. "Ready as I'll ever be," I say following her into the back, where our clock-in machine is and quickly put my things in my locker. She says, "So we'll be upfront today." While waiting on me to fasten my apron. Great.

She begins showing me the ropes of the store and where our boss usually hides when he doesn't want to be bothered. I know I will not remember most of this by tomorrow, but I nod and shake my head, anyway. Before I know it, it's my break time.

I don't bother taking off my name tag or apron, grabbing my employee-discounted coffee and cell. I sit in the cafe instead of the break room, thinking the sunlight through the windows will help me feel better. I text Jackie when I hear the cafe door open. Natalie walks in laughing along with some friends and I quickly look elsewhere, hoping she didn't see me. I look back seeing Mateo walk in behind them, my heart sinks.

Now I regret getting a job so close to campus. I hope this is not what every day will look like. He isn't paying any attention to what they are laughing about. He seems lost in thought, continuously glancing at his phone.

As they approach the register, I quickly grab my things, go into the back, and walk through the swinging door with a loud swoosh. I turn around to watch them. I see his face perfectly clear through the small plastic window. He's casually looking around every few seconds. Searching. God, I feel like a creep watching him like this. As I'm about to turn around I hear Cynthia's voice.

"Enjoy your break?" Cynthia startles me as she stands there with a bright smile. She has a mop and bucket in hand. I simply nod my head, knowing I probably have a few minutes left. "Perfect, we clean the bathrooms every other hour and it's about that time," She hands them to me and continues, "There is a sign-in sheet by the door in both bathrooms." I mentally gag at having to clean public bathrooms and tossing my half-empty drink in a nearby trash can. I walk back out, trying not to find his face, but I can't help it and see that they're sitting at a table, not far from where I am standing.

Natalie's back is facing towards me as Mateo is sitting on the other side. Both bathrooms are single stalls, so it really doesn't matter which I clean first. As I walk into the bathroom door closest to me, I look up once more and we lock eyes.

Warmth in my stomach arises as I enter the first bathroom. I hate that I react to him like this, my inner voice yells as I analyze the small room. I check the toilet paper and paper towel rolls, which are semi-full, and begin mindlessly mopping the floor.

I sign the paper Cynthia was telling me about and place a wet floor sign before moving to the other bathroom. This time, I don't look up as I walk inside. This one doesn't look as used as the other, so I don't bother checking the rolls. I'm about to take the mop out of the bucket when I hear the door quickly open and close. My heart rate picks up as I immediately swing around, preparing to use the mop as a weapon. "You look adorable in that outfit," Mateo says, standing by the door, smirking.

"It is not an outfit, it is my uniform," I take a deep breath, trying to steady my heart rate. "I am mopping, nonetheless working, get out," I say harshly. "But you look so cute working, can I watch?" he says playfully, leaning against the bathroom door. "I can get in trouble, plus you've made your choice. So leave," I say, but he makes no move to leave. Instead, he walks toward me with a facial expression I can't read. I step back, feeling the sink behind me.

The mop is still in my hand and as he gets closer, I try to use it to keep what's left of the small distance between us. He stops right when it touched his chest. He is less than two feet in front of me. "You can't have your cake and eat it too, you know," I say breathlessly as our eyes meet once more. This lights a fire in the pit of my stomach that burns through my heart and into my throat. His honey eyes look dark in the dimly lit room. He speaks, his voice low but amused, "It depends on the cake."

He grabs the mop, slowly taking it from my hands and letting it hit the wall. He closes the distance between us without taking his eyes off mine. For the first time, he was close enough that I could smell him. I took a quiet sniff. He smells like fresh linen. He then cups the side of my face, "Melina." He says my name in a way that creates a pool of desire. "You've made it so difficult," He trails off and moves his hand under my chin. I don't understand what he is saying, let alone process what's happening.

He pulls me close and whispers seductively, "I want to taste you, in many ways," then he kisses me. His tongue exploring mine. His hands seem to pull me closer as if we aren't close enough and I kiss him back, melting into him. He bites my lips in response to a tiny moan that escapes me.

His hands start to explore my body. This makes me panic, clearing my head so I pull away. "Please stop," I barely manage as he freezes with his hands still around me. I slowly look up at him. He looks like he's in a trance.

The look in his eyes screams at my girl parts and it kills me. I can't stand how much he's affecting me. I need to process why I want him so badly. He slowly pulls away from me, "Here." Mateo grabs my phone out of my apron pocket, putting his number in, "Text me when you're off," and with that, he leaves the bathroom. A smile erupts on my face as I turn to look at myself in the mirror. What the hell? I quietly laugh, touching my lips where I could still feel him. What have I just done?

After finishing my original intent in the bathroom, I was back behind the counter, taking orders and making drinks. I can't focus, though, every time I look up. He is staring with a new light in his eyes. After a while though I see him leave alone.

***

"Oh, my god!" Jackie yells. "You did what?" excited, Jackie jumps up and down on our living room couch.

I try to shush her as if people can hear, "Calm down!"

"Do you know what this means? You have to text him! But not tonight. You don't want to seem desperate," She stands now, pacing with joy, "Please tell me you're going to text him. Better yet, call!"

"Okay, Jackie let's take it 10 steps back here, okay, it was just a kiss," I say, trying to reel her back into reality. "And he gave you his number!" She sits back down next to me. I sigh, asking, "What about Natalie?" Why would he kiss me if he chose her?

She rolls her eyes, "To hell with her!" Turning towards me, she continues, "If there was anyone on this earth who deserved a chance at something real, it's you. You deserve a chance to redefine sex and love, so take it."

"Oh, Jackie, I love you." I hug her as unwanted images flash before my eyes, making me shiver. I pull away before she can notice. "I should get some sleep," I say. She agrees and leaves my room. I know that I'm in a good mood and I don't want to ruin it.

After I hear her door shut, I jump up and pull out a blank canvas, grabbing my favorite paintbrush. I begin with black paint, swishing this way and that way across the canvas. I add a little gray and white, trying to create a marble effect.

After a couple of hours, I analyze my painting, Seeing my heart, although disfigured, a marbled, broken heart. I want to add color, so I create a red string dripping blood as it sews the two pieces back together. I stare in awe. It is a graphic piece, but it makes me happy.

I check the time. It's 3:45 a.m. It's still too early to make noise in the kitchen, so I pull out my copy *of Milk and Honey.* I let the lines speak to me as I can feel sleep threatening to break my peace. I move around my bed, trying to delay what I know sleep will bring. After a while, I can't fight it anymore and I succumb to my tiredness.

It's Saturday, but I wake up in a rush. I get up and take a shower, reviving myself. I check the time as I decide on leaving my wet curls as is today. It is 8:46 a.m. I know Jackie isn't going to be up this early, so I tiptoe to the kitchen, making sure not to be loud as I make some coffee. I have an essay to write for one of my other classes and I know I am going to fail it miserably, still I know I need to work on it.

I sit at the kitchen table with my green mug typing and erasing. I type in a few extra lines when I hear a knock at the door and Troy's voice soon after. I move to open it, "Morning, you're here early."

"Yeah, Jackie agreed to spend time with my family this weekend."

"Did she?" I ask, feeling bad. I don't remember her telling me about this. "Well come in, she's still sleeping I think," I say moving for him to walk in. He walks straight to her room, knocking before entering, as I reclaim my seat at the table. As I stare blankly at the unfinished assignment, I get a message from Elijah;

Elijah: Hey Dad's going to fire up the barbeque today. Want to come over?

Me: sure... I could go for your dad's BBQ chicken. What time?

Elijah: Be here in 30 minutes

Me: Okay.

I respond happily, knowing I am going to eat *good* today. Meanwhile, I hear Troy trying to get a very cranky Jackie out of the house. "Okay, I'm coming," she whines as he shuts her bedroom door behind them. "Sorry, I forgot to tell you, I'll see you later, okay," she hurries over to hug me. "Okay, let me know how it goes," I say, waving them out the door.

I decide to wear something quick and comfortable, which is yoga pants and a zip-up sweater. I make a quick batch of coffee to go, grabbing my keys, and heading out the door, locking it behind me. I settle into my car when I realize I left my stupid phone on the table by my computer. I go back inside and grab it and head back out, quickly getting in the car and taking off.

The drive from our new house to Elijah's house is a little further from my grandparents, but I find the drive peaceful. When I arrive, Elijah is waiting out front for me. "Hey," he says as soon as I get out of the car. "Hi," I respond, and he leads me to the backyard where his father is already on the grill. Michael's face lights up when he sees me. "Melina! Hey!" He waves wiping his hands on apron.

I've known Michael since I was a little girl, he practically raised me. "Hey, how are you?" I ask, matching his energy. "I'm doing good, especially with the news and all," he says bubbly turning to flip a patty. "I heard," I say, moving to sit at the already set table. I smile, "Congratulations!" I look over at Elijah, who's sitting in a nearby garden chair, "It'll be nice for Elijah to have a sibling to play with." Elijah rolls his eyes and says, "I thought you said no more kids, anyway."

"Well, things happen, kid, besides I've already got you two, what harm will one more do?" He says looking at me and Elijah and we both roll our eyes. I know Elijah does not see me as his sister. Even though I told everyone in middle school, we were twins once. We were closer back then.

"Hello Melina," Hope says walking outside from the house. Her little bump is barely visible. "Hello Mrs. Grim," I say nervously. Michael injects, "Now you know there is no need for formalities."

Every time we greet each other, Michael always says this, but, unlike Michael, *she* never said I could call her Hope. She completely ignores him and asks, "Michael dear, I forgot to grab the chips, and I'd like to sit for a moment. Do you mind getting them?" He swoons at her voice and kisses her before heading inside the house.

"How have you been? I haven't seen you in a while. I thought maybe you'd forgotten about us," she says, sitting across from me.

"I've been good, Jackie and I are officially in our own place, and it feels like time is flying by," I smile. She agrees, saying, "That's good. Time seems to go by faster as you get older." She pauses, asking, "How's Jackie? You never bring her over with you anymore?" I reply, "She's good, she's just doing her own thing, I'll ask her next time if she'd like to join me."

Michael comes back with the chips, setting them on the table and moving to the grill. "The Chicken and patties are done!" He cheers, taking the tray and sitting on the table. "Oh, please do. It'll be nice to see her again," Hope says to me as she moves to help Michael. Elijah moves to sit next to me as his parents hand us plates and we quickly fill them. "Can you hand me the ketchup?" He says and I pass it after putting some on my bun first.

After eating more than I can bare, the sun disappears into the night. "The food was delicious as usual," I comment with a plate for Jackie and I in my hands. Elijah and his father walk me to my car, and I continue, "You have to show me how to barbeque chicken like that."

"Oh, don't flatter me," Michael says playfully and continues, "Don't be a stranger Melina." They stand on the sidewalk as I place the plates in my car, saying, "I'll make sure to bring Jackie next time." Michael smiles, "Later kid." He walks back to their house as I wave bye.

I walk to the driver's side door and Elijah is beside me as I open it. "Thanks for coming. You know they love you," He smiles briefly pointing back at the house. "Text me when you get home," He takes a step back as I sit and shut the door. Starting up the car I reply, "Okay." He walks back to the sidewalk but doesn't go inside until I drive off.

I message Jackie that I'm on my way home and she lets me know she isn't home yet and to not wait up. The neighbors seem to be throwing a party as I hear music grow louder as I get closer to my house and there are plenty of cars parked on the street. There's a blood-red car parked on the curb in front of my house, but it doesn't bother me too much as I pull into the driveway.

I quickly grab the plates and head inside, switching on the lights in the living room. I nearly have a heart attack "Oh, my god!" I say as the lights reveal Mateo sitting mindlessly facing the door. "What in the world, how did you get in here?" I ask as I go to place the plates on the table and gather my boggled thoughts. "What are you doing here?" I finally ask. He watches me intently before speaking, "You left the door unlocked and no one was home, so I thought I'd wait for you."

7. No Key No Problem

Crap I thought I locked it. "Okay you clearly don't know boundaries," I say as my heart settles, and he watches me in amusement. I don't remember seeing his BMW out front either. "Why are you here?" I say noticing how casual he looks. He sits there calmly wearing gray sweats and a loose black short sleeve top, "I like being around you, plus you were supposed to text me."

He's still sitting down as he speaks. How can someone make sitting look so attractive? "Yeah well, that was before you declared your love for Natalie," I speak softly, trailing off towards the end. "I didn't say that," he stands and begins walking towards me, "I merely said we fuck." He stops right in front of me.

"Well if sex is all you want then maybe she's right for you," I say crossing my arms feeling a sudden jealousy as he speaks about *them*. "It was at first, that's how it was supposed to go, and then you came along," He lightly touches my face. His words confuse me, so I walk away shaking my head, before turning back around to face him, "What does that mean?"

"I've told you, we are promised to each other," he says. I don't like the way he says that as if they are bond together. "What? Like an arranged marriage?" I question in disbelief.

"Yes, but then I met you and now," He sighs.

"Why do you say that like it's a bad thing? Is it a bad thing?"

"Yes, actually" he laughs but shakes his head "Unfortunately I am the son of a very powerful man. Natalie and I's arrangement was a part of a deal my father made when we were younger, If I break said deal very bad things will happen."

I stand in disbelief "Your joking, right?"

"Not in the slightest, Melina. I come from a very respectable and dangerous family," He speaks calmly. I, on the other hand, didn't know what to make of this. How can some High handed out of my league guy, come into my life and make me feel things...and then tell me I'm the problem.

"Is this what you were trying to talk about the other day?" I ask. He nods his head. "I don't know what you want me to say..." I trail off. He gets close to me again, "I expect you to tell me to leave, to tell me I should do the right thing and forget about my interest in you." His eyes pierce mine, but I don't respond still unsure if he is telling the truth, "Melina, I'm sure this is a lot to process, and I know it's not fair but-"

I cut him off, "I want you to do the right thing." His face falls and it tugs at my heartstrings, I continue, "But when I'm around you, I feel like everything's not so bad, and that I never want that feeling to go away. But that's selfish of me." I question my mortality as I take in the situation that he's in, that I'm in, "When are you supposed to be be-wed?"

"The day after your graduation," he rubs his temples stress-fully. I take a moment to respond, fear and excitement spilling from my pores as the words leave my lips, "Then, we have until Graduation." He doesn't reply at first, frowning in confusion. "We can convince your family to change their mind," I'm not sure I believe the words coming out of my mouth as I say them. He looks doubtful even, but he takes a deep breath and smiles, "Well then, let the chaos begin."

I smile back although I can't help but feel like I've sealed the fate of innocent lives. Suddenly I realize how close we are. I can feel his breath on my face. He's looking at me intently. Standing here, I know or maybe I don't, but I want this, whatever this is, I want it to be mine.

I breathe quietly as I slowly move closer to his lips, he continues to watch me, slowly wrapping his arms around me as our lips finally meet. They begin to dance in sync as I focus on his scent. He begins to rub on my ass, though it spikes my adrenaline, I refuse to pull away. His lips move lustfully and his hands wander farther than I can handle. I softly pull away resting my head on his chest. He wraps his arms around me and playfully says, "You know, you're becoming a tease."

"I don't mean to be," I say innocently, and he laughs. I move to look at the time, it's getting late, and I remember where Jackie is.

I ask, "Do you want to stay the night?"

He arches his eyebrows, and a smirk appears on his face "And do what?" I rise and drop my shoulders, "I don't know." I don't want to lead him on. Still though, he smiles and proceeds to pull out his phone to send a text before replying, "Okay, but you're not going to make me sleep on the couch are you?" This makes me laugh, "No, I guess you don't have to, but I'd like to shower so could you maybe wait out here." He agrees and I grab my phone quickly and head into the bathroom. I turn on the hot water as the excitement sets in and send Jackie a text:

Me: Mateo's staying the night!

It takes a few seconds before she responds.

Jackie: What! I leave you alone for one night and you've already bagged him in your bed! Mamas so proud!

I roll my eyes, but I laugh at her response before setting my phone on the counter and getting in. I scrub up pretty quickly, but

I linger glancing at the door every so often, I cringe at the idea of him walking in here, but a part of me kind of wants him to.

After a few minutes of soaking, I get out and dry myself off. I quickly dry my wet curls in the towel before tying my hair in a low bun. I quickly get dressed in simple grey pajama shorts with a loose t-shirt, but not before putting on some body lotion.

I walk back into the living room, Mateo's now sitting with the green cup of coffee in his hand, "I hope you don't mind." He takes a sip, continuing, "I made us some coffee." He hands me the pink cup as I sit down next to him. "Are you hungry?" I ask.

He grins, "I also ordered us a pizza."

I smile and lean my head against his shoulder, "This is nice." He laughs, "Depends... I've never stayed the night at a girl's house without the full intention of having sex." I laugh and shake my head, "Well Mateo allow me to be the first to disappoint you."

"Why do you insist on calling me that?" He speaks kindly although annoyance laces his voice.

"Because that's your name."

"That's my *grandfather's* name, not mine," He sighs. "That may be his name as well, but you are *not* him," I try to give him a reassuring smile and the doorbell rings. That must be the pizza as I watch him open the door and pull out his wallet. His phone lights up, and I can't help but read the text that pops up

Natalie: I'll kill her, Mat. Don't try me!

This raises every hair on my body, I feel goosebumps all over me and the pit of my stomach drops. Is Natalie really capable of such a thing? As he sits back down, He immediately sees the text and my expression. Sitting the pizza box on the table he moves closer to me, "I won't let anything happen to you, Melina. Natalie is bluffing."

"How do you know that?" I question quietly. "If you're serious about your family being dangerous, about the arranged marriage, how the hell do I know she won't actually kill me!" I say, the panic in my voice is nowhere near the actual fear in my soul, and not because of Natalie's threats, well partially.

But if she could say something like that and mean it, has he? Has he ever...killed someone? The thought of the answer to that makes my stomach turn.

"Melina, the moment I decided I wanted you; you were safe, I will keep you safe."

I melt at his words, he wants me. I try to calm down and he kisses my forehead, "Now. can we eat, before the pizza gets cold?" I nod in response.

My nerves are still scattered but we manage to eat in comfortable silence, soon we are both tired and for the first time since he's been here, I'm nervous.

I've never wanted someone in my bed before. But here I am guiding him to my bedroom as my heart thumps in my chest. "Are you okay?" he asks as we walk into my room, shutting the door behind us. "Honestly..." I begin "I'm scared."

His face shows concern and a glimpse of pain, "I'd never do anything to you, without your consent Melina, I'm not that guy." I reply quickly, "No, I know. I'm sorry I didn't mean to offend you. I've just been through a lot. I've been guilt-tripped into doing a lot of things I didn't want to."

"I'm sorry that happened to you, Melina. I promise I don't have any bad intentions, okay," he says speaking softly. "Okay," I respond. I turn towards my bed and plop down without undressing, quickly climbing in and wrapping the blankets over my lap. He doesn't turn off the light as he takes off his shirt. He's definitely fit. I notice there's a bulge imprint in his sweats and it makes me hot.

I turn away almost embarrassed like I've seen something I shouldn't. He turns off the light. "Wait, can you lock the door please?" I ask. He stands there a moment, but I soon hear the click of the lock.

I take a deep breath as I feel him slide in bed but doesn't get too close to me. I lay there motionless, and he reminds me, "Nothing will happen if you don't want it to, baby girl." This calms me and excites me all at the same time. I debate a few minutes before I softly scoot closer to him, and he opens his arm for me to lay on his chest. I breathe out in contentment as I begin to count along to the sound of his heartbeat drifting off to sleep.

I wake to the sound of a phone conversation, Excitement shoots through me as I recognize Mateo's voice, he's still here. I slowly sit up and he's already watching me as he continues his conversation, "We'll sort it out." He hangs up and addresses me, "Morning." He smiles. "Hi," I reply softly, still a bit tired. "You talk in your sleep," he says moving to sit beside me on the bed.

My heart races, not because he's inches away but because what the hell did I say? What did he hear? How did I not know this, Jackie's never mentioned sleep-talking. "Oh god, what did I say?" I ask as I notice he's all freshened up in a completely different outfit from last night. "You kept saying you were sorry," he pauses but doesn't take his eyes off mine, "You even sounded like you were crying at one point."

"I'm sorry," I look down and begin fiddling with my hands, embarrassed. He moves to grab my face forcing me to look at him again, "Don't be. We can talk whenever you're ready, but just tell me this, is it still happening?" I don't know why his concern pulls at my heartstrings.

Maybe because no one ever spoke about it after it ended, simply swept under the rug and the only person it seemed to affect was me, "No" I answer quietly. "It will never happen again, not while I'm here," He says reassuringly. His face is only inches from mine, and I can't help myself as I lean forward, kissing him. He doesn't miss a beat as he kisses me back.

Immediately my body reacts to the space between us growing thin as I lean more into him, placing my hand in his lap. I want to drown in this bliss, the good butterflies to never end. My lips part as his tongue begs for entrance. A light moan escapes me at the same time he pulls away, "Melina." He speaks softly, "You're making it really hard for me to contain myself. What I would give to flip you over and..." he trails off, closing his eyes momentarily before looking at me again.

My breath catches in my throat as I realize where my hands are, and I feel his dick pulse under my palm. He speaks roughly as if he truly is trying to contain himself, "So unless you want me to go there, I suggest you get dressed, plus you have morning breath." He smiles, regaining his composure, "I'll go make us some coffee." He doesn't move though, not until I get up removing my hand from his lap. I stand awkwardly in front of him biting my lip. "Melina," he says my name.

"Yes?"

"Get dressed," he says again. I feel like a child as I nod in response and move toward my closet, I quickly hear the door close, and I take off my night clothes. I grab another loose t-shirt, along with some flared jeans, and head into the bathroom. My hair looks a mess as coils spring in any which way.

I wet my brush and tame them in a low bun with side swoop bangs then finish my other bathroom formalities. As I walk out and finally check the time, it's ten o'clock. At that moment I realize I slept all through the night, without waking up in fear. I can't help but smile as I hurry out of my bedroom. I like this feeling. Just then my phone dings and I see a message from Jackie;

Jackie: Just checking in! You okay?

Me: Yeah I'm good, He's still here!

Jackie: Did you fuck?

Good grief Jackie, I power off my phone choosing not to respond to her last text.

Mateo's leaning against the kitchen island silently drinking his coffee. "Hey," I smile. "Spend the day with me?" He asks as he hands me a cup and my heart flutters at the idea, "Okay." I take a sip. "Mmm," I verbally moan as the strong flavor slides down my throat.

"I want to make you moan like that," He moves to sit down at the table and I almost choke on the hot liquid. He laughs and checks his phone "We've got to get going, do you want your coffee to go?" He puts his finished cup down and I shake my head taking one last sip before setting my cup down, "Do we have time to stop for food?" I follow him to the door as he holds it open for me saying, "We'll stop for brunch."

Confusion knits my eyebrows as I don't see his BMW, "Where's your car?" He continues to walk past me and points at the blood-red car. My eyes nearly pop out of my sockets, that is so not his car, "What happened to *your* car?"

"Melina, I have lots of cars," he's already on the driver's side as I hear the doors unlock. This car is bulky and looks dangerous like the ones in those car racing films, I nervously get in. The inside is very spacious. The leather seats are a bit warm, but at least my thighs won't stick due to my jeans. He starts the car, and it roars to life. "We're not going racing, are we?" I ask, nervously.

He laughs but doesn't reply as he throws it in Drive. We take off and I can't help but close my eyes as he hits the gas and flips the car. "Mateo," I say nervously. He laughs, "I'm kidding." Then begins to slow down.

Soon we were climbing up a ramp onto the freeway in silence, the only noise being the wind "Have you always disliked music?" I ask. "No, not always" He answers as he rolls the windows down a little. I debated a moment before asking, "What happened?"

He doesn't respond at first so I turn my head out the window watching the city move by in frames.

"My mother," he begins, "She and my father were dancing one morning." He smiles at the memory, "They were always dancing in the morning to some tune, always laughing completely devoured by each other's company. I used to sit at the top of the staircase and watch, they never knew of course. One morning..." He trails off as he seems he is no longer present, here in the car.

"It was like watching a scene out of a movie, watching them dance like any other morning to my dad's favorite records. Hearing her laugh at my dad's shit jokes. To see her body fall lifeless to the ground. You think the lights will cut back on you know, like it was a play, a scene, and the director will reveal himself, but no. Men dressed in black were crowding them in seconds."

He takes a deep breath, "I couldn't tell where the shot had come from, if it were inside or outside. Every passing minute felt like hours, everything happened in slow motion." I wait for him to continue but he doesn't so I speak, "I'm sorry Mateo. How did your father handle her death?"

"Surprisingly, my father made peace with it very quickly."

I wait a moment before speaking again, "Well she sounds like she was a beautiful soul." We are now getting off the freeway into what looks like a very wealthy area of restaurants and gift shops. "She was," His smile returns as we continue in the unknown area.

"Are you going to tell me where we're going?" I ask again as my stomach rumbles. He shakes his head, his voice amused, "You don't like surprises, do you?" I guess I don't. I don't respond as we finally pull into a casual restaurant and he quickly parks, "Do you have any siblings, Melina?"

Confused, I shake my head and he responds, "Lucky." As if on cue a small thin woman pops her head in his side window "Hey stranger!" she yells. "Hey sis," he replies, unfazed by her loudness and unbuckles his seatbelt. He has a sister? I don't move as she tilts her shades down and looks over at me. Her brown hair almost covers his face, "Who's this, hmm?" I smile shyly as he grins at her, "My girlfriend." He bats her hair from in front of his face. My stomach bursts with butterflies but I don't say anything because I think he is just teasing her, still, I would love to hear him say it again.

His sister rolls her eyes, "Yeah right tell father that." She then moves, and he opens his car door, "Come on Melina." He is still laughing as he gets out of the car and I follow behind him cautiously. We're now standing in front of his car, and I can't tell if his sister is sizing me up or frowning upon me, either way, I'm nervous as hell.

"Melina, this is my older sister Sofia."

She waves, "The one and only!" She takes off her shades and she is absolutely beautiful. Her hair falls down to her thighs and her skin is lighter than his, and I see a very large wedding ring on her left finger. The outfit she's wearing looks more expensive than the ring.

Did he say, big sister? She looks so small, still, I didn't know he had siblings. I give a friendly smile but don't say anything and she responds, "Is she usually this quiet?" Well, she's very forward. Mateo notices and says, "Leave her alone, Sofia."

God, I probably seem like a joke to her. Mateo laces his fingers through mine, pulling me from my thoughts, and making my stomach do that butterfly thing again. We settle at a table near a window, and I embrace the warmth from the sun as Mateo orders our food. I sit there mindlessly as they talk. I mostly drown them out watching some nearby birdies.

In no time the waiter returns with our food and I'm thankful to see a cup of hot coffee. "Melina," Mateo calls my name. "Yes?" I reply, reaching for a fry but his phone rings. He smiles apologetically before dismissing himself from the table.

As he leaves, I turn back to my food only to see Sofia staring at me intently, I fiddle in my seat not sure what to say. I suddenly don't have an appetite anymore as my stomach knots, so I take another sip of my coffee and quietly say hi. She hisses, "You have no idea what you're doing don't you?"

"What do you mean?" I ask.

"Look I don't know how you met my brother, but you are probably just a temporary fling so don't get so attached to him okay," She looks away and takes a sip of her soda. Ouch. I don't know how to respond. I kind of wish Jackie was here. She'd never settled for disrespect. Speaking of, I should probably check in with her.

"God wait until," she cuts herself off and sighs, "Why can't he just follow the rules like the rest of us?" Before she can vent about anything else, Mateo returns and Sofia registers the look on his face. She immediately starts getting up and tossing some money on the table to cover the bill. "What's wrong?" I try to ask but Mateo grabs my arm causing me to panic as he tugs me quickly back to his car.

He nearly shoves me in, as he shuts the door behind me quickly getting in himself. "What's going on?" I ask again as he starts the car and reverses within the same second, I try taking a deep breath feeling a tremble in my hands as I realize I haven't put my seatbelt on and reach for it, I nearly yell this time, "What the hell is going on Mateo!"

This catches his attention, and he responds impatiently, "They're following us." He presses the gas speeding through the red light to get back on the freeway and I look in the rearview mirror seeing an all-black vehicle with extremely tinted windows. I can feel my breath hitch, each breath getting harder to take. "Mateo," I whisper as he continues to speed, weaving through cars.

At this moment, I realize, I really don't know what I've gotten myself into. "Take me home," I nearly cry. He continues weaving through cars. "I can't," he says, shaking his head. "Take me home!" I finally yell as my vision blurs from my tears filling my eyes.

"I can't take you home Melina! It's not safe right now!" he yells back in frustration. "They were there! Of course they were fucking there," He hits the steering wheel, "I should have known this shit would spread like fire."

I don't respond, I can't respond, my house was being watched? Were they inside my home? What about Jackie? I close my eyes as fear spreads throughout my body and the sound of him speeding floods my ears. I open them to warn Jackie but I'm shaking so badly and the car is moving so fast, I can't type correctly, so I power off my phone, reclosing my eyes, feeling helpless.

I'm unsure how much times has passes, but I don't open my eyes until I feel the car slow down. Mateo's frowning and I look back to see that no one is following us anymore. He takes a deep breath, speaking softly as he glances at me, "I am so sorry baby girl." Mateo drives silently as I collect my thoughts. "Where are we going?" I ask half-heartedly, knowing he probably won't answer but he does. He replies, "My Dad's house."

8. House of Crows

The sun is setting, and I'm sure we are pulling into what looks like a gated community, but as the gates open, a dozen men in all-black stand guard, which makes me a little nervous. As they close the gate behind us, a single modern home comes into view, well more like a small mansion, if that was even a thing. The car comes to a slow as we pull into what looks like a 3-car driveway. The outside of the house is plain, simple gray panels with black trim. Neatly cut bushes are placed on each side of the entrance.

He turns off the car but makes no move to get out. "I don't think your sister likes me," I sigh, looking down at my hands; I feel exhausted since the adrenaline has passed. "She's just over-protective," he says. Lifting my face to look at him he continues, "She's also a bit jealous since she didn't get to choose." He whips a lingering tear from my face, and I lean into his touch, "I'm sorry, baby girl."

We sit like that for a moment, the earlier events fading away as he stares into my soul, "I know you've been through a lot today, and

I really am sorry about that, but we have one more hurdle." My stomach knots because I don't want to endure anything similar to what just happened. He laughs a little at the expression on my face, "My Father wants to meet you."

"He knows?" I question underestimating how quickly words travel here. He nods his head in response and gets out of the car, quickly rushing to my side to open my door. I wish I could have the butterflies from this morning and the happy bliss I felt when he called me his girlfriend, but right now, all I feel is doom; considering the events from today, this man is powerful and dangerous.

"Mateo," I ask as he grabs the door and opens it for me. "Yes?" He responds. "Has your father ever killed anyone?" My question takes him aback, but he answers honestly, "Yes." I take a deep breath, refusing to let his answer make me turn around and run for the hills, and I mean that literally. This place is isolated and surrounded by nothing but greenery.

Mateo places his hand on my lower back to guide me in. The house is warm, and we are immediately met with a black staircase in the main hall. "Dad?" Mateo calls. It's surprising to hear him call him that; I assumed they had more of a strained relationship. Mateo moves to hold my hand in his while still resting a hand on my lower back, which I'm grateful for since I feel I'll faint at any given moment.

His father's voice booms from our right, "In here, son!" and Mateo guides me into the kitchen area. If I didn't know that he was Mateo's father, I would immediately assume they were twins; they stood equally at the same height, with the same sharp jaw structure & frame.

Is *all* of his family good-looking? I wonder what his mother looked like. I'm too busy rambling in my head to notice at first, but then I realize he's staring at me with a strange expression, "It can't be. Lilian?" He's almost inaudible, but I know what he said, the name I haven't heard out loud in years. A name that shatters my soul. My mother's name.

Before I can respond, Mateo says, "This is Melina." I look at Mateo; did he hear it too? "Ah yes, Melina. My apologies...you look like someone I once knew; my name is William." Something makes me reach for my necklace and press against the cool pendant. I smile wearily, "No worries, nice to meet you." I ask, "Can I, um, use the bathroom?"

"Of Course, back into the main hall right under the stairs," he gestures, and I quickly dismiss myself. What the shit? I'm so confused at how calm he's acting, aren't I supposed to be terrified, isn't he supposed to be mad? I quickly find the bathroom, which doesn't fail my expectations; it's spacious despite being under the stairwell. I look at myself in the mirror and close my eyes.

They could have been friends or closer. Oh god, I hope they weren't that kind of close. I never knew my father, his name or age, or if he had other children. My grandparents refused to tell me anything about him. My thoughts crowd my mind so loudly I don't notice Mateo opening up the bathroom door, "You okay?" he treads lightly as he stands in the doorway.

I'm sure I look horrified. "Yeah," I lie, of course. "I just, didn't realize my mother actually knew people; I mean, of course, she did. I don't know. I'm sorry, I just need a few minutes; my grandparents never really talk about her, and hearing her name just took me by surprise." He gives me a supportive smile, "So that's her name, Lilian?" I lightly smile at the sound of it, "Yeah."

"If it helps, I didn't know my father had friends either, only enemies," he says the last part more to himself. "Take your time," he says, leaving. I take a deep breath. Okay, get your crap together, I suddenly have the urge to actually use the bathroom, so I do so quickly, washing my hands. Sofia is standing in the hall waiting for me, "they're out back, come on." The rudeness from earlier is no longer present in her voice.

I completely forgot she had was with us, so I ask, "Are you okay?" She's surprised by my concern. Still, she answers kindly, "Yeah, I'm okay. I'm sorry for my attitude earlier, but you have to understand they're all I have. I'll do anything to protect them." She grabs my hand, "Come on." It is dark out as she leads me to the backyard, revealing an outdoor hot tub and pool.

It looks like a gym pool, maxing at 10 ft deep. This backyard could easily be mistaken for a retreat, from the beautiful pebble paths to the tall lights alongside them. Four tan pool side chairs lay in sync and nearby them stands a tan pavilion with a small fire pit lit in the center.

Mateo and his dad stand alongside a new face; his father has a drink in his hand now. "Adam, this is Melina," Mateo introduces me as soon as we get in earshot. He grabs my waist, which takes me by surprise, and he holds me in front of him, pressing against him, which gives me a sense of happiness.

"Adam Cruz, a pleasure to meet you," Adam says, lifting his drink to me. Adam stands about my height; he had short black hair and playful brown eyes; unlike Mateo, he's dressed more like a civilian, in cargo shorts and a loose t-shirt. I shyly say hi just as Sofia walks over to kiss him. "This is my Husband, Adam," she says possessively as if Mateo hadn't just introduced us.

Meanwhile, his dad has this undeniable grin on his face as he says, "I feel like I haven't had the family together in ages; your mother would be so happy." He raises his glass and takes a sip. I feel a slight sadness for Mateo, but the warmth from the fire feels nice against my legs.

I try not to think about what was said earlier, but I can't help it. I need to ask how he knew my mother. I barely register the way Mateo is lightly caressing my hips, and I turn just a little to look up at him, and the look on his face lights a fire deep in my gut.

His father interrupts our trance, "Dinner should be ready if you all care to join me?" He takes a swing of the last of his glass as we all move to follow him. I stop, and Mateo turns to me. "Hold on. I need to check in with Jackie," I say as everyone continues to walk ahead of us. I sent her a quick text, asking if she's okay. I click the side of my phone without waiting for a response.

I lace my hands with Mateo, and he guides me back into the house. We walk into the kitchen, and everyone is sitting at a very long and large dinner table; I see servers placing food down that I haven't noticed before, and Mateo opens the chair at the end of the table next to his father for me, before sitting down next to me.

Sofia is now across from me, with Adam at her side. She smiles at him as he reaches for her hand. "Are you okay?" Mateo asks me once we all have plates of angel hair pasta in front of us. "Yes, I'm okay," I squeeze his thigh in reassurance, and he bites his lip briefly, causing me to squeeze my legs together.

"I would ask you how you met my son, but that does not matter. I'm more interested in you, Melina," His father asks while picking up a spoon and fork to spin his pasta. "What are you studying for?"

I feel kind of embarrassed as I answer, "Well, I'm an art major."

"An art major?" He repeats with interest. "You know Lilian," He stops himself, pausing for a moment to take a sip of his champagne. There he was again, saying her name; he definitely knew her. He begins to change the subject, but I cut him off, "No, please tell me about her."

I look over at Mateo, he has an unreadable expression on his face, but I'm not letting it go; no one talks about her. He begins again, "I was just going to say she liked art as well." He leaves it at that, refusing to continue the conversation.

Sofia senses the strange atmosphere and speaks to change the subject, "Adam and I went out to this beautiful Art Museum, called the heart of stars. Maybe we could all plan another trip." Suddenly, Adam and Sofia have a mouth full to say about Museums and art galleries. We continue to eat in light conversation.

I have to remind myself that it's okay that servants or other people are cleaning up after me, each time I finish my drink, there's another fill, or when my plate is empty, I'm not told to clean them myself. Still, I find myself wandering into the kitchen to help, but everything is clean by the time I make it there and the servants disperse. I set my hands on the large island and softly sigh.

"You look so much like her."

William startles me as I turn to see him staring back at me with a glass of whiskey. I don't respond at first, and he moves closer but keeps a respectable distance. "Were you guys, Did you," I begin, but I can't find my words or decide which questions to ask before he shuts me down again, "Are you," I sigh, frustrated; why can't I ask a simple question. "Am I related to you in any way?" I finally ask. He almost laughs. "No, Unfortunately, we didn't get that close," He speaks into his glass as he takes a sip.

I let out a breath of relief. Thank God. "Okay," I respond, feeling calmer, yet weirdly, I am a little disappointed. I change the subject. "Please excuse me if this sounds rude, but aren't you supposed to be upset? Didn't you arrange for Mateo to marry Natalie?"

"I did," He doesn't deny it nor sound offended, "and I was mad at first, until you walked through that door, then everything changed."

"I don't understand," I say, confused; what does he mean by everything's changed?

He sips the last of his whiskey and says, "I guess destiny has a weird way of presenting itself."

Suddenly I notice Mateo standing off behind William. Was he there this entire time? "Sorry to steal her from you dad, I'm going to give her a tour of the rest of the house," He dismisses us without waiting for a response. I don't know why, but his dad's words stick with me. "Are you okay?" He asks.

"Yes, I'm fine," I reply as he calmly guides us up the black staircase, "Where are we going?" I ask. "There's a guest bedroom upstairs," He smiles shaking his head as we reach the top. I follow him to the right as Mateo opens the door for me, which reveals a bedroom just as modern as the rest of the house.

The night sky dimly lights the room. It's spacious, in the center sits a California king bed with black bed sheets. There are no pictures, clutter, ruffled sheets, or shoes, which weirdly saddens me like there's no life in here. I slowly enter, and he lingers by the door. There's a door that leads to a large bathroom with a walk-in shower big enough to fit three people, and of course, there is a walk-in closet.

There is a single large window with a bench that you can lay on while watching the world outside. That seems nice, I think to myself as I suddenly feel his arms wrap around my waist, the warmth of his body pressing against mine as he nuzzles his head into my neck. The electricity I feel from his touch goes straight between my thighs. "Mateo," I say, but he does nothing else, simply resting his head on the swoon of my neck.

That's all it takes, and suddenly there is that need, that fire in the pit of my stomach that travels down between my thighs, and I don't want to fight it off anymore, so I slowly turn around in his arms, taking in a quiet breath, I gently lift my lips to his, closing my eyes to kiss him with courage. Desire floods my mind as he kisses me back slowly, moving his hands from my upper back to my ass and gently squeezing it.

I ignore the panic rising in my chest, but Mateo seems to notice, slightly pulling away but not releasing me, "Melina, we don't have to." He speaks in the softness of tones as I take a few seconds to steady my breathing. "But I want to," I whisper.

My admission lights a fire in his eyes, "Do you know what a safe word is?" A safe word? "It's like a code word, right?" I question. His voice is low, "Yes, it's similar. When you are uncomfortable or scared, or you want something to stop, you can use a safe word. Everything stops, no matter how far we're into it."

"Okay," I respond.

"I need you to pick one."

I don't respond as I rattle my brain for a moment before saying, "Roses. I want our safe word to be Roses." Mateo leans into me again, "Promise me you will use it as needed, no matter what."

"I promise," I say, and he quickly kisses me again. At first, I don't notice, but he's slowly moving us toward the side of the bed. Once at the edge, he pushes me onto its side, wasting no time hovering over me, reconnecting our lips once more.

Mateo moves hungrily as he bit my bottom lips, causing a moan to escape from me. My mind is so clouded by this desire; sure, I've been horny before, but to crave someone so deeply, to want them inside me, to bond myself to him in every way possible. That's a path I've never crossed until now. He pulls back again, "Tell me your safe word, baby girl." The way he looks into my eyes calms me more than it should. "Roses," I say breathlessly.

"That's a good girl."

I want this man to claim me, to recreate the meaning of lust and desire. Our lips find each other again as I dig my hands into his hair, and he begins laying sweet kisses down my neck. All too soon, he rises, moving off to stand over me. I sit up, unsure why, when he removes his shirt, "Take your shirt off."

I feel like it takes my brain a second too long to process his request as I stare, admiring his body, but I move quickly, removing the loose fabric over my head. I bite my lip, what he wants…What I want is most evident in his jeans; his boner pokes through, making me move faster to remove my bra, revealing my 38Ds.

I hold them in my hands, feeling a little self-conscious, but he's on me like a moth to a flame, quickly removing my hands from my chest and speaking softly, "Don't do that, don't hide from me." He kneels in front of me as he cups them together. "Okay," I say, and he takes me by surprise as he begins kissing them, then brushing his fingers lightly against my nipples.

"You are so beautiful, Melina," he says moving to take my jeans off and my panties with them. Mateo lingers with my panties, closing his eyes and taking a whiff as he puts them in his pocket, "I'll be keeping these." My pussy pulses at his actions and he smiles, moving to stand between my thighs, "I want to taste you."

"Okay," I say shyly. He pulls me to the edge as if I am the weight of a feather and kneels again, pulling my legs over his shoulders while wrapping his arms around them, locking his head in, hovering his face right over my clit.

"Promise to tell me if it's too much." He says. The feeling of him so close to me makes my pussy pulse again, "I promise." He takes in a deep breath of me. "Mmm" He hums, slowly licking me, and I moan, throwing my head back at the contact.

I try to contain myself as he begins swirling his tongue lightly over my clit. I'm trying so hard not to move against him that I whimper. "You like that baby," he breathes over me in a calm voice as he sticks a finger inside of me and starts pumping, causing me to roll my hips. I moan in response. He doesn't look up as he says, "Such a wet girl."

I raise my hips, wanting him to go faster, but he doesn't pick up the pace, and I whine as it nearly drives me mad. "Mateo," I moan his name, he rises to kiss me, making me taste myself. "I like the way you taste," he says, pulling away again.

He doesn't bother removing his jeans as he pulls down his zipper, pulling his dick out, it's too dark to get a good look at him. Mateo pauses as his tip gently lays at my entrance, and he repeats himself, "Tell me if it's too much, baby girl, I want you here with me, okay." He doesn't move until I respond, "Okay."

He slowly pushes it inside of me. "Oh," I whisper as I feel every inch of him as he slides deeper. He pauses momentarily, allowing me to feel how thick and girthy he is. "Shit," he mouths under his breath. Panic rises again, but I don't say anything; instead, I tell myself this is different because it is. I want this.

He looks at me softly, asking, "You with me, baby girl?" I take a second to respond, "Yes," and I close my eyes; I don't want him to stop. He pulls out slowly, his voice full of desire, "No, Baby, open those eyes, here with me, okay." He speaks so gently that it soothes me. I open my eyes, "I am."

He's looking at me in a way that makes me wonder if his vulnerability matches mine. "Such a sweet, wet girl," he says, pulling my legs straight up to his chest. "Your mine now," and he immediately pushes back inside of me. I cry out, lifting my head briefly, and he pauses until I lay my head back down.

Not taking his eyes off me, he does it again but doesn't stop. "Say it," He asks in such a demanding tone. Through every thrust, I huff, "I am yours." I know what I'm saying. I know what this means. I hope I know what this means.

He moans as he continues to pump into me, "That's a good girl. Look at you, so thick and so beautiful." I melt at all the praise. "Yes. Please," I try to speak through the moans. It seems like he has an easier time doing so. "What?" he asks in an innocent voice. "You like being called a good girl?" He questions, pounding me so hard I can't muster words, so I moan in response.

He takes my legs in one arm and begins circling my clit with his finger. "Oh god, Mateo," I whisper; the combination of the two is more than I can bear. He takes this as motivation to thrust faster.

I feel tears threaten the brim of my eye as I feel my orgasm coming close. "Come for me, baby girl," he says, and I feel it; I do, just a little more. He continues this tortures pleasure and I bath in the sound of his voice.

"Yes, oh god, yes," I say out loud as what feels like a wave of paradise washes through me, my pussy clenches around him as I come. "You're such a good girl," He says in praise. Mateo keeps thrusting as my moans fall to whimpers, "How do you want it, baby girl?"

The thought of feeling his warmth filling me, claiming me, changing me, is too good to deny, "In-Inside." He thrust a final few spilling his cum inside me, before collapsing on my chest. We lay like that for a moment catching our breath, coming down from the high.

He slowly pulls himself out of me and watches as his cum seeps out. I sit up on my elbows and push as he continues to watch, letting more come out, and he smiles at me. "You did such a good job, baby," He kisses my forehead and moves to button up his pants. "Don't move," He leaves out of the room.

I can't escape the feeling of loneliness. Is he really going to leave me lying like this? But before I can let my thoughts jump off into the deep end, he's back with a glass of water and a small pill. He sets it on the dresser and grabs his shirt from the floor, and begins to clean me up; I sit still staring at him embarrassingly as he wipes away the evidence of him.

I sit up completely on the side of the bed, and he hands me a pill. "Plan B," I say, popping it, grabbing the glass of water, and drinking it. I sigh. "I've taken one too many of these," I say this mostly to myself, but when I hand him back the glass, he looks, sad.

Way to go, Melina; a great way to ruin the mood. "I'm sorry, it's just bad memories, I guess," I say. "I'm sorry too," he says, moving to remove his pants and climbing back into the bed. I don't move, unsure what to do, until he says, "Come here." So I move to cuddle up next to him in the blanket.

"You're mine, Melina," he says those words so simply, yet I feel ever thread of truth behind them. It makes me feel safe, but also turns me on again. Gosh, what am I now, a whore? "I like the way that sounds," I say softly. He smiles and kisses my temple, then rolls me over so that he's spooning me, and a little laugh escapes me because how is this man able to move me with ease?

"My weight doesn't bother you?" I question. "Baby, it doesn't matter what you weigh. You're mine now, I will gladly devour you in any shape or size," He presses himself against me as he pulls me closer. Resting his arm around my stomach. Although this warms me, I remember the events from today, "What are we going to do about Natalie?" It seems like he stops breathing for a moment, as I'm sure he's forgotten about today as well. He kisses the back of my head. "Don't worry; I'll deal with her." I take a deep breath as I nuzzle under him, drifting off to sleep.

9. What am I

I wake in a rush, sitting up in a heap of breath, clutching the blanket. I look around the dark room, slowly remembering where I am. I turn to the side of the bed and notice Mateo's place is empty. I rest my head in my hands, taking a final breath and sighing. I reach on the nightstand for my phone, which reveals it's six a.m.

I begin thinking about what we did and how it felt, then I smile to myself and almost laugh. Is that what good sex feels like? Of course, I've made myself cum before, but to have someone else do it while inside you. That's a blissful feeling.

I hear the room door open, and in walks Mateo holding a cup of coffee; he pauses as he notices me. "Did I wake you?" He asks, and I wonder how long he's been awake. "No," I respond noticing he's now in black sweats. "Want some coffee?" He asks lightly, lifting his cup.

"Yes, please," I smile, and he walks over, taking a quick sip before handing it over to me. I cup it with both hands and take a sip, "Thank you." He sits beside me in bed. "How are you feeling?"

"I'm okay," I say, still processing everything that's happened, but I am okay. "It's six in the morning. You're not going back to sleep?" I ask, taking another sip. He sighs, moving to sit at the window, "I like to be up early," he says playfully.

Hmm. "I guess that makes two of us," I realize that I'm still naked, and I set the coffee down. I ask, "Can you hand me my shirt, please? It's on the floor somewhere, along with my bra and pants." He shakes his head smiling as he gets up and soon hands them to me, and I quickly put on the soiled clothes. "Is it safe to go back to my house? I really need a shower and a change of clothes," I ask, now standing in front of him.

"We can go, but I'll have some men following us, okay."

I sigh, "Yeah. Okay," I pick up my phone and see Jackie hasn't responded. "She hasn't texted me back yet."

"She's okay, Melina," he says, placing his hand gently on my cheek. I look up at him, "What do you mean she's okay, she hasn't responded to me, and she checks in with me pretty freaking consistently." He cuts me off speaking slowly, "Melina, she is okay." His voice is stern but not aggressive. "She's enjoying her weekend very much by the looks of it," He adds, trying to calm me.

I believe him; I do. A part of me wants to ask how he could possibly know this, and another feels like I already know the answer. Such a statement should weird me out, but I find myself more relieved than anything. I realize how close we are, and it takes me back to last night, causing me to bite my lips.

He raises his hand, lightly brushing his thumb across my bottom lip, and responds, "Are you sure we need to go to your house to shower?" He then leans into me, and I can feel his breath as he speaks seductively, "I'm sure you look just fine in my one of my shirts."

I laugh lightly, "I don't think your father would appreciate me walking around his house in your clothes." He takes a moment to respond, "Yeah, I guess you're right, come on, let's go."

We make it there safely, and Jackie finally messages me back along the way. Jackie's response is simple: she is okay and enjoying her time with Troy. I want to tell her about my time last night with Mateo, but I much rather tell her in person. So, I reply that's good to hear.

The sun is now up as Mateo follows me in, and even though I know it's my house, I feel like a stranger wandering into someone else's home. "I'll be quick," I say, setting my things down. "Can I watch," He smirks as he begins to follows me to my bathroom?

Before I can respond, my phone rings, and we stop still in the living room. I answer, "Hey, Grandma," I say. Her voice purrs through the phone. "Hey, Sweetie, how are you doing?"

"I'm okay."

"Well, I'm calling because I miss you terribly, dear; come have dinner?" She asks, and I look up at Mateo, who can't hear a word she's saying. "Yeah, I think that'll be nice. What time?" I ask. She responds quickly. "Okay, sounds great, see you then...love you too bye," I hang up the phone, and Mateo waits patiently for a response. I speak slowly, "So we're going to have dinner with my grandparents." I guard his expression as I continue, "Is it too early?"

He laughs. "No, it's fine; I think it'll be fun, as long as they don't beat me with a cane or something."

"Yeah, my grandpa might," I say jokingly. "The last boyfriend I had, well, he scared him pretty bad." Amused, He responds, "Oh really, what'd he do?" I laugh, "He caught us kissing on the front porch and threw a beer can at his head; it nearly knocked him over."

"He must have a good arm then, huh."

My laugh dies down as I remember what happened afterward. "Yeah, I guess," I look away momentarily, closing my eyes to shake away the memory. "She wants us there around seven, so we have plenty of time to spare, but I still need to shower," I leave him in the living room as I hurry to my room. I plan to take a quick shower as I get in, wash up and get out.

I feel much better as I pull a pair of panties out of the drawer and throw on a sports bra. Putting my hair in loose bun, I quickly throw on a pair of button-up jeans. When I leave my room, Mateo is right where I left him. "Next time, I get to watch," He smirks and stands, "Now, as much as I'd like to have some fun before we have to leave later, there is the business to attend to."

"Okay," I sigh.

"I'd like you to join me," he says. I respond, knowing my reply before it leaves my breath, "Of course." I make us a quick bite to eat before we leave and remember to lock the door.

As we leave the house, instead of getting into his car, he heads towards one of the Black SUVs that followed us here. He holds the back door open for me as I get in and he climbs in beside me. The windows are just as tinted as they are on the outside; it was kind of unsettling.

I fasten my seatbelt as the driver takes off and whisper to Mateo, "Can we ditch them when we go to my grandparent's house." He smiles at me, "We can ditch one; as much as you're worried about what they'll think, I care about your safety more. Especially with Natalie acting out of character. I want you protected at all times."

He moves to place his hands on my thigh, "Besides, I'm tired of driving." I take a deep breath, knowing I have no idea where we're going. I try to relax, looking around the vehicle at nothing in particular. Mateo's thumb circles my thigh in a calming motion as I continue to find something to do. After being unable to see what's passing by, I look over to Mateo, "Play a game with me?"

"A game?" He raises his eyebrows.

"Yes, a game. It's called What am I?"

He doesn't respond immediately before choosing to entertain me, "What's the rules?" Excited, I explain how to play, "So you choose an item, or feeling, anything you want really. After you give three short descriptions of what you chose, then the other player has to guess by asking yes or no questions."

"Okay, you go first," He nods towards me. I take a second to think of something, "Most people spend their entire lives trying to attain me. A different version of me exists in everyone's mind; I belong to the eye of the beholder. What am I?"

He smiles at me momentarily before briefly repeating what I've just said and then answering, "Money?" I shake my head, "No," and he continues, "Love?" "You're close," I laugh, and he takes a moment as he thinks before smiling at me. "Beauty?" "Bingo," I smile, placing a kiss on his cheek. "I thought I almost gave it away with the whole eye of the beholder thing."

"Hmm, is that so," he responds playfully, "my turn."

"You turn indeed," I say patiently as he thinks for a moment. "You need me to live, both figuratively and physically. Sometimes you'll give me away, and sometimes I break. What am I?" I repeat his words quietly in my head, mildly getting distracted by the smirk on his face. I ask, "Hope?" He moves further, relaxing in his seat, "No."

I continue, "Is it Love?" He shakes his head, and I repeat his words out loud this time, but before I can answer again, the car stops moving, and the driver calls Mateo by his last name. Mateo turns to me and smirks, "Game over."

He opens his car door, holding out his hand out towards me, and I take it nervously as I still don't know where we are. I whisper as we begin to follow his men from the car towards an unmarked building, "Can I at least know the answer?" He places his hand on my lower back, moving to whisper in my ear, "My heart."

Two men guarding the front door let us through. As we walk inside, I still have no idea where we are, but I feel uneasy as the light immediately dims. There are people casually standing around, however, none are casually dressed. It looks like a hole-in-the-wall bar, and I notice there are almost no other women here.

Mateo's attire fits in with his dark plaid pants and white button-up shirt. He stops us a few feet in front of the threshold of the room and turns to me, "Baby, I need you to be a good girl while we are here. Can you do that for me?" Mateo states in a soft yet demanding tone that scrambles my brain cells, but I manage to nod my head in agreement.

Only after I agree, he grabs my hand and leads us over to an empty rectangular table. It has a single light bulb hanging above it. The bar isn't that big, with a couple of chairs and tables around the room, with a small bar off in the corner. Whatever is happening here, I'm not about to draw attention to myself.

As Mateo sits in the chair at the head of the table, he swiftly pulls me down in his lap, completely unbothered by my weight on him. Suddenly the men standing around slowly sit in the remaining chairs around the table. "Mat, nice to see you here; we were under the impression your father would be meeting with us today," A pale-face man speaks nervously to Mateo. "Plans change. I'm here now. What's the news?" Mateo says coldly, which surprises me a bit; I'm unsure where to look, so I play with my fingers while mindlessly looking toward the ground.

As a low, raspy voice pitches in, "The River Family took out two of our men last night at the Bowling alley off of Main Street." "Dammit," Mateo curses sharply in response. The man continues, "Jose's little brother, Johnny was one of them. Jose's seeking revenge, he wants blood."

Somebody was killed? Mateo slowly places his hand on my lower back, which heightens my senses, saying, "Of course he does, where is he now? We need to keep him contained until we can track these guys, leave it up to Jose and the whole town will pay for this. Is this all?"

"One more thing, boss," The man says but doesn't continue, looking at me. As if reading his mind, Mateo asks, "Are you thirsty baby girl? The Bartender's name is Leo; he'll get you something nice." I smile lightly and stand, knowing this is not optional; I make my way over to the empty bar and quietly take a seat on one of the stools. "Hello," I say shyly.

"Hey Darlin, what can I get for you?" Leo's voice is cheery and doesn't give off the vibes of the men at the table. He's short with dirty blond hair and a bright smile. It's so odd seeing Mateo like this. It makes me realize how little I know about him; I'm even more curious as to why he wants me here, "Umm, I'm not sure; something sweet, I guess." He smiles, "Non-alcoholic, I'm sure."

I nod in response, and it takes him a few moments before he sets a strawberry virgin martini in front of me with a lemon on the rim. "Thank you," I said before lifting the glass and taking a sip. I glance over at the table of men, I'm no longer in earshot, but something isn't good by the looks of it. Soon they all stand and shake hands.

Mateo then walks over to me, "How's the drink?" he asks, stepping behind me and wrapping his hands around my waist, causing warmth to spread between my thighs as I respond, "It's sweet."

He removes his arms and holds out his hands, "Come on, let's go." Without another word, I place my hand in his and follow him out the door. Soon we're right back in the back seat of the SUV.

"Mellow Rd," he tells the driver, and we immediately take off. Some time goes by before I finally ask, "What was the purpose of that?" His brows knit in confusion as he asks, "purpose of what, baby girl?" I shift in my seat to face him better, "Why was I there?" He pulls me close and laces his fingers through mine, and I patiently wait for a response.

"Each of those men belongs to important families. I'm sure they've heard about us. Which I know has spread like fire by now. I'm just sending a message, that you are mine, Melina." He says not breaking eye contact as he speaks.

I'm not sure what I expect his answer to be, but at least he is being honest. I am his. I lean over to kiss him, and he grabs my face all too fast. He's crashing his lips into mine and I don't know what it's like to want to be owned, to want to belong to someone, but if this is it, then I'm spoken for. His lips move in hunger, and I still have no idea where we are going, but I want to get there. Any longer in this enclosed space, and I think he'll have me right here. I pull away to catch my breath.

Mateo flashes a smile when we make it to wherever we're going saying, "Come on, I want to show you something." He opens the door and holds out his hand for me. When I step out of the vehicle, I'm face to face with a one-story contemporary home, the driveway looks at least half a mile from the street, and there is a koi pond near the front door. "Where are we?" I ask as the black SUV slowly pulls away, leaving us alone in the driveway, "My place," he says, once again taking my hand.

The house is large and modern looking. I notice there are no neighbors, and it is not as heavily guarded like his father's home. I seem to never know what to expect, but I am surprised the inside actually looks like he lives here. A heavily packed bookcase takes up an entire wall in the living room. Two couches face a center coffee table but no TV.

Mateo speaks, "I'm going to go change but make yourself at home. I won't be long." I nod in response as I feel my stomach ache from hunger. He disappears down the hallway, and I quickly find my way into the kitchen.

A long glass dining table with two chairs on each end, and a silver two-door fridge sits in between a sliding door and grey countertops. I head to the refrigerator and pull out some lunch meat, a head of lettuce, tomato, and loaf of bread, finding comfort in the kitchen, I finish making two sandwiches and sit at the dining table. I devour my food and drink down a glass of water.

Soon, Mateo comes into view in casual jeans and shirtless "If you're hungry, I could have ordered us something to eat," he says as he leans against the threshold of the kitchen. The way he is so casually confident makes me warm, "No, it's fine. I made you one too."

He makes no attempt to move as he watches me set my plate in the sink. "Melina," He calls. I don't skip a beat as I respond, "Yes?" I look over at him innocently as he starts walking towards me. I wait patiently as he stops behind me moving to whisper in my ear, "I want to be inside you." My breath gets caught in my throat. He grabs my waist and presses into my ass, "I want to feel your warmth around me."

He snakes his hand into the front of my pants, quickly finding my clitoris, and I release an involuntary moan. "Is that what you want?" he asks as he moves his fingers in slow circular motions. I moan again, "Yes, please."

I close my eyes as he picks up the pace, and I feel his cock harden against me, causing me to press myself more into him. "Fuck" He groans as he slips a finger further down, revealing how wet I am.

He turns me around, crashing his lips into mine; I throw my arms around his neck as I feel him reach for the button of my jeans. He struggles slightly, trying to take them off. "No more pants," He growls once he finally gets the button undone and shoves my pants to the ground, which causes me to laugh, but my laugh turns into a gasp as he's quickly on his knees in front of me and his lips meet with mine. "Oh my..." I trail off as his tongue flicks against me as I shiver from the pleasure.

He switches between kisses and licks, and I feel my legs going weak, and muster nothing but moans. He stands smiling with the glisten of my juices on his lips, "I don't remember chocolate tasting so good," He reaches for my hips and turns me around again, gently pushing me forward so that I'm bent over the sink; his pants quickly meet mine at our ankles and he slides inside me bare, "Fuck baby girl." He starts off by slowly pulling out before going back in again. I breathe out, "Oh god."

"You like that?" He picks up the pace and slaps my ass, causing me to moan again. I pant breathlessly, "Yes."

"That's a good girl," he feels so good inside me, and the way he talks to me, ugh, it is almost hard to explain. I don't want this feeling to stop, I reach down to rub my clit, and the combo only causes me to moan louder. "Your mine baby," He moans. "Yes Mateo," I gasp. He spanks me again and growls, "Say it!"

"I'm yours!" I cry out and start to gasp as my body begs for a release, but he slows down. "Not yet, baby girl," He completely pulls out of me, and I poutingly turn around to face him. He discards his pants entirely and walks over to the fridge. He pulls out whip cream & caramel drizzle.

I quickly kick my feet out of my jeans, leaning slightly on the counter. I try not to think about how half naked I am in his kitchen. "What on earth are you planning to do with those?" I ask as he sets only the whip cream down on the counter. He smirks, "adding toppings to my dessert."

He's standing completely naked in front of me, I reach out and run my hands down his chest to his torso. This man feels like a sculpture, like the gods took a little extra time on perfecting him, and here he was looking at me with hunger in his eyes.

After a moment of me exploring, he takes off my shirt and bra, then opens the lid of drizzle and pours it on my breast; I laugh, "I'm going to be all sticky now." He smiles, quickly setting the bottle down and wraps one arm around my waist, and cups one of my breasts, pulling me into him. I can feel his cock press against me, let alone his entire naked body flat against mine. He follows the caramel drizzle first near my collarbone and onto my nipple. My head goes back as I release a soft breath at the contact. "oh," I gasp as he cleans one boob and moves on to the other.

"Mateo," saying his name causes him to groan. "I want to taste you too," I say, and he leans in to kiss me, wrapping his arms around me; we slowly trade places.

He's now leaning against the counter, allowing me to move at my own pace. I move to my knees, trying not to take my eyes off of him, and he whispers something about a pretty face.

Grabbing his cock first, I feel the thickness of him in my hands. He is hot and heavy, and I already wanted him back inside me. I grab the whip cream and spray some on the length of his cock. I begin to take him in my mouth; I can taste myself on him, as well as the cream, as he moans.

I lick and swirl my tongue until I've completely cleaned his cock, then I pick up the pace and start to close my eyes. He raises my chin slightly, "No baby girl, I want to see you; I want to see those beautiful brown eyes while I'm deep in your throat." I whimper as I feel his cock throb in my mouth, this man and his words.

I can hear the sloshing of my saliva as I quicken my pace. "Fuck" he moans again, "I want to fuck your pretty little face," he groans, grabbing my head and begins pounding into my mouth. I whimper, the only sound I can muster. "Fuck yes," he says, not taking his eyes off me. I try to focus on breathing as he praises me, "Such a good girl." Before I know it, he's pulling me off my knees and up to his lips.

I can get lost in him, I am getting lost in him. "I want you inside me Mateo," I beg, quickly leaning over the counter. He spreads my legs and slips inside me with ease. I begin to circle my clit as he takes no time pounding into me. "Come for me, baby girl," he says.

"Oh, yes!" I respond, trying my hardest not to lose rhythm. He slaps my ass, "Mine!" I feel myself getting closer, "Oh, Mateo!" He spanks me again as he keeps a rhythm, "Yes, baby girl, let it out for me."

I whisper desperately, "Just a little more." His huffs and puffs fill my head, "Oh, god!" Each stroke brings me closer until I reach the edge, finally toppling over, "Mateo, oh god! I'm coming!" He holds me as my legs start to give. "Yes, baby girl," He doesn't stop thrusting, soon following behind me, "Such a good dirty girl." He moans before pulling out, grabbing himself, and spilling onto my ass. Then collapsing over me.

We stay like that for a few moments catching our breath and regaining the energy to move. He grabs his shirt and wipes his cum off of me. We stand still, completely naked, and he's grinning at me, still taking deep breaths, "We should shower if we're still going over to your grandparent's house."

10. Questions that Need Answers

We had to stop at my place again because I was uncomfortable wearing my soiled clothes to my grandparents' house. Mateo is apparently serious about me not wearing pants anymore, as he was frustrated to realize I was low in the skirt and dress department.

He said we'd be going to the mall first thing in the morning, and truthfully if it means easier access, I'm not to upset about it. It's nightfall as we arrive, and as promised, only one SUV followed us here and was not so noticeably parked nearby.

"Are you okay?" Mateo asks as we reach the porch. "Just nervous," I respond, trying to shake away the actual fear of how my grandfather will react. "It'll be okay," he says, grabbing my hand as my grandmother opens the door.

"Hi, Grandma!" I say as her face breaks into a smile once she sees me. "Hey, Baby," she says excitedly, reaching to wrap me in a hug. She looks at Mateo, "And who's this bright young man?" She steps back, eyeing him. I lace my fingers back into his, "This is Mateo." She grins, "Well, you look like a handsome young man.

Come, come on inside. I've just placed dinner on the table!" She opens the door, and I guide Mateo inside.

My grandfather is already sitting at the table, sipping his beer. He does a double take and nearly spits up his beer when his eyes land on us. "Who the hell is this!" He barks but doesn't get up from his seat.

Mateo reads him well and says sternly, "Hello Sir, my name is Mat Crow. I'm Melina's boyfriend." I don't know what it is, but as my grandfather continues to stare at him, something changes in his eyes. My grandmother cuts in, "Now honey, you be nice, go on dear, sit." Mateo and I quickly take a seat.

Christ, I know this wasn't going to be fun, but the tension in the air is choking me. As if he can read my mind, Mateo places his hand on my thigh, giving me a light squeeze, then proceeds to rub my thigh as he turns to speak to my grandmother, "You guys have a lovely home." she replies, "Oh, thank you, dear." she places the final dish on the table, "It's not much, but we love it anyway."

My grandfather doesn't take his eyes off Mateo, but Mateo's confidence doesn't waiver. Me on the other hand, I feel like an ant when I'm around him; I wish I could lie about something coming up so we can leave. As my grandmother sits, he finally speaks more calmly, "Melina," he calls my name, "How's the new house?"

Discomfort rises in my chest as I respond, "Umm, it's okay. It's nice." He looks at me as I try to look everywhere else. "Hmm, you sure you don't miss your *old* bedroom," As he says this, my heart drops into my stomach, and a bile builds in my throat. I reply quietly, "No, I don't." He stares at me a moment more before turning to Mateo, "So Mat." Venom laces his voice, "I'm sure there are plenty of women you could have chosen. Why my granddaughter?"

"Honey!" My grandma quickly taps him, glaring at him. He snaps, "What women?! I want to know how they met; can't I be concerned for my granddaughter's safety?" She tsks at him before saying, "My apologies, he doesn't know how to speak to people; I blame the old age." Mateo responds unfazed, "Oh, rest assured, she is very safe with me."

My grandmother changes the subject, "That's great to hear. Anyway, who's hungry? This food is not going to eat itself!" She begins picking up grandfather's plate and loading it with chicken and green beans. "Pass me the cornbread, dear," She asks and I reach for the bowl as Mateo's hand still rests on my thigh.

Leave it to my grandfather; he doesn't back down so quickly, "Crows aren't good company, you know." He begins eating the chicken on the plate in front of him. Mateo laughs, "Well, that depends on how you've acquainted them." Mateo watches him with just as much intensity. I've learned that if you ignore him, he eventually stops talking. But Mateo keeps engaging him, and it's making my heart race.

"Umm, Mateo," I whisper. When he hears the unevenness in my voice, he turns to me, and his face softens. "Can we get a little air?" I ask sheepishly.

"Excuse us," Mateo says politely, not taking his eyes off me as he stands, taking my hand and leading us out into the front yard. As soon as the front door closes behind us, I take a deep breath, "It feels like a pissing battle in there." I watch him pace the yard. He's opening and closing his hands and running them through his hair, "For fuck's sake, does he always act like that?"

I don't respond. "I can see why you got out of there; I just wish you'd left sooner," he says, taking a deep breath. "He's just trying to get a reaction out of you," I say, continuing to watch him pace. He sarcastically laughs, "He's trying for much more than that." He finally looks at me, "He makes you uncomfortable, doesn't he?"

When I don't reply, he rushes over to me, anger and sadness taking over his features at the same time. "Oh baby girl," he whispers, clasping both sides of my face, looking me dead in the eyes. He asks ever so lightly, "It's him, isn't it?" My vision blurs as water pools in them, and he continues, "He's the reason for your nightmares, isn't he?"

"They're not nightmares," I try to defend myself. Mateo sees right through me, "Baby, I know nightmares when I see them. You talk in your sleep as well, remember?" We've only slept together twice. Has he really read me like an open book? "He blames me for her death, you know, my mothers," I croak, not holding back the tears any longer, "and he's punished me for it."

"Come on," he says, quickly tugging my hand as he signals the SUV to pull in front of the house. "We can't just leave!" I'm sobbing as he continues to pull me. "Melina baby, I can't sit here and do nothing, knowing what he's done to you," He trails off, and I can see the anger taking over. "Please don't hurt him," I beg, even though I know he deserves whatever's coming to him, but it'll hurt my grandmother.

"I can't promise you that."

"Mateo," I say, but he forces me into the car. "No, please!" I beg as he shuts the door and tells the driver something. I'm too busy trying to pound on the glass, "Mateo, don't! Please!" I knew this man was dangerous; after all, he warned me. "Mateo!" I yell one more time. Mateo pulls out his phone, and I hear him say, "Dad, I have a problem." I can't see him through the window, but I know he's still there.

The car pulls off, and I don't turn away until I'm sure we're far from view. "Oh god!" I cry, looking for my phone, realizing I left it on the table in the house; I cry more "No, no, no."

I put my head in my hands before yelling at the driver, "Where the hell are you taking me!" but of course, he doesn't respond. I feel helpless, and I sob more. I lay down on the seat and cry uncontrollably until I can't cry anymore.

I think I cried myself to sleep as I'm suddenly awakened by one of his security guys as he opens the door. "Where are we?" I ask again with less energy, but they ignore me. I slowly slide out of the car and realize we're back at his father's house. It's dark out and I don't know what time it is.

Sofia greets me at the door, "Come inside, hurry." We walk silently into the living room and sit on a couch. "I know he deserves it," I whisper. "I just don't want it to happen like this," My eyes start watering again as I look at the floor. "I'm sorry you have to see this side of our family," she says.

"Mat's a great guy, but after losing our mother, He does not take disrespect, let alone harm to our family, lightly," She lifts my face to look at her, "And the moment he took an interest in you, you became our family." I sniffle at her words, "Is he going to kill him?" I ask.

"I'm not sure," She says half-heartedly. I don't like how fast news travels here; I wrap myself in a hug, suddenly feeling exposed. "Do you have a cellphone?" I ask her, remembering where mine is.

She nods but hesitates before putting it in my hands. I sigh, "I just want to check on my grandmother." She hesitates more before saying, "I hope you understand what you're a part of now." Then she lays it in my hand.

I ignore her subtle threat. I just want to know if my grandmother is safe. I dial her number, and it rings. Once, twice, a third time, but it goes straight to voicemail, making me cry more. I need air.

I quickly hand Sofia back her cell phone and head back into the backyard, taking a gulp of the fresh air. I walk to the edge of the pool, looking up, noticing I'm not really alone; men in suits keep their distance, but they're still nearby.

So I sigh rolling up my jeans to stick my feet in the water. The cold water hurts my feet, but I don't take them out, knowing my feet will adjust soon. "It'll be okay," William's voice startles me. I turn to look at him in surprise, "Aren't you supposed to be with Mateo?" He laughs lightly taking a sip of whatever's in his cup, "Mat is a grown man, Melina; he can handle his own."

"Somehow, that doesn't make me feel better," I cross my arms, looking back towards the water. William laughs again, "It's amazing how much you resemble her, Lilian." The mention of her catches my attention, "You thought I was her when we first met, didn't you?"

"Yes, that I did," he takes another sip.

"Please, tell me about her," I ask quietly.

There's no way he can keep bringing her up and expect me not to ask questions. "Well, she was...she was everything to me," He smiles sadly as he joins me by the pool continuing, "We met at a bar; she was a server, and I was technically there on business." I sit quietly, not daring to interrupt. "She had brought me three complimentary shots by the time I figured she was digging me. I'll skip the details, but it wasn't long before we became inseparable. My father approved, and my mother loved her. Soon My father struck a deal with her father; I was going to get the woman of my dreams," He sounds so sad as he speaks of her.

"That was until she found out about my family's lifestyle. She didn't want any part of it. She said she didn't want to live in fear for her life or her children's." He takes a breath and his voice cracks a little, "She was a free spirit. I'll give her that. But a deal was a deal; before I knew it, she had run anyway. My father never told me what happened to her, but I always suspected he wasn't being truthful. Soon after, I met my late wife and had two beautiful children," He trails off.

This is the most someone has ever talked about her, "Do you know how she died?" I ask, curious if he knows. His face drops as he stands back up, "I'm afraid I'm not the right person to tell that story." He starts to walk away, but I can't accept that response.

"I was told she died because of me, some medical complication after delivering me."

He nods towards me once more, "If that's what they're telling you." My mind wraps up in the new novelty of my mother; I try to picture her being a waitress and sadly smile to myself. What does William mean by that, though? I realize just how tired crying has made me.

I get up from the pool and sneak away into the spare bedroom; comfort washes over me as I can still smell Mateo's scent in the room; I quietly undress and slowly sink into the covers. The bed feels much larger now that I am lying in it alone. I sigh, closing my eyes, allowing sleep to wash over me.

***

It's been two days since I was forced into that damn SUV, and I've heard absolutely nothing from Mateo or my grandparents. I sit quietly in the living room by myself. Sofia keeps offering me something to eat or drink, but I can't stomach anything.

I still haven't heard from anyone I care about, and doing anything other than sitting absolutely still is only going to make me cry. So much has happened in the past few days, let alone the classes I've missed, but that is the least of my worries. "Melina," A familiar voice calls me nervously from the door.

I look up, and there stands my bestfriend, "Jackie!" I run towards her, thankful if anything that she is okay. "Have you been in this mansion the whole time? Is that why you haven't answered your phone?" She asks. Relief washes over me, as we crash into a hug. Whatever's happening must not be too bad, right? After all, who else could have sent Jackie here?

"I'm so glad you're okay," I breathe out. "Yes?" she stretches the word in confusion. "Why wouldn't I be?" She asks, taking a step back to examine me. Coming to the realization she's unaware of what's going on, I put on my best smile, "Of course you are, I've just missed you."

"I miss you too. Now If you don't have a juicy story to tell me about your whereabouts, I will walk right back out that door," Jackie says jokingly. I smile, "Of course, I have so much to tell you." Her face lights up in excitement. "Let's go somewhere a little more open," I take her hand and lead her to the backyard. "Oh my god! You sure know how to pick them!" she praises, looking around the house, as we walk to the backyard. I don't bother mentioning, it's his dad's house.

We plop down on a couple of suntan chairs by the pool, and she waits patiently for me to begin. "We had sex. Very good sex, I might add," I start off, and she squeals like a high school cheerleader. "Oh my god! Yes! Tell me everything, every little detail!"

So I do. I tell her about the first night we slept together in my bedroom, the night in the spare bedroom. I even tell her what I learned of my mother, Lilian. Though, I don't say anything about Mateo finding out about my grandfather or what he has or has not done to him.

When Jackie's caught up, Sofia walks up to introduce herself, "Hi, I'm Mat's sister." She says, waving to her and then sitting with us. "Oh my god, and he has siblings!" Jackie squeals, waving back. One of the servants brings us tea and a small charcuterie board. It is still very weird having people bring you food or drinks; I feel like I'm being rude. "Wow, Melina! You landed a good one; I am so happy for you!" She squeals with more excitement.

I finally relax a little, coming to accept not knowing what's happening outside of this house. Of course, I get her to talk about her time with Troy, and she's grinning the entire time she speaks about him.

"I'm glad you had fun, Jackie," I force a smile; I mean, I really am happy for her; I just hate sitting here with no contact with anyone, especially him. She looks at me, "Melina are you okay? I mean, really. It's not like you to miss class?" I nod, "Yes, of course, I'm okay; I'm happy. Here with him, I mean."

Sofia's phone rings, and she steps away to answer the call. Jackie places her hands on mine, "If you are happy, then I'm happy." She then gets a text, "It's Troy, he's asking when I'll be back. Should I tell him tomorrow morning?"

"No, no, it's fine, you can go," I smile. "Are you sure?" She stands excitedly. I nod, "Yes, it's fine." I move to stand up, "I'll walk you out." We walk back in giggles as she awes about how spacious the house is or how fancy something looks.

When we reach the front door, I say, "Be safe, okay? I'll text you when I can." She smiles, giving me one final hug before turning to get into the back seat of the SUV. I stand in the doorway of the threshold, waving her goodbye as the car begins to leave. I shut the door when she's out of view, and Sofia's waiting behind me, "That was Mat, he's at the hospital." My heart drops, and I can't help but think the worst.

We hurry into the back of another SUV. He really killed him, didn't he? How could he do that to me? We sit silently the entire ride as my mind gets the best of me. This hospital is one I haven't been to before; We approach through a private entrance before following the driver in as two men in black follow close behind us.

After reaching the desk, Sofia guides us through the halls before we stop in front of a patient room door, "I'll be out here; you go on it." I take a deep breath before reaching for the door handle and walking in.

It's a little surprising how spacious the room is, the walls are tan with white trim, giving off warmth and homey vibes. I walk inside, immediately seeing my grandma sitting beside the patient bed, in tears. There's a little couch by the door that faces the patient's bed, as well a 5ft luscious green plant near the wall.

I finally look at my grandfather, expecting to see him in the worst condition, but he doesn't have a single bruise on him. "Grandma," I say quietly as she raises her head. "Oh, Melina," She gets up and quickly embraces me into a hug. "Are you okay?" I ask as she releases me. "Yes dear, I'm fine, just worked up is all," She turns to point at him, "Your grandfather went into cardiac arrest, later that night after dinner, after you left."

"Cardiac arrest?" I say in confusion. "Yes, the doctors said he took one too many sleeping pills," She's wiping her tears away and moving to sit beside him again. I refuse to look at him; even in this quiet state, he has something over me. Besides, I have questions that need answers.

11.No excuses, No messages, Nothing.

She's been sitting beside him for the past thirty minutes now as we wait for more information from the doctor. I grow impatient, and I am still waiting to hear from Mateo.

I stand from my seat on the couch, "I'm going to grab something to drink. Would you like something?" She responds, "No, thank you, dear," without taking her eyes off my grandfather.

I leave the room quietly, and Sofia is nowhere to be seen. Mateo's security is still here, so she should still be here. I walk towards the lobby, where little to no other people are waiting. Passing the desk, I head for the cafeteria to grab a coffee. I still don't see her anywhere, so I return to the room.

As I approach, I see Mateo standing there, slowly pacing in front of the door, and a wave of different emotions wash over me as I begin to fast walk towards him. My eyes start to water, feeling relief and anger all the same.

"Mateo," I say as he closes the distance between us, wrapping me in a hug. "Hey, baby girl," he speaks softly. "How could you-"

I begin, but he places a finger over my lips, cutting me off; he grabs my hand and pulls me into a nearby empty patient room.

He locks the door and shuts the blinds as I move to sit on the bed. "I'm so sorry, Baby girl," He begins, and I can't help but sigh in relief. "I didn't know you left your phone in the house; I didn't mean to leave you in the dark like that," He stands by the door running his hands in his hair. "What happened to him?" I ask, wiping my face. He huffs, "Nothing, unfortunately."

I look at him in disbelief and notice the bruises on his knuckles as he opens and closes his hands. He sighs, "Natalie has caused more problems. Her father now wants my head. I had to deal with him first. We gave your grandfather a sedative, which his heart reacted negatively to. I brought him here and left." I take a deep breath of relief, but somehow feel a small pang of disappointment.

"Did her father hurt you?" I ask, still looking at his bruises. I want to be near him, to touch him. The space between him and the bed feels all too far, so I walk over to him as he speaks, "I'll spare you the details." He places his hands around my waist and I move to touch his face. His eyes look so tired, yet they burn into mine. "Did you know about my mother?" I ask curiously as my hands wander to his hair. "Yes," He responds. He knew? "For how long?" I question scrunching my nose and removing my hand from his face.

He begins, "Since you met my father. The way he kept looking at you. It didn't sit right with me. It kept me up all night." Wow, and he didn't tell me. "Do you know how she died?" I'm expecting the same response as his father, but he doesn't say anything. I move to take a step back as the feeling of dread creeps up my throat, but he doesn't release me. So I ask again, "Mateo. How did she die?" His eyes silently plea as he says my name, "Melina." Panic rises in my chest as he continues, "I don't think this is a good time."

"A good time?" I question him trying to wiggle out of his arms. I huff, "There's no such thing as good time." He finally lets me go. "What happened to her?" My voice trembles, as I try to hold back from crying again.

"You have to understand. I didn't lie when I said my family is dangerous. There are rules to follow, Melina. Your grandfather made a deal with mine, and she broke it," His voice is pleading along with his eyes.

My vision blurs as the tears unwillingly build in my mine. "Oh god," I whisper as my heart sinks. He continues, "He felt she had spit on the family name, took him as a joke." I take a step back, bumping into the bed, "Don't say it." I feel like my heart is tearing out of my chest.

His eyes are just as blurry as mine as he whispers, "My grand-father had your mother, murdered." I broke, I mean, I physically broke down; my heart is so overwhelmed by all of the emotions, all the highs and lows over the past couple of days, my knees go weak, and my vision grows dark; I hear him yell my name before slipping into darkness.

***

I wake to the sunlight on my face. I try to move only to realize I am hooked up to a bunch of medical machines; I gasp, sitting up, realizing I'm still in the hospital and now in a hospital gown. I recognize the room I'm in and everything that's happened comes crashing down on me. Some machines start beeping loudly, and a couple of nurses rush into the room.

My eyes instantly lock on Mateo as he enters the room after them. He looks like he's been in an accident, his hair is a mess, and his eyes have dark circles around them. His shirt seems stained, and his pants are dirty. After they check to confirm my heart rate, they encourage me not to work myself up, and they leave the room.

He stands by the door, closing it behind them. I am heartbroken. I want to be mad at him because what are the chances, all I want right now is for him to tell me it'll be okay. But I don't believe it will be.

"You fainted," he says, breaking the silence. Is that what that was? "How long was I out?" I ask rubbing my forehead. "For a few hours," He takes a deep breath. "Were you ever going to tell me about her death?" I ask, exhausted. He cautiously walks over to the edge of the bed, now speaking softly, "I wanted to, but I thought if I did... you'd leave."

"I don't think that was your choice to make," I say lowly. What kind of person would want to stay with someone who was a descendant of their mother's murder anyway. I shake my head, not wanting to answer that question, not yet, anyway. And if Mateo's father isn't my father, then who is?

"Where are my grandparents?" I ask, trying to stand up. I feel a little shaky at first but quickly gain my balance, I begin pulling off the cords, and he tries to stop me, "Woah, what are you doing?" He reaches for my hands, forcing them into his. I struggle, "I need to see them." His grip doesn't budge, "and if you faint again?"

"I'm not going to," I huff, still trying. "Why are you being difficult?" He says in frustration. I look up at him, "Difficult? I'm being difficult. You were just ready to kill my grandfather-"

He cuts me off, frustration clear in his voice, "He assaulted you!" We stare at each other, tears threatening my eyes again, frustration in his. But I won't back down; I need to hear it from them. "Get these off of me, or I will never speak to you again," I say, tugging again, and he releases my arms.

He curses the entire time but helps me remove the cords and some needles from the machine. Still in the gown, I begin looking for my clothes. He picks up a small bag and hands me a flowy black dress as if he knows what I am looking for. "Where are my clothes?" I ask, confused.

"The nurses cut them off of you."

"Great," I say, putting on the dress feeling less exposed than in the gown. "Where are my grandparents?" I ask, and he opens the door and quietly leads me back to their room. Before I enter the room, he stops me.

Slowly he lifts his hand to my face, and I rest against his cool palm before he brings my face close to his, wrapping me in a kiss. His lips move urgently against mine, not lustfully but intently, like it's the last time.

He releases me slowly and reaches into his pocket pulling out my cell phone. Saying nothing, he places it in my hands.

I feel a knot in my throat as I force myself to turn away and into the room. As much as I want to check it, I know it's not going to help right now. My grandmother is right where I saw her last, sitting at his bedside. Seeing him now makes me sick.

My grandmother doesn't notice me entering the room, so I sit quietly beside her, "Has the doctor said anything?" She doesn't reply immediately, and for a moment, I really think she isn't going to. "They said all his levels seem to be in good shape, now we just have to wait for him to wake up," she finally responds. I try to comfort her, but I know I don't mean it, "I'm sorry grandma."

"It's okay dear," she finally turns to look at me, and her eyes are bright red from crying, "They said it happens to over 80% of patients."

"How are you holding up?" I ask her.

"Oh, I'm fine dear," she says, but the red in her eyes hint at otherwise. I know this is the worst time to try and probe her for answers, but I do anyway. "What really happened to my mother?" I ask. She sighs sadly, "She fell in love." Looking back at my grandfather, she continues, "Your mother had such a strong personality. She drew everyone in, even the bad kind of people."

She refuses to look at me as she continues, "Anybody could easily fall in love with her, Melina, and everyone she met, did. Instead of doing the right thing, your grandfather saw your mother as a dollar sign when the wrong people showed interest. I tried to tell him that she was exploring, she was young, but he was a stubborn man. And sure enough, when he realized he made the wrong choice, we tried to hide her from them, and we did, for a few years-"

I cut her off, "So you knew who Mateo was?"

"No, I never saw them or even knew their names, but I knew my daughter and my husband were in real trouble. So, we moved here and tried to keep a low profile, but Lilian was too impressionable. Years later, she met another man, and then she got pregnant with you. We knew the pregnancy wouldn't be safe, considering her having a bunch of doctor appointments, which meant constantly being in public. But she wanted you."

She pauses, tears threatening her eyes once more, "We tried to keep our eyes on her, we really did, but they must have known where we were. I left her for five minutes to check on you in the hospital's nursery. Five minutes." Tears are running down her face, and as she realizes the weight of her words. She quickly wipes them away, "Excuse me dear, I need a breath of air."

Shock is an understate as I stand, trying to run over everything I now know. As everything falls into place, rage takes over me. I looked up at the man I feared my entire life. "This is all your fault," I whisper. When he doesn't respond, I stand and yell, "You selfish bastard!"

The rhythm of his heartbeat doesn't change as he lay motionless, "And you blamed me?! You made me think this was my fault! My mother is dead because of you!" I know he can't hear me, but I am so furious he doesn't respond, "You took advantage of me, you took away *my* childhood, all because you fucked up!" I slam my hands at the edge of his bed.

"You don't deserve to wake up," I croak as tears take over and weakness fills my bones. I allow them to fall, as a new wave of sensibility washes over me. After a few minutes, I wipe my face, "I hope you rot in hell." Just as I spur the last of my venom, my grandmother re-enters the room; she pauses at the door, taking in the scene.

Still angry, I turn to her, "Did you know?" She slowly shuts the door and I continue, "Did you know he used to creep into my room every Saturday night when I was a little girl?" She calls me, "Melina, baby," and slowly walks towards me.

"Hmm, did you? Did you know why I hated every time you worked overtime? Didn't it concern you as to why your eleven-year-old granddaughter suddenly went mute for six months?" As she gets closer to me, I stand to move from her reach. "I'm so sorry, Melina, I just," She began as her eyes water again.

That's all I needed to hear; I feel my blood run cold as I move towards the door, "You knew." I shake my head, my voice cracking as I speak, "That's why you always took me for ice cream Sunday morning or bought me every Barbie doll I wanted for Christmas. Buying my love to make up for the guilt?"

As if my heart can handle any more, she tries to make an excuse, "I didn't want to believe it." I wipe my face cutting her off again, "Oh, you didn't want to believe it." I shake my head sarcastically in agreement, "You're just as bad as he was." I leave, not wanting to hear anything else from her.

I look around through blurry eyes. I just want to escape from here; everything I thought I knew and loved, I had it all wrong. I keep walking, wiping away tears as I look for Mateo. I notice most of his security guards are gone, except one.

He approaches me as I make it to the lobby, "This way, Miss Sky." I don't protest as he leads me out of the building and into another SUV. I cry quietly, allowing myself to grieve.

After a while, I finally decide to check my cell phone. I see a bunch of texts and missed calls from Mateo that night, as well as missed calls and messages from Jackie, the most recent one from her was 30 minutes ago:

Jackie: Hey love, you said you'd text me. All good?

Me: Yeah, sorry, all good

I reply, riding in silence until the vehicle stops. When the door opens, I am surprised to see we are back at my house, "Is Mateo coming?" I try to ask, but of course, the man in black simply opens and closes the door for me.

As I walk inside, everything is exactly how I left it. Nothing seemed affected or bothered by all this new knowledge I had. I shut the front door behind me and decide a shower would help.

I let the hot water run down my head and back. I stand there for a while, replaying all my experiences in my head. I almost don't notice when the water starts to run cold. I turn it off and ring out my hair; grabbing the nearest towel, I wrap myself in and recheck my phone:

Jackie: Okay, good to hear!

Me: Yeah, I'm back at the house

I close out our conversation and open Mateo's, but there's nothing new. So, I send a quick message asking where he is. I sit my phone down and begin drying off and putting on some lotion. Walking back into my bedroom to my dresser, I notice the picture I have of my mother and reach for my necklace. I whisper, "I am so sorry." I stare at the frame differently now. I am so sad for her.

Getting dressed, putting some pajama pants on and a spaghetti strap, I tie my hair in a low bun as it is still dripping water. I walk into the kitchen, thinking food might help. Seeing the tub of ice cream Jackie and I shared, I settle for that. I sit in the living room and turn on a random R&B playlist. I wait and wait, but there is still no response from him.

So by the time I finish the remainder of the tub, I decide to call him. The line rings three times before going to voicemail, and I can't help but panic, so I call again. I hold my breath as it rings, once, twice, three times, voicemail. I don't know if he is purposely ignoring me or if something happened to him, and I have no way of finding out.

***

Weeks went by.

Still no contact. I zero in on my classwork, catching back up on my classes and supporting Jackie by being her test dummy every time she has to submit a fashionable outfit for class. Doing anything distracting, I pick up as many extra hours at work as I possibly can—anything to keep me from thinking of him. None of the guys have seen him in weeks.

My grandfather never woke up, eventually flat lining sometime in the night. I blocked my grandmother's phone number, but she still tries to write me letters and has popped up once or twice at school and my house.

"The funeral's tomorrow, are you going to go?" Jackie asks as I sit on the floor in front of her, letting her play with my hair. "I don't want to go," I say truthfully. "But I feel like I should," I sigh.

"Well, if you do decide to go, I support you," She says looking at me and placing a hand on my shoulder. I smile weakly at her, "Okay."

Later on, I find myself drawing in my sketchbook; thirty minutes in, I realize I am drawing *his* face, and by the time I realize it's him, I complete his eyes, and they are now staring back at me.

I can't help but cry. It's been so long since I've seen his face or heard his voice. Each day that passes is forcing me to accept the realization Mateo left me with nothing. No excuse, no message, no reason, nothing.

12. I'VE HAD ENOUGH

Jackie knocks on my door, all dressed in black, "Are you ready?" I turn to face her in a black short sleeve, mid-thigh, tight dress, "Yes, I'm ready." My black stockings make it bearable to wear as I keep fiddling with my cleavage showing. She walks into my room to lightly pop my hand, "Stop messing with it, it's fine, you have big tits, now let's go."

I grab my cross bag as She drags me all the way out of the house. I get into the back seat of her car as Troy sits in the passenger seat. I don't really want to ride with anyone, but Jackie refused to let me drive alone.

The funeral home is conveniently across the street from the cemetery where my mother's buried in. I feel chills as we pass. Thankfully we aren't early; everyone starts taking their seats as the ceremony begins. Sitting down in the back, I can see the back of my grandmother's head up front.

I see Elijah's family a few rows closer, and Jackie's Dad is even here. The pastor begins, "We have joined together on this day to celebrate the life of a loving husband and father." I fight the urge to roll my eyes as Jackie places her hand on mine.

The pastor continues, "He was a valued voice in the community, helping a neighbor in need, head of the neighborhood watch committee five years in a row. Always headstrong and fought hard against the economy to provide for his family, working long days to ensure food was on the table. If there ever were a man we could aspire to be, it would be him."

I eventually zone out the rest of the ceremony until I hear my grandmother's voice. She stands over his casket with watery eyes and a tissue in hand. Her dress is ankle length and hugs her body loosely. She doesn't focus on anything specific as she turns to face the crowd, "First, I'd like to thank you all for coming. It means the world to me. I won't talk about how great he was; you all knew that."

She pausing lightly smiling, "We were lucky enough to watch our baby girl grow up, and we thought we'd be able to watch our grandkids grow up as well while we sat in rocking chairs on the porch of our dream home, but the world had different plans." She looks over at his casket, "Kiss our baby girl for me." She kisses her fingers and then plants them on his coffin. Her eyes land on me when she turns around, and my heart sinks.

I can't stand sitting here, listening to them talk about him like he was so great. "I'll be back," I whisper over to Jackie, and she gives me a sad smile. I quietly leave the building.

I can feel the cool morning air on my cheeks and hear the quiet songs of the morning birds. I feel like someone's watching me as I walk across the street through large metal gates. I feel the atmosphere change as I walk pass gravestone after gravestone. I still remember where she rests; reaching her doesn't take me long.

My mother's gravestone is clean and small. A fresh bouquet of lilies lay across her. I breathe out, "Hi, Mom." Tears brim my eyes as I stare, "I'm sorry it took so long." I slowly sit down in front of her, "I wish we could have gotten to know each other. Maybe things could have gone better for us." I sigh, looking around before continuing, "You stole William's heart, and his family ruined your life."

The tears begin to fall from my face, "and I fear Mateo has stolen mine." I wrap my arms around myself as saying his name physically hurts, "He left me, just like you left *him*."

I lean into my shoulder and take a few breaths trying to stop myself from crying so hard, "But I'm not going to let it ruin my life, and I'm not going to live in fear, or regret." I wipe my face as I sit, letting the time go by as I try to calm down.

Suddenly I hear footsteps behind me. I stand up, turning around to see my grandmother. She stops a few feet away from me, "You know your grandfather hated visiting her grave; she reminded him of his guilt."

I don't respond as I'm trying to collect myself. She sighs, moving to close the distance between us, "You've stopped taking my calls." I stay silent, and she continues, "Well, anyway, I'm not sure if you've been getting my letters."

"I haven't," I lie.

"Melina, I am so sorry. Whenever you're ready, I'll still be here, and I love you," Now, in front of me, she places a closed envelope in my hands. She says nothing else, and I watch as she walks away. Looking past her, I see everyone flooding out of the building. I turn around to face my mother's grave, "It was nice seeing you again, Mom."

I tuck the envelope in my bag and make my way out of the cemetery to find Jackie and Troy. I walk back, feeling that weird feeling of being watched again. I casually look over my shoulders, but I don't see anyone else around me.

Jackie stands at the entrance of the building, patiently waiting for me; as soon as I approach her, she says, "I'm so proud of you, Melina," and hugs me. "Come on; The Reception is at Elijah's house," She takes my hand, and we head back to her car. "Can we stop at the house first? I want to change and take my car," I say, getting into the back seat again. She gives me a parental stare but agrees.

Pulling up to the house, I quickly get out of the car and wave to them, "I'll see you there."

I head inside and into my closet; since I've volunteered to be her design model, Jackie has made me a few beautiful pieces. I scan through a few outfits and decide on a matching skirt set she made for me. I keep my stockings on as I head to the hallway bathroom. I use the toilet and move to wash my hands.

I notice a pink box in the trash can. I quickly wipe my hands on the towel and reach for it. "Oh my god!" I say as my heart skips a beat. I grab a tissue and pull out the used stick, and there are two clear blue lines. "She's pregnant?" I say out loud to myself.

Why hasn't she told me? Have I been that shitty of a friend not to notice? "Oh my god, my best friend is pregnant!" I say excitedly and rush to head over to Elijah's house.

When I pull up, I have difficulty finding a parking place as cars line the streets. Elijah's dad is the first person I bump into when entering the house. "Hey, Melina," he says softly. "Hi Michael," I briefly smile at him and scan the room. "I just wanted to say I'm here if you need me, okay kid," he says. I nod, trying not to ignore him as I look around the room. "Thank you" I say, quickly dismiss myself and walking towards the backyard.

I see many faces I don't recognize, including Elijah's and his mom's. I walk back inside, and just as I walk down the hall, the bathroom door opens, and Jackie comes out while wiping her face; she stops in her tracks when she sees me. I immediately push her back into the bathroom, closing the door behind us. I lock the door and whisper trying to contain my excitement, "You're pregnant!" Her eyes bulge a bit before she sighs. She re-wipes her face, "I just found out last night."

"Oh my god," I gasp. "You're pregnant, and I didn't notice!"

"To be fair, your mind has been wrapped up in a lot these past few weeks, and I didn't know either," She moves to lean against the sink and takes a deep breath, "Troy doesn't know."

"Are you going to tell him?"

"Yes, just not right now."

"Are you going to keep it?" I ask.

"I want to...I just don't know if he wants to."

I lean against the door, saying, "You won't know until you tell him." She sighs, moving to lean into me, "I know." I wrap my arms around her head and lightly brush her hair, "Whatever you choose, I support you. Okay." I whisper to her. Sshe nods, "Okay."

When ready, we return to the living room, where more people have gathered. "I'm going to go find Troy," She squeezes my hand as she walks away. I look around and see Elijah talking to his dad; I walk over to join them, "Hey, Elijah," I wave, "Hey Michael, sorry about early. I just had to use the bathroom."

"Don't worry about it," He smiles. "I'll be right back," he says walking away.

"Hey Melina, how are you feeling?" Elijah asks as I take a seat next to him. "I'm okay," I reply. "Do you know if my grandma is here?" I ask, curious as I have yet to see her. "She was here earlier but didn't stay too long; she said she was tired." Hmm.

"Are you sure you're, okay?" Elijah asks again. "Yes," I try to say intently, "I am fine, okay."

"Okay, just making sure. My dad said he saw you leave the ceremony early; he saw you walk into the cemetery across the street."

"Yeah, I did; I just wanted to say hi to my mom."

The reception went well, people came and went, but I wasn't ready to go home, so I lingered and helped clean up. It is well into the night now, and I am exhausted.

I find myself sitting on the porch, staring at the stars, lost in thought when Michael comes out to join me. "There you are," He says, handing me a cold soda and cracking open another. "Thanks," I respond, remembering what Elijah said earlier.

I crack open my soda and ask, "Did you know my mother?" Michael laughs, "Everyone knows Lilian." Seeing the sad expression on my face, he straightens his face and continues, "She was an amazing woman, Melina, just like you are."

He takes another sip of his drink, and I do the same, "Do you know who my dad was?" He looks around and sighs, then speaks into his drink, "I know him very well, unfortunately." I stare at him, as he's suddenly avoiding eye contact with me.

I sit and wait for him to elaborate, but he doesn't and continues to look everywhere else but at me, "Please tell me. I'm so tired of all the secrets." I plea setting down my soda. He takes a moment to respond speaking slowly, "You know I mean it when I call you mine, kiddo. You and Elijah, you're half siblings because you really are mine Melina."

A wave of shock fills me as I analyze every memory I have of him. From being at every birthday party to every doctor's appointment. Introducing me to Elijah, Stepping in for conferences and parent meetings when my grandparents couldn't. Every important moment in my life, He's been here all along. He's been with me all this time.

"My god," I whisper. I can't muster the energy for anger. I am emotionally exhausted. But relief and comfort oddly wash over me. "Michael," I say feeling a wall crumble inside of me. He guards my reaction, "Yes?"

"Please...Can I have a hug?" I ask. I think we both didn't expect that reaction, his eyes widen a moment, and he sets down his soda can before he moves to wrap me in a hug. "I am so sorry for not telling you Melina," he says, and I rest my head against him, as warmth fills my chest.

"Why didn't you?" I ask quietly. "Your grandparents didn't want me to. They only allowed me in your life as Uncle Michael," He responds still holding onto me. "Does Elijah know?" I ask, now pulling away from him. He takes another deep breath, "No, he doesn't."

"I think you should tell him," I stand feeling weight fall from my shoulders. "Good night, Michael and thank you," I say feel a little lighter now as I walk towards my car, sending Jackie a text that I'm on my way home. She left earlier with Troy, but I'm unsure where they went.

***

I didn't think I'd make it to this day. I stare at myself in the mirror. Seeing myself in the cap and gown makes it all too real. I'm finally graduating. Underneath I am wearing this beautiful emerald green hourglass dress. It's short-sleeved and glittery, designed by yours truly, Jackie Green.

We are touching up our faces and outfits in the auditorium bathroom. "Jackie," I laugh as she won't stop worrying about her little baby bump, "No one can see it, I promise. I mean, you look beautiful either way, but nobody will see your belly."

She finally sighs, looking at herself in the mirror; Her dress is bright red, floor length, and flowy. "Okay, okay," She zips up her graduation gown and fixes the tassel on her cap. She's curled her hair, framing her face beautifully. "We need to go!" I say, waiting for her impatiently.

She rolls her eyes as she grabs her phone, "I know." We walk out of the bathroom, soon joining the other graduates. "Good luck!" she squeals as we walk to our seats. Jackie is a couple of rows ahead of me, and Troy's only a few people ahead of me. I look at the crowd and try to see if Elijah made it, but I can't tell.

As the ceremony begins, sadness pulls at me, but I try to ignore it. We sit through a bunch of speeches from professors and two valedictorians. It feels like forever when they call my name. Adrenaline rushes through me, and I can't hear any specific voice as all the noise conjoins into a hum; I feel like an animatronic as I walk to the stage to receive my diploma, I shake the dean's hand, and we pose for a picture.

Looking at the crowd, I see Elijah, Michael, Hope, and Jackie's dad cheering in the stands. I'm overcome with joy and sadness all at once. I thought maybe he'd be here, if not for me but for Natalie, but I haven't seen her around campus since everything happened. It would hurt if they were here together, but at least I'd know. At least I'd have an answer. Getting my diploma was the highlight of the day; everything after feels like a crash course downhill.

We're out celebrating over dinner, sitting in a crowded restaurant waiting for the rest of our party to show up, "Oh my god, I still can't believe we did it! We freaking did it!" Jackie's screaming as a waiter brought out a pitcher of water. I cheer sarcastically, "Woohoo Now we have the rest of our life ahead of us to pay off our debt." Jackie's belly laughs, and Troy butts in, "Don't get too excited, we don't want to hurt the baby" He moves to rub her belly, and she rolls her eyes. Soon, Elijah and his family show up, bearing gifts.

"Hey, sis!" Elijah calls while taking the seat beside me, and I laugh, "I told you not to call me that." You can imagine just how Elijah reacted when he learned we were half-siblings. He didn't want to see or speak to me or Michael at first. Hope already knew, and maybe that's why she doesn't like me, but she'll never admit it.

Hope's belly is much more noticeable now as she sits next to Jackie, waving at us and immediately asking Jackie about her pregnancy. Michael stands in front of me with something behind his back, "Now, I know what you're going to say, but your grandmother personally asks me to make sure you read this one, so if you don't, I will," He reveals a white envelope with my name on it from my grandmother.

I don't know if she came to my graduation since I wasn't actually looking for her, "Okay, I'll read it." He slowly hands it to me, "I'm serious, don't yank my chain Melina." I lay out my hand, "I'm not; I promise I'll read it."

Once he hands it to me, I immediately put it in my cross bag, "I'll read it later." He frowns for a moment but lets it go. "So, what are your plans now that college is over?" Michael asks as he takes a seat next to his wife.

"I don't know about you guys, but I created a web page to start my clothing line, and thanks to Melina, we have a full and ready plus-size collection," Jackie unconsciously rubs her belly as she speaks, "Troy and I also have decided to move in together, we want to try and settle in before the baby comes." Everyone cheers and congratulates them.

"That's so good to hear," Hope says, happily. "If you need anything, anything at all, I'm here for you," she continues, resting her hand on Jackie's in reassurance. "I'm so happy for you, Jackie," I say, trying not to get teary eyed. "You've accomplished so much. I'm so proud of you," I say. Her eyes start to water, "Oh gosh, stop. You're going to ruin my makeup." We laugh and enjoy the rest of the night, discussing our plans for the future and reminiscing over the past.

The next day, Troy and Jackie were not kidding about being prepared for the baby. We spent the whole morning discussing how we'll rearrange the house, and the things Jackie wants to get rid of that could harm the baby. When I have an excuse to leave the house, I don't second guess it and leave almost immediately.

Jackie asks me to stop at the nearest baby store to pick up their gender-neutral bassinet. I quickly make my way in. The tiny baby clothes are too cute. It's tempting to pick out a few, but they still won't know the baby's gender for a couple more weeks, so I refrain. "Hi, my name's Melina. I'm picking up an order for Jackie Green!" I say to the cashier.

"Okay, I'll be right back!" She left for a few minutes before returning with a medium-sized box, "May I just see your ID," She asks while scanning the barcode. I smile briefly before reaching into my cross bag. I pause as I see the little white envelope from my grandmother still in there.

"Miss?" The cashier questions, and I laugh nervously, "Yeah, sorry." I quickly pull out my ID showing it to her as she asks another associate to help me load it into my car.

Surprisingly it fits with ease as I sit in the driver's seat, locking my doors as I put on my seatbelt. I reach to start the engine as my mind wanders back to the envelope. I sigh; I might as well get this over with. I pull the letter full of wrinkles out of my bag and carefully rip it open. I unfold two written out papers in my grandmother's handwriting, it read:

Dear Melina,

I cannot begin to imagine how hard life has been for you, and I'm partly to blame. You're such a strong woman, just as your mother was. She would have been very proud of the woman you've become. If it's not bold of me to ask, I pray you find it in your heart to forgive me. I'd like to think your grandfather is just as sorry; On the next page is the routing and account information, That he's put in your name. Written in his will, he asks only you have access as it was the money for your mother. I'm sure she'd like you to have it as well. I don't know how much is in there, and I know money can't buy happiness, but maybe this is a start.

I'll always love you, Grandma.

13. You Do, or You Don't

Three Years Later

It's almost midnight as I sit patiently at my kitchen counter. The night sky lights the room as the view from my apartment overlooks a beautiful central park. The city's usually alive at night, but tonight, you can only hear the rain as it hits the window. The clock on my bookshelf finally strikes twelve. "Happy Birthday," I whisper to myself before blowing out the purple candle on my chocolate cupcake.

I put the cupcake in my fridge, not in the mood to eat sweets this late. I begin to shut the door before briefly changing my mind, "Maybe just a little." I quickly swipe my finger in the frosting before closing the fridge completely.

Twenty-five years old, and I still feel the same, although I've gained a few more stretch marks. I walk over to the bookshelf and smile at the picture of my mom before reaching for my red notebook. My little apartment sits on the second floor, with white walls and small living room connected to a modernized kitchen.

Although I've added some vintage decor to minimalize the modernness, you can only do so much when you're renting.

I snag the pencil laying on my coffee table before settling on my coffee-stained couch. I quickly open to a blank page. I begin sketching mindlessly of what I thought at first to be set of balloons but I turn it into a tree, with new roots and old ones. I write next to it; New roots and old ones, our journey and paths forever changing but your true self will remain the same.

I know I'm avoiding my bedroom; I'm just not ready for tomorrow. I have the honor of presenting our newest addition to the art gallery and give a speech, well more like a few lines but all the same. I get goosebumps thinking about it; I've rewritten it over three times. I should head off to bed soon, though; I have to be there before the doors open. I sigh, closing my book and heading off to bed.

I wake to the sound of the rain still hitting the window; I slowly rise, stretching at the edge of my bed. I continue my morning rituals before heading into my walk-in closet. The one thing about having a fashion designer as your best friend, all your clothes are tailored to fit and one of a kind.

I pull out a black dress Jackie has specifically made me for this occasion. It's a short, wrap-around dress that shows off some of my boobs. Since being her test model, I've grown to love how confident her clothes make me feel; I've worn nothing else since.

I briefly examine the tag that says JackieGreenCo before pulling off the hanger. I put on black stockings to help fight the cold, along with a coat. Once I'm all dressed up, I receive a video call from Jackie. "Hey!" She says excitedly; she has the phone propped up while she's in the bathroom doing her makeup.

"Morning," I say, heading into the kitchen to brew a cup of coffee. "Happy Birthday! I know it's early, but I just want to wish you luck! I wish we could be there; why'd you have to move so far!" Jackie pretends to pout.

"Thank you and oh don't do that, you know I visit," I blow an air kiss through the phone. I used most of the money from my grandfather's will to move as far away as I could. "How's Tristen?" I ask, and she rolls her eyes dramatically. "Tristen's fine. It's me you should be worrying about. The more he grows, the more reckless he gets. He's getting into everything, always finding something to tear up," She vents.

I reach for a to-go coffee cup as I scold her, "Oh, he's not that bad, he's just curious, and he's got a lot of energy." She sighs, "Luckily, Troy's taking him out to see a baseball game today. So I'll get a couple of hours to myself before today's show. Have you made a decision yet, about Henry?"

I set my phone down to fill my cup with coffee, "Jackie, you know I can't answer that." Jackie moves to the living room, setting me down somewhere, "What do you mean you can't answer that? You guys have been dating for two months now," she says.

I reply, "Yes, I know, but that doesn't mean I'm ready to give up my personal space, and anyway, he hasn't responded to my texts since yesterday afternoon." Which is kind of nerve-racking considering he's supposed to be helping me set up for the new art piece today. I quickly mix in my sugar and creamer before snagging my keys and heading for the door.

"Oh Melina, you're full of shit; you don't date anyone for almost three years, then you jump into a relationship with the first guy who impresses you, let alone a two-month relationship with him. Then you don't know if you want to take it to the next step? Or do you mean you thought dating again would make you forget about the name we shall not speak of, and now that it hasn't, you're just going to ride it out. Am I right?" She says, picking up the phone again.

I stutter, feeling like a deer in headlights, "A-aren't you the one who said dating would help, gosh give me some credit. At least I'm trying." I get a message from the gallery and sigh. "They need me at the gallery; I'll talk to you later," I say. "This conversation isn't over, Melina; text me later," she says before hanging up the video call.

I head out my front door, now more frustrated than when I went to bed. I lock my door before skipping down my little set of stairs. I glance at my phone, noticing a text from Elijah wishing me a happy birthday. I quickly respond, stopping in front of my car. There she sits, holding on strong. She's coming up on five years old. I quickly get in and hurry to get to work.

As I pass the front entrance of the Art gallery, I notice a bunch of black SUVs out front, even a limo, which stresses me out more. I really hope no one important is coming to see this art reveal. I take a deep breath and say to myself, "You got this." I pull into the employee's parking lot and head inside through the back entrance. It's already warm inside which tells me Henry made it to work. "Thank god," I say as I hang up my coat.

I worked my ass off to become the assistant manager at this facility, so I know I'm dancing with the devil by dating my boss, and I know it's entirely unfair for him dating someone not fully committed. It's nice though, having someone who wants your attention even if your withholding everything else. I quickly pass by some of the guys setting up the new piece before heading into Henry's office.

I knock twice before opening the door slowly, "Morning, Henry." I smile as he's sitting at his desk in the center of the room. I shut the door but don't move from it. He looks up happily, "Hey, Beautiful" He stops writing and stands. Henry's hair lay messily upon his head, his light complexion and blue eyes are enhanced by the brightness of the room. He's handsome no doubt.

There's no trace of our last conversation laced in his voice, "Everything ready for our newest addition?" I nod, "Yes, they're hanging it now." He begins walking towards me as he glances at his watch, "According to one of the journalists, this piece could sell anywhere from five grand to 30k."

When he stops in front of me, he lifts my left hand and kisses it, "This could bless the art gallery greatly, Melina. Shall we?" He then opens the door gesturing for me to go first. I don't move, time to rip the band-aid off, "Look, Henry, I like what we have going on; I just prefer to take it slow." He smiles, "We can take it at whatever pace you want as long as we're on the same page."

I force a smile in return before taking a deep breath and walking in front of him, "This could go really good or really bad, Henry." We walk down the hall at a slow pace, "Oh, relax, the response from the previews say otherwise." He rests his hand on my lower back as we make our way to the main entrance.

The glass doors of the entrance show a line of important people and paparazzi. I take a deep breath, trying to calm my nerves. The painting now hangs with a dark sheer cloth covering it. "Good luck," Henry tells me just as I receive a text from Michael wishing me luck and a happy birthday. I smile, quickly typing in thank you.

He remains next to me as he turns towards our small staff that's now gathering in front of us and the new painting, "It is with great pleasure to welcome this new addition into our lives, as much as we'd love for it to have a permanent home here in the gallery, the world loves it more, so let's pray for its success. Doors open in two minutes, does anyone have any questions?" Everyone remains silent, so he clasps his hands together, wishing us luck, and moves to open the front doors. I rush towards the other side of the room as he opens the doors, and people start rushing in.

Everyone immediately gathers around in front of the painting; excitement on their faces, and others look in awe. I make my way to the front of the art piece as everyone settles down in silence. "This piece is called a man and his shadows. Let his fears consume you all the ways it has consumed him," I remove the cover with the pull of a string, and light gasps and murmurs bubble in the crowd shortly before the applause. I move out of the way and towards the back of the crowd as cameras begin to flash.

I stare at the painting of a man in the night, walking down a dark alley. The shadows of his mind are strangling him. His face, unclear, twists into a blur as the shadows decide which personality will arise. This is the artist's depiction of schizophrenia; he committed suicide shortly after finishing this painting.

My phone begins to ring, so I momentarily look at the caller ID before deciding to answer as I move farther away from the crowd, "Hey, Dad."

"Hey, hon!" Michaels's voice rings through my ear. "Listen, I know you've got that big event at the gallery today, so I'll be quick; your grandmother isn't doing too well, Melina. She's losing more of herself as the days pass. I think you should visit her. If you want, I'll be your moral support."

I sigh, this is the third time this month he's called to tell me this. "I'll try to plan a trip or something, okay," I say, lying through my teeth. I hear him sigh of relief before he responds, "If you need anything, let me know, kid. We miss you."

I pause for a second, remembering our last visit. He'd be ecstatic to find out I was dating someone, but I'd rather not give him the satisfaction. Not yet at least, "I have to go; I'll talk to you later, okay." I hang up the phone Just as Henry approaches me.

"It sold!" He begins in disbelief. "For how much?" I question as excitement floods my veins. He boasts, "For seventy thousand dollars!" I try covering his mouth as my eyes widen, "Jesus!" We silently celebrate. He smiles against my hand before removing it to continue, "Oh yes baby, dinners on me tonight!" I smile as we share mutual happiness, "That's really freaking great Henry!" Henry moves to kiss me which takes me by surprise, "Marry me, Melina!"

***

That's all it takes; those three words have me on the next plane to my best friend's hotel room with nothing but wine and the intention of never returning. It's well into the night, and I'm almost fearful she isn't going to make it back in time from the fashion show, but she rolls in a little after midnight.

"No, he didn't say that!" She dramatically sits down beside me on the suite's sofa, "Well, you could argue that was the money talking. I mean, holy cow, seventy thousand dollars, I'd want to marry the assistant that helped me bag such a deal myself." I lay my head in her lap, "I'm serious, Jackie. I feel like a pup with its tail between its legs."

She says sadly, "It's because you are, Melina. The way I see it, though, you have two options; I'm not saying marry him but be with him physically and learn to be with him emotionally or break it off right now because nobody deserves to be a placeholder." I swear, even well into our adulthood, she's always lecturing me.

"I hate that you're right," I say, sitting up. "Yes, I love you too; now order us something from the hotel's restaurant while I call my son and finance," She moves to grab her cell from her purse, and as I head out the door and down to the hotel's restaurant. She's right, I tried to move on, but I'm just not ready yet.

How can a man I haven't seen in three years, let alone completely ghost me and apparently disappear from planet Earth, still hold so much over me? I sigh to myself as I approach the hostess; I have to end things with Henry.

14. How Theatrical of You

Jackie let me stay the night in her hotel room, but I know I have to be back as soon as possible to deal with this as quickly as possible. I make it back to the art gallery, just after sunset. I head to my office, where I hope Henry is waiting, but no one's there. In fact, there's no one else in the building.

Where are the guys that should be setting up the next portrait or the janitor who's usually mopping the halls by now? I nervously walk down to his office, the lights aren't on, but I knock anyway. No one responds, so I slowly open the door, and suddenly the little light on his desk flicks on.

I gasp at the scene in front of me. Henry kneels on the floor with his hands tied behind his back and tape over his mouth. Above him on his left stands a tall man dressed in a black suit. He's wearing black leather gloves as he holds a blade to Henry's throat. The light only illuminates Henry's face.

The man standing behind him is practically a shadow, along with two other men I can barely see standing off to the sides of him. I turn to run back out the door and get help, but suddenly two men push me back inside, closing and guarding the door as they stand outside, "Hey!" I bang on the door.

"Nice to see you again, Baby," The dark and deep voice travels from across the room, causing my heart rate to spike. Confused, I ask, "What do you want?" His voice is deep and strong, demanding even as he says, "Only what's mine, of course." I have no idea what he's talking about, so I look at Henry, but he's just as terrified.

The man speaks again, "Henry, I've got to tell you, you've picked a good one. Isn't she beautiful? Just look at her." He moves Henry's head to face me as if he wasn't already. Henry whimpers in response, and I don't know if I should move forward or stay where I am.

"I'll make it easy for you, baby," The dark voice moves to the right side of Henry, and one of the guys, takes his place with the knife. The man in black doesn't move any closer to me. The room is so dimly lit I can only see his body frame and the mere shape of his face, and I clearly don't have a fighting chance.

"Come with me willingly, and I'll spare the guy. If not, I'll decorate this entire room with his blood."

I still can't really see his face from across the room, is he bluffing? "Doesn't seem like much of a choice," I manage to whisper. He smiles, flashing a perfect set of white teeth. Who on earth is this man, and what does he want from me? "Suit yourself." He smiles as he moves to pull another knife from his back pocket, but I yell, "No, wait! I'll go, I'll go with you." He smiles again and slowly walks up to me.

Fear consumes me as I try to take deep breaths, but as he approaches me, I begin to see his facial features. His eyes look familiar, and that blackish brown hair. As he stops directly in front of me, recognition floods my brain, and all the memories I have tightly locked up in the back of my head flash in front of my eyes. "Oh my god," I whisper in fear of saying it too loudly. I visibly see him relax, and he says, "Eyes closed, baby girl." Suddenly, a blindfold goes over my eyes.

***

I don't go quietly, even if I may know him. I try to be as difficult as possible, but they end up tying my hands together. After being dragged around from multiple vehicles. I'm tugged through a building, as I hear multiple doors open and close.

When we finally stop walking, someone forces me to sit down on a leather couch somewhere quiet, the blindfold still covers my eyes as I hear the door close, and a single pair of shoes walk over to me. Hands touch my face as the blindfold falls. My eyes adjust to the light as I'm met with those familiar brown eyes again, but they were different somehow, darker.

I don't speak as he bends down in front of me, "I'm going to untie your hands. Are you going to give me a hard time in doing so?" He looks up at me and waits for a response. I shake my head, unsure what to do; This can't be the same man who left me three years ago. He is so much more defined and good-looking. This isn't right, "That was theatrical of you," I say as he unties my hands.

"Baby girl, you're lucky I didn't kill him anyway."

My eyes widen at the thought, and he laughs, "Oh please, He isn't innocent; he has a full collection of much darker things on his laptop; I tossed him to PD; they'll give him a lesser fate." My gut drops. Oh my god. There is no possible way he's talking about Henry; he's been my boss since I started working there, "You're lying."

"I won't lie to you," he says, walking over to sit at his desk. That's when I realize we're sitting inside a well-stocked library, an office maybe. "Yeah, you've already done that," I say, looking at the bricks lining the walls up to a high ceiling. He responds, "I'm sorry, Melina, for not telling you about your mother. I only wanted to protect you."

I don't react and continue to analyze the room. It almost looked like an older building, renovated, no doubt but still old. "What am I doing here Mateo?" I ask instead, finally meeting his face. He eyes me like candy; that's when I remember I'm still in a dress. So I look down to make sure my tits were still covered and my stockings still in place.

"Oh, don't worry, baby, as much as I wanted too, I haven't peaked at anything."

My face heats up, and he continues, "Although, giving you look rather sexy in that dress, I'm willing to bet there's something sexy underneath it." He gets up from his desk with a growing bulge in his pants.

He stalks over to me, and I have no idea how to react, I mean good grief. I'm not sure I like how his words are affecting me, so I stand to try and move further away from him, but he simply smiles and follows my direction. I head for the door, and of course, it's locked.

By the time I turn around, he's right up against me. This can't be the Mateo I knew; this man here scares the hell out of me. I press my back into the door, whispering, "What happened to you?" He moves his head closer to mine. I can feel his breath inches from my face, "Tragedies change people."

I'm startled by a knock on the door. "Mr. Crow," a male voice calls. Mateo looks at me a second longer before responding, "What is it?"

"Business, Sir," the voice responds. Mateo looks at me again now agitated, "Stay here." I move as he reaches for the doorknob. When he leaves the room, I notice I don't have any of my belongings, and I roll my eyes, getting Deja vu. I sigh and yell at the door, "Can I at least have a change of clothes!" Unsure if he hears me, I turn back towards the room.

The large space is intimidating compared to my one-bedroom apartment; I wonder how big the rest of the place is. I'm unsure what to do with myself, so I walk towards his desk and sit in his brown leather chair. I wish I hadn't worn this dress as I'm getting cold. The drawers have locks on them, but there are a few pieces of paper scattered on the top. I pick one up, and it read:

The subject exited the home at 0800...Returning at 1700 Subject visited Dawn Ave three times this week...Point A 153 North...

I gasp, reading my whereabouts on the paper. Oh my god. Is he stalking me? The second is a picture of me leaving my front porch in the outfit I wore just a few days ago. I don't know what happened to him, but this... This can't be Mateo Crow.

A few hours have passed, and I'm too tired and cold to move, so I wait on the couch, curling up as comfortably possible. When the door finally opens again, A pushcart of clothes comes through, but nothing I recognize.

If he was going to have me here against my will, I'm going to give him hell about it. He shuts the door as the gentlemen leaves, and before he says anything, I speak, "No, I want *my* clothes, JackieGreenCo. That's my brand." He smiles at me, picking up a dress from the rack, "You don't think I know what you wear."

I reach for the tag of another random dress, ignoring the one in his hand, and there it says JackieGreenCo, plus size collection. I roll my eyes at him and turn to the rack. I'm cold, so I grab a pair of plaid Bell bottoms and a black long-sleeve top. I walk over to his desk, placing the items on top, "Can I have some privacy?" I ask with my back facing him. He smirks, moving to sit at his desk so that I'm forced to look at him, "No," he says, amused.

"Fine," I reply, "I'll make you a deal." He leans back in his chair, "Go on."

"For every piece of clothing I remove, I get an answer." Why am I prepared to make such a stupid deal, I'm not sure but if he's getting a free show, I'm at least getting some answers.

He hesitates for a moment before responding, "Start undressing then." I nervously reach for the bottom of my dress, immediately wishing I wore more. "Why did you leave me?" I ask the first question that's been burning my tongue as I slowly pull up my dress over my head and let it drop to the floor.

I stand there, stomach and all, wearing my black lace matching bra, cheekers, and stockings. He licks his lips before leaning forward, "To protect you." To protect me? Of course, Classic. "You left me in a hospital; I'm sure that was one of the safest places I could have been."

He doesn't respond, so I sigh and begin to slide down my stockings and throw them at him, but he doesn't react as they quickly fall to his lap. "How is leaving me going absolutely ghost, no text message, no calls, nothing," my voice breaks a little, "How was that to protect me?"

He stands up slowly and walks around me; I'm still facing the desk as he moves directly behind me. Mateo lightly presses himself into me, causing me to gasp as he puts his face by my ear, "It was the safest decision for the both of us at the time. Sometimes the less you know, the better." He doesn't move his head away as he slowly snakes his hand around the right side of my belly before placing his cool hands on my hips and pulling my ass against him.

My breath grows short, and heat spreads through me, but I have another question. I move to slide my straps off my shoulder and unclasp my bra. I watch it fall to the floor as his hands immediately cup my breast, he groans as he caresses them.

I speak softly, trying not to get distracted, "Why now? Why do you want me now?" I put up so many walls, I sought out therapy. I fought so many silent battles to not want him, to not want to breathe him, I moved, for crying out loud, and here he was, destroying my work by the second.

"Baby," he speaks softly in my ear again, sending chills down my spine.

"I've always wanted you," He kisses my shoulder, "but I thought I could keep you safe by letting you be. Giving you a chance at a normal life." Then he kisses my neck, "To sacrifice my desires for the better good." He stops just above my ear, I feel myself pooling in my panties, "But I've realized I am not good, and then when I found out that lowlife asshole asked you to marry him, I nearly snapped. Your mine, and you always will be, and this time, I'll kill anyone who tries to take you away from me." How'd he find out so quickly about Henry's proposal? Was someone watching me and for how long? His words and my thoughts, it's just too much take in while he's so close to me, touching me. I can't handle it.

All my emotions are front and center, and I want to do nothing more but to touch him. I whisper, "I want to feel you. I want you." I couldn't have said those words fast enough as he bends me over his desk. Before moving another inch, he asks, "Are you sure, baby girl?"

Am I sure? I'm not completely, but that doesn't matter. The man that stole my heart is standing right in front of me, and I want him. "Yes," I speak softly, and he moves my panties to the side, only pulling his cock out of his pants and sliding into me. "Fuck" He moans, throwing his head back. For a moment, he pauses as he flexes inside of me, then pulls out and slams into me. "Oh god!" I whimper as a combo of relief, sadness, and pleasure wash over me.

He moves in and out with rhythm, "Such a beautiful girl." He grabs a handful of my ass as our moans fill the air, "Your so wet, baby." Reaching for my throat he pulls me close to him, changing his pace, "I want to savior you, all of you." Holding me there, he continues, "God, I've missed you. You're mine you hear me." Moaning is my only response as he pulls out and turns me around, "Lay down," He commands, and I lay down on his desk stupidly obedient.

I'm having sex with the man who broke my heart, only moments after seeing him again, I can regret it later, but for now, this man is mine. He stands between my legs, slips back into me, and smiles, "I want you like this for eternity." He begins pounding into me as I try holding onto the edge of the desk. "Yes, oh fuck!" I cry out in pleasure, as he moves his fingers to my clit and begins circling. "Mateo," I moan, relishing in hearing his name fall off my tongue.

He pulls out again and moves to his knees, "I'm going to make you come for me, and then you'll come again like a good little girl. Do you hear me?" I nod and he dips his head between my legs. I let out a gasp for air and move my hands to grab my boobs.

He flicks and licks as I feel that high building up in me. "Oh yes, oh fuck!" I moan more, and he continues his pace. I feel myself reaching the brim of ecstasy as he pops a finger in, which does it for me, sending me over, my orgasm washing over me in waves.

He stands, resuming his position inside me, wiping my juices from his lips onto on his thumb, and says, "Here, baby girl, taste how good you are." He begins rocking his hips in and out of me as I lick myself off of his thumb. He curses under his breath, and I feel his dick pulses inside me. Using that same hand he starts rubbing my clit. I truly don't think I can come again, but he keeps going.

"You may not believe me, but you own my soul Melina. You always have," he says looking down at me. I can't listen to his words, I can't accept them, I just can't. So I focus on his body and the pleasure. He moves one hand to my stomach, then up to my breast all while not breaking his rhythm, "Tell me your mine baby girl." His hand moves to my throat as he begins pounding me aggressively.

I cry out in moans purposely ignoring him and in that moment, I realize, I was always his. I never truly stopped wanting him, from the stupid bookshelf I bought that reminded me of him, or never changing my phone number as these years went by, because just maybe, maybe he would call, but I'm not giving him the satisfaction of knowing that. "Just keep fucking me," I moan.

He removes his hands and rests them on each side of me as he leans down to kiss me. I wrap my arms around his head as his lips dance with mine; he slows down his pace and begins deep stroking me. I moan into his mouth as the pleasure becomes unbearable. Looking into his eyes, I beg, "Please, Mateo, make me come." He smiles, "As you wish, baby girl." Leaning back up, he resumes his hand over my clit and the other around my neck.

He starts pounding into me again, and soon I feel it reach the pit of my stomach; he doesn't stop as I moan incoherently, releasing another orgasm. I don't get the chance to allow my body to calm as he pulls out, but continues stroking himself.

He says quickly through gritted teeth, "On your knees, baby; I want to see it all over that pretty face of yours." I move fast, plopping on my knees in front of him. He moans profanities as he releases his cum all over my face. I shut my eyes as he strokes the last of it out.

I hear a light shuffle, and he wipes my face with a warm cloth; when my vision is clear again, He's staring at me, smiling, now shirtless, using the other side of his shirt to wipe what remains off of his cock, "I like decorating your face."

I smile briefly, saying, "My face feels all tingly now." He smirks in response.

I continue, "I'd like a shower now, or are you going to keep me locked in here like a sex slave?" I stand to remove my soiled underwear. He responds sarcastically, "That's an option?" I roll my eyes at him as I put my dress back on, now completely naked underneath. He holds out his hand, "Come on," and I childishly take it.

We leave his office, and there's no way I could prepare for how beautiful this house is. It's a large old Victorian home; you can tell it's been renovated, but it's still beautiful nonetheless. Dark brown maple wood covers the floors and dark panels line the walls. It's nicely decorated with a cozy warmth to it.

I'm sure Mateo is annoyed by my compliments as he shows me where the bathroom is. "Erica will bring you a proper change of clothes," He says, and my eyes bulge at the thought of another woman here. Mateo quickly restates, "Erica is my maid, Melina; she's been with the family for years."

He walks over to kiss my head before turning on the water, "You having nothing to worry about baby." He tilts my chin to look up into his eyes as the hot water starts to heat the room, "I have a business to attend to. I'll meet you in the dining room for dinner." He says nothing else as he leaves, closing the door behind him.

I sigh and look over at myself in the mirror; I definitely look like I've been riled up. I begin to take off my dress and get in the shower. I let the heat of the water caress me as I recap the past few hours. God, I can't believe I let him have me just like that; I put up no fight whatsoever.

I reflect on the first sight of him; his eyes seem to carry pain behind them; I wonder what he's been through over these past few years. It's clear he's become a dangerous man, but how dangerous? I let my mind wander until I hear a knock at the door. "Come in," I say cautiously, pulling back the shower curtain to see who it is. Just then, a little old lady walks in and places some clothes on the counter from the rack, "Erica?" I call, and I recognize her. I remember her face from his father's house. "Hello dear," she smiles before leaving the bathroom. Relief washes over me as I resume my shower.

15. Baby Crow Grew Some Balls

After changing into the nightgown, I let my damp curls hang against my shoulders and work up the courage to leave the bathroom.

Immediately I can smell fresh pasta from the hall, I follow the sound of movement into the dining room, which reveals someone setting the table. "Evening," he says while pulling out a chair for me to sit in. I thank him, and he continues, "Dark or light?" He holds two bottles of wine in front of me.

Before I can respond, Mateo enters the room, "Stop trying to woo her, Jasper." He's not smiling, but Jasper laughs as Mateo chooses the red wine for me. I take a deep breath noticing Mateo is no longer shirtless; He's wearing dark sweat pants and a black polo. Causal always looks so hot on him. "Hi," I say, reaching for my now full glass of wine. Instead of sitting at the other end of the table, Mateo walks over behind me, leaning down into my ear, "I'd like to spread you out on this table, baby girl."

I nearly choke on the wine as he continues, "Would you like that?" I don't respond in fear I might not deny it, and he runs his hand through my curls to the back of my head before pulling my hair, forcing me to look up at him. "Mateo," I begin nervously, but he kisses me briefly before releasing me and my hair all too soon. He walks to the other end of the table and sits.

The table displays a mouthwatering meal; in front of us sits a gourmet fettuccine pasta, a rectangular plate of bread rolls, and a large salad bowl sits in the center of the table. He watches me as I reach for my fork. "What are you staring at?" I say right before taking a bite. "Mmm," I moan in satisfaction. The food is delicious. As I take another bite, Mateo replies, "I've missed your face." He finally moves to eat his meal.

We eat our dinner intimately. I'm nearly soaking by the time I drink the last of my wine, his eyes burn through me the entire time. "You don't expect me to give up everything I've worked hard for, just to let you possess me like some trophy, do you, Mateo?" I ask boldly, although I'm sure if he wanted to, he would.

He sets his fork down as he finishes his chewing before reaching for his wine and downing it, "No, that would be poor of me to assume. After all I put you through anyway." He sets his now empty glass down, "I don't expect you to *want* to drop everything for me but alas, I've become a selfish man, Melina. So now here you are. Of course, you can still see your friends and family but do understand; This is still a dangerous game; your old life and freedoms, consider them dead."

I wipe my lips with a napkin, thinking of my response carefully. After all, what the hell am I supposed to say? My old life? My freedoms? Gone? All because baby Crow grew some balls? No, "So I suppose you want me to sit at your beck and call and have little Crow babies." This response gets him to stir, but he quickly composes himself. "Crow babies," He mocks me. "That's quite the term," he says with amusement dancing in his eyes.

He stands walking over to my end of the table and takes my hand, "Come let me show you something." Still upset, I huff as he pulls me from my chair. We head out of the dining room back towards what I believe is the living room, although it looks more like a room for decor. He guides me down the hall until we stop at the end. On the wall in front of us hangs a large Painting.

"You remember my father," He states. As I look closer, the painting is actually a portrait of William Crow; He's standing near a window looking off into the distance. The red wallpaper in the painting stands out against his black suit. I can only imagine how long this painting took as you could see the detail of the patterns on the wall and the texture in his shoes. I ask, "Why didn't he get a professional picture taken?" Mateo responds sadly, "Paintings honor our deceased."

My heart sinks as I look over at him. "What happened to him?" I ask quietly. He's silent a moment before he speaks, "The Cortes, Natalie's family. They were consumed with making a lesson out of me." He speaks slowly, guarding my expression, "They killed my father." I gasp, feeling a pang of sadness, "Oh my god...and they just, they got away with it?" He smiles sickingly, walking away, "No, of course not."

I hesitate before moving to follow him and wait for him to continue, but he doesn't, and I don't pressure him to for fear of what I might hear. I follow him into the main bedroom, where a new phone and my handbag lay on his bed.

He states, "You're not a prisoner here, Melina, but I will keep you safe at all costs. Do you understand?" He hands me the new phone only after I agree, "I uploaded some of your old contacts and things from your old phone." I frown, saying, "My old phone works perfectly fine."

He doesn't respond and moves to the bedroom door. "Where are you going?" I ask as I power on the new phone, still sitting on his bed, "I have a couple of things attend to; I'll see you in the morning." With that, he shuts the doors behind him.

You're not a prisoner, my ass, I mock as my first thought is to call Jackie. She doesn't answer the phone at first, but when I call again, and she hears my voice, I explain I got a new number. "So, did you talk to Henry?" She asks, and I remember what Mateo said about him, "Yeah, I did. He agreed, actually," I lie.

"He agreed?" She repeats my words.

"Yup," I respond.

"So that's it? No explanation?" She doesn't sound convinced, so I say, "Yeah, he said he felt like he was rushing into it anyway."

"Okay, that went easier than I expected; how are you feeling?" She asks. I wish I could be honest with her, but where do I even start? "Jackie," I begin. "Yeah," she responds. I pause a minute before sighing, "I think I'm going to be okay."

"Well, I hope so," she replies in light laughter. I smile, "I'm going to go to bed; I'll talk to you tomorrow." We wish each other a good night, and I hang up. I look around the room, still in awe of his home, but I don't want to go to sleep yet. I scroll through my contacts and see Mateo's name, so I call him, and he answers on the first ring, "Yes, baby girl?"

"Is this how you woo women into sleeping with you, making them sleep alone?" I say. He sounds amused as he replies, "I don't have to *woo* anyone, and I certainly didn't have to woo you, Miss Sky." I pull away, making a face at the phone as if he can see me before responding, "Are you saying that was a mistake on my part Mr. Crow?"

"No, of course not," I can hear the amusement in his voice as he continues, "Just a slight short-sightedness, on your part." I huff, "Well, rest assured, Mr. Crow, it won't happen again." I gasp as the bedroom doors swing open, making me drop my phone in my lap. Mateo walks in, "We'll see about that." He shuts the doors behind him. "Oh my god! Don't scare me like that!" I can feel my heart pounding in my chest.

He laughs, and I notice the bulge imprinting on his sweats, I fight the urge to bit my lip, "What kind of business requires you to wear sweats?" I ask, unfolding my arms as he pulls back the blanket. "None." He says simply getting into bed, and I hesitate momentarily before laying down next to him. I haven't slept next to anyone in such a long time. He speaks softly, "Come here, baby girl." I snuggle into him as he pulls me close, making me feel warm inside. I sigh, relishing in the comfort and drifting off to sleep.

By morning I wake alone in his bed. I sit up, looking around for him. My eyes lands on a note left on the nightstand;

Go to the closet and find something to wear; I'll meet you for lunch at noon.

-Mateo

I stand up, grabbing my new phone; the time shows 10:45 a.m. I had a little over an hour to get dressed. I quickly shower and find myself in the walk-in closet. To my surprise, Mateo brought my clothes from my apartment here. They're all neatly hung up as if they belong here.

Do they belong here? I wander deeper into the closet, settling on a cream-colored matching skirt and sweater set with a black top & black thigh-high tights. It's still pretty cold out, but I'm sure I won't be leaving anytime soon. After getting dressed, I walk into the kitchen.

Jasper is standing over an island stove. "Good morning, Melina," He calls to me as I approach. "Morning," I smile. "How's an omelet and toast for breakfast?" He asks, and I nod, sitting at the table where we ate dinner last night. He quickly makes me breakfast, and I happily dig in. "This is delicious, thank you," I compliment him, and he smiles graciously. "No problem, my dear, let me know whenever you're hungry, I'm usually here from seven a.m. to seven p.m. I'm off on weekends." I nod in acknowledgment, and he leaves.

I finish my food, still wondering what Mateo has been up to these past three years. I wonder if he's been with anyone else. I place my dish in the sink, quickly washing it. After I look through the cabinets for a coffee machine, When Jasper startles me, "Let me get that for you." I immediately take a step back.

"Light Roast or Decaf?" He asks, pulling out a coffee machine from a cabinet I hadn't checked yet. I move further back, realizing this is *his* space. "Light Roast, please," I decide to wander the house, checking my phone; I message my dad and Elijah, my new number, in case they've tried to reach me the past twenty-four hours.

This house feels so empty when you wander it alone. I creep down the hall and open a random door. This room takes my breath away and pumps fear into my veins. A Dark wooden crib sits in the corner, across from that sits a brown rocking chair, and there's even a changing table. Oh my god. Mateo really does want me to have little Crow babies.

I panic, shutting the door behind me. I stand against it for a few moments before walking off as if nothing happened. I head back down the hall; that's enough exploring for one day. I make my way to the common areas, but not before grabbing my coffee first.

A few bodyguards stand against the walls, quiet and motionless. It's almost noon as I check my phone and sit on a nearby couch. Michael responds to my text asking what happened to my old phone, which, I say, got water damaged. I wait quietly. It feels so weird, with so many silent eyes watching me.

After a while, I hear Mateo walks in, as his voice startles me, "There she is." He smiles at me as I look in his direction, he approaches me laying out his hand in front of me. "Hi," I say as I grab it, standing before him. "You look breathtaking Melina," he says kissing my hand. I smile in responds and he pulls me in for a kiss.

His lips devour mine as I wrap my hands around his waist. His hands find my face as our kiss deepens, and I involuntarily moan into him. Mateo pulls back and fire blazes his eyes, "A beautiful sound from a beautiful girl."

He looks down into my eyes, moving his left hand to caress my cheek, "Stay here with me Melina. Let me take care of you and your body." His right-hand trails down to my ass. I take a deep breath as his words send electricity right to my pussy, but I think about the nursery I happened on and say, "Not a chance." Just then his phone rings and he curses under his breath before stepping out of earshot to answer it. He paces for a minute before quickly returning to me, "Lets take a drive baby." He grabs my hand.

He doesn't let go as he leads me through the house again, "Where are we going?" I ask as we find ourselves in his garage. The cold gives me goosebumps, and I regret my choice of clothing. There are two cars parked next to each other. We approach one, and he opens the door for me, He taunts, "It's a surprise, don't you like surprises?" I roll my eyes as he shuts the door behind me and gets in himself. "Relax, Melina. Enjoy the ride," he says, starting the vehicle.

We find ourselves on a quiet car ride, and I can't help but think again about the nursery, but I refrain from bringing it up. Soon we pull into the driveway of a quiet restaurant. It's bright and open, with tan a white themes and it doesn't look too busy. After getting out, I'm not surprised to see a black SUV following behind us; at least, that hasn't changed. Mateo doesn't bother properly parking the vehicle, and he leads me inside. I notice everyone here is dressed in their Sunday best.

A waitress guides us to a table in the back, as people talk in a low buzz. Mateo opens the left chair for me, and instead of sitting across from me, he sits next to me; I ask, "Did we really need to leave to have brunch?" He responds, "This isn't just brunch." and as if on cue, a man and another woman approach our table. Mateo smiles, "Hector!" He gestures at the table, "Welcome, sit!"

"Mateo! Thanks for having brunch with me!" Hector says, sitting the woman first, then sits next to her. "This is my wife. You remember her," he says turning to the woman, "Amalia baby say hello." She smiles, and briefly says hi. Mateo nods respectfully to Amalia and places his left hand on my thigh.

Mateo begins to introduce me, but Hector cuts him off, moving to kiss my hand over the table, "No need to remind me, Mateo; I couldn't forget such a face as hers even if I tried." This response makes Mateo twitch. I mean, I literally see this man twitch beside me. He takes a deep breath and flexes his hands under the table.

"Excuse us for a moment," Mateo states as he stands, retaking my hand and leading us to the nearest bathroom. Horror strikes my face as he pushes into the women's restroom, tugging me in with him. There are a few shrieks as Mateo snaps, "I want everyone out of here now!"

Immediately, women scramble out of the bathroom, and I can't decide if I'm more horrified at his confidence and visible rage or the fact that a bunch of women listen to him, without question.

As soon as they're all out, I snatch my hand away, "What the hell is wrong with you!" He doesn't respond. I continue, "Why are we in the women's bathroom Mateo?" He snaps, pacing, "Would you prefer to be in the men's?" I don't respond as he continues to pace and slams his hand on the wall, "Damn Nunez, He is a fortunate fucker!" I jump and move back a little, this catches Mateo's attention. He pauses, looking me over. He's clearly developed a sense of rage.

He tries to take a deep breath and struggles to speak calmly, "Hector remembers you from the first time I took you to a meeting with me. That's fine; however, he's fucking you with his eyes right in front of me!" He yells the last of it, and I want to call out how ridiculous he's acting. Hector simply gave me a compliment, "Mateo, you're over-exaggerating. Besides, his wife is sitting right next to him."

Mateo laughs, "That's his third wife, Melina. How do you think he found her." He finally stops pacing, "Hector better be grateful he's part of a loyal family, I would have killed him for such public disrespect." He takes another deep breath composing himself, then suddenly pulls me into him.

His lips, only a centimeter away from mine, he says, "You are mine, baby girl. I own you; do you hear me?" What? I try to pull away, but he has a stone grip around me; this man is out of his mind, "Mateo, let go of me!" He doesn't budge, "Say it."

"No," I respond. I Press my hands against his chest, trying to create some distance, "You don't get to claim me."

"Why not?" He asks innocently, and his hands begin to loosen, but then he pushes me into the wall, resting his arms on the sides of my head. I look up at him as a wave of unreliable expressions flashes behind his eyes, "You left me, Mateo; you don't get to reclaim something you left, for three years might I add."

He softens as he sighs and steps back, saying, "I never left you." I scoff, "Yeah, whatever helps you sleep at night." He looks at me intently, "I'm serious, Melina; I never left you; I was there the day of your grandfather's funeral. I watched you sit at your mother's grave. On graduation day, I watched you walk across the stage. Even when you moved to your apartment in the city, I never left you, baby girl."

"And that's supposed to make me feel better?" I question as tears begin to swell, "You watch me like a stalker, and I'm supposed to suddenly not feel alone? You abandoned me, Mateo. If you want me, you'll have to try harder than kidnapping me and trying to force me into submission or having Crow babies." I take a deep breath, successfully not allowing the tears to fall. His face looks confused at the last part, so I continue, "I saw the nursery, Mateo. I am not here to pop out children for you or anyone else for that matter." I finish strong, and he laughs. He freaking laughs at me.

Before he can actually respond, though, his cell phone rings, and he takes a deep breath, recollecting himself, "What?" He pauses, listening, "Get all of them together. I'll be there in thirty minutes." He hangs up the phone and finally speaks to me, "Melina, if I wanted a surrogate, I would have gotten one. You are here because I want you here. Now, take the SUV back to the house. There will be company waiting for you when you arrive."

16. Life, Death, and Love

I sit in silence on the ride back, sending Jackie a message;

I miss you.

I type, pressing send before clicking off my phone. When we arrive, there is more security surrounding the yard than when we left, and it makes me nervous. I walk inside, immediately smelling the aroma of pasta sauce and garlic bread. I hear voices of laughter coming from the dining room. I cautiously make my way over as the voices grow louder.

"Melina!" Sofia's voice is full with happiness, and a beautiful baby boy lays in her arms. I smile as she stands to hug me. "Hi Sofia!" I side hug her trying not to disturb the baby. "Oh my gosh, I haven't seen you in such a long time, and who is this handsome boy!" I say, the last part cooing at him in her arms. She smiles, "This is my son, Carter."

"He is so precious," I say. I finally look around the room and see Adam chatting on the phone in the corner; they both look the same, yet different. Sofia's features look more defined and her hair even longer than I remember. "Well, what are you guys enjoying for lunch?" I ask, hearing my stomach turn.

"Just a light chicken salad. Would you like to join us?" She asks, unconsciously swaying the baby.

"Yeah, I'd like to change into something more comfortable first."

"Of course, I need to lay Carter down for a nap, and I should probably pump too, so take your time," Sofia walks towards the nursery, and I feel a little dumbfounded. I hurry back into Mateo's bedroom, embarrassed. How was I supposed to know the nursery is for his nephew? That sounds so odd, I feel like I've missed so much of his life in just three years. I undress and redress into a simple black house dress. I receive a reply from Jackie soon after;

Jackie: Miss you too! Is everything okay?

Me: Yes and no; I'd much rather tell you in person.

Jackie: Is it bad?

Me: No, not bad, just complicated

Jackie: Okay, let me know so I can clear my schedule

Me: Okay, I'll figure something out; love you

I head back to the dining room, where Sofia now sits alone; Adam is no longer in the room. Jasper quickly hands me a full plate and pours me a glass of wine, "How have you been?" I ask.

"I've been good," Sofia responds. She pauses before asking, "How have you been? Mateo told me you moved from your hometown."

I smile, "Oh yeah, I moved to an apartment in the city; I thought a change of scenery would be nice."

She agrees, eating the last of her food, "When Adam and I found out we were pregnant, we thought the same thing." She paused for a moment. "Forgive me if I sound rude, but why are you here? I haven't seen you in years, now you're suddenly here again," She asks boldly. I smile briefly, reaching for my glass, "You should probably ask your brother that." I take a long sip of my wine before Adam reappears in the room, "Sofia baby, it's time to go."

He acknowledges my presence, "Nice to see you again, Melina." I smile in response as Sofia heads off to get the baby. I stand and meet them at the front door, "Well, it was good seeing you guys!" I wave as they leave and immediately shut the door behind me. My mind runs to Mateo as I lean against the door. What am I doing?

***

A week has gone by since I've been here in his home. Still unsure of Mateo's intentions and my feelings, I haven't let Mateo touch me since that first night, but God, he is tempting. It certainly doesn't help waking to your backside being poked in the morning; however, he's up before me most days. Mateo brings me along on most of his business trips, only to have one of his guards babysit me somewhere nearby while striking deals and proposals.

Today I sit at a bar watching him from afar as he laughs and plays pool with a bunch of other men. I am bored, and the alcohol is making me hot. I down the last of my third dirty martini and pull down my short black bodycon dress, while going over to the empty pool table in front of theirs.

As I grab a stick off the wall, the chatter from their table falls to a low hum. I focus on the cube to dust the tip of the stick as my back faces the edge of their table.

Bending over slowly just enough to make sure they can all see the edge of my cheeky, red-laced panties, I align my cue with the white ball. I turn my head briefly, making eye contact with a rage-burning Mateo.

I smile, turning my head to easily break the set, and move to randomly hand my cue to one of them. As I walk back to the bar, I can hear Mateo dismissing himself. He catches up to me, snagging my wrist as he tugs me out of the building and into his waiting limo. After nearly pushing me onto the floor of the limo, my chest is pounding as he snaps at the driver, "Drive!" He shuts the door, hitting the privacy buttons and sits looking down at me. As the little window rolls up, he begins, "Do you remember your safe word."

My safe word? I'd be lying if I said I didn't, but there was a time I desperately wanted to forget it. "Yes," I whisper as fear and excitement flood my chest. Mateo loosens his tie, "Good. Since you'd like to act like a brat, I'm going to treat you like one. What's your safe word, baby girl?" My eyes widen as I reply, "Roses."

He smirks, unbuttoning his slacks, "Kneel in front of me." It takes me a second before I agree to scoot closer, kneeling in front of him. He immediately tangles his fingers in my curls, as he shoves his cock down my throat and begins rocking my head with quickness giving me no room to breathe. I place my hands on the seat on both sides of him as he speaks through gritted teeth, "You want to let all those filthy men get a glimpse of what mine, huh baby?"

I don't respond, I mean it's not like I can. Feeling him move in out of my mouth, while leaving me no room to breathe or even flex my jaw, all I can do is focus on short breaths and not passing out. "What's the matter, baby? Cat got your tongue?" He pauses his cock in the back of my throat, causing me to whine before forcing me to suck him again. All his shit-talking is making me wet, and I hate it.

"That's it, take it like a good girl," He coos as I try to breathe with every stroke, I gag on his cock, and I feel his dick flex in my mouth, "You're mine, baby, and if you ever pull a stunt like that again, I'll bend you over my knee, and spank that pretty ass of yours until it bruises." He strokes faster as water pools in my eyes, and my jaw begins to ache.

He moans in pleasure just as I think he's going to pull out and cum on my face, He doesn't. Instead, He holds my head in place and releases it in the back of my throat; I protest in moans as light tears fall from my face as I'm forced to swallow and struggle for air.

He pulls out slowly as I remain kneeling in front of him, finally taking full deep breaths. He quickly grabs a water bottle from the side of the door and hands it to me, "Are you okay, baby?" He wipes away a tear near my eyes as he waits for a response. I take a small sip before nodding my head, still in shock from the experience.

I'm not telling him how an act of pure dominance like that only makes me want him more. I speak softly, "That was different." He smiles and pulls my lips to kiss me softly. His phone rings, and he pulls away from me.

Mateo tells the driver to stop the car as he answers the phone. He opens the door to the limo, which causes me to pout, "You're just going to leave me hot and bothered?" He smirks, "Be a good girl, and we'll find out." He turns to continue his conversation over the phone, and I sit down in the seat miserably.

The next day I wake in an empty bed of dissatisfaction and boredom.

So I call Mateo, knowing he already has a start on his day, and he answers in one ring, "Yes, baby girl?"

"Are we done playing games, Mateo. I have a life, you know, a job, that I've most likely lost at this point. I'm done playing prisoner." I say sternly. I hear him grinning through the phone, "I'll clear my schedule, and we can do whatever you'd like."

"No, I don't need you to babysit me, Mateo," I say, and he sighs. I wait, but he says nothing, so I continue, "I want to visit Jackie."

He responds, "I'll arrange it."

I protest him accompanying me to no avail, not even a distant compromise. Jackie will have a heart attack when she sees Mateo let alone seeing him *with* me, even without knowing all the details, she knows he left me. So I can only imagine how horrible this will play out.

The driver slows as we approach Jackie's modern two-story home; I sigh as we arrive in front of her house. My heart rate quickens as we approach her doorstep, and I ring the bell. Almost immediately, Jackie's assistant answers the door, "Hello!" Maryann lightly smiles at me before turning to Mateo, "Welcome in!" she smiles brighter at him.

He immediately places his hand on my upper backside as we walk in. I never actually met Maryann in person before, but I've seen her on plenty of video calls. Jackie's house is beautiful and it's got every detail of her personality, the entrance is wide, with a white light chandelier hanging in the middle. Beautiful modern paintings line the walls of her home, a white staircase is off to the side, and an archway in front of us leads to the sound of a TV and childlike laughter.

"Jackie?" I call loudly.

"In here!" she yells back. Mateo and I follow the sound of her voice. Her back faces the entrance to Tristen's playroom as she watches him play with a few toys. "Melina!" She squeals, turning around to hug me. "Hi," I say nervously. Her face falls. "What the hell?" she questions glancing over at Mateo, still pulling me into a quick hug. "What the hell is he doing here?" she says, frowning as she pulls away. Mateo only smiles in response, "Good to see you, Jackie." She does not return the gesture, "It's Miss Green."

"Jackie, come on, stop it." I scold her.

"Can I have a moment with Melina, please," She demands as she pulls me out of the playroom, "MaryAnn? Can you please watch Tristen for a moment?" She asks, shutting the door of the playroom. Leaving Mateo in the room with MaryAnn and Tristen. Turning to me she yells, "Do you care to explain what the hell Mat is doing here? I thought he was dead for god sakes. Need I remind you he left you Melina, High and Dry!"

I allow her to finish before responding, "I know. I mean, I don't know." I sigh, "He found me in the city, and...we just got to talking."

I lie not in the mood to explain everything right now. "You just got to talking?" She repeats. "That's it? He just happened upon you after not even existing for the past three years!" She questions, definitely not believing me.

"I know this is strange, but he's here now, and we've talked-"

She cuts me off, "No, I don't like this, Melina. You can't just forgive him after one conversation." She crosses her arms as she begins to pace the room. "I haven't forgiven him," I defend myself. She side-eyes me, "Oh really, have you fucked him already?" I don't answer, and she huffs, "You are unbelievable."

I stay quiet, knowing she is right, but when have I ever held her hot and cold monthly whiplashes with Troy over her head? She stares at me briefly before speaking more calmly, "So what are you doing with him?"

Before I can reply, Maryann opens the door of the playroom, peaking her head out. "Miss Green," she states. Her face is bright red from blushing, "Mr. Crow says he can hear you, and he sincerely apologizes for what happened to Miss Sky. You also have a client on hold, they said it's an emergency. Something about a stained dress." Jackie sighs in frustration before pointing at me, "This conversation isn't over."

Mateo responds, walking towards me, "Maybe you'd like to settle this conversation over drinks, in a calmer setting perhaps." I glance at him with wide eyes, before turning towards Jackie. She takes the phone from Maryann as she still eyes Mateo, "Drinks sound necessary right about now." She turns to me, "Troy took me to this beautiful club just a few weeks ago. I have a few things on schedule today, but I'll message you the place Melina." She answers the line and walks away.

Mateo smiles when Tristen runs up to me excitedly with a toy in his hand, "Auntie Melina!" He wraps around my legs, and I laugh, "Hi! Tristen." I move to floor level when he releases me. "Whatcha got there?" I ask with extra enthusiasm. He holds up his action figure and says in his tiny human voice, "This is Superman!" Then he starts pretending to fly around.

"Wow! How cool!" I entertain, "Listen, I've got to go, okay, I'll see you later." He nods his head and happily runs back into his playroom. I stand and turn towards Mateo, who's got this amused look on his face. "Let's go," he says, holding his hand out for me to grab.

We make our way back to the SUV, and after I tell Mateo the location, he makes a smug look but informs the driver anyway.

He pulls out his phone, looks at something briefly, and puts it back into his pocket, "There's an important event taking place tomorrow night. Would you like to go?"

"An event?" I asked.

"Yes, kind of like a charity event, except there will be a lot of important people there," he says. A charity event? "Yes, we can go," I answer excitedly. He replies, "I'll call a stylist to come by tomorrow." I look at him and before I can say it, he says, "Yes, I know. I'll make sure it's all JackieGreenCo." I smile to myself. "Pull over," Mateo tells the driver before checking his phone one more time and silencing it. The car quickly comes to a stop so I ask, "Where are we?" The driver puts the car in park and Mateo tells him to take a break.

He turns to me pulling me into him says, "We have a few hours to occupy." This lights my core like a match to a flame. "Mateo," I begin knowing damn well If he starts something I won't be able to resists. "Yes baby?" he says ushering me into his lap. He rests his head against the seat as I stare into his eyes finding myself getting lost in them.

Sighing, I say "Why do you have so much control over me?" He smiles, pulling my face closer to his lips before saying, "You have control over me too, Melina. More than you realize." He pulls me into a kiss before I can respond or react to his words.

***

Soon we approach the club. The driver does not pull in front, but rather in the back. I notice there are a few more SUVs parked here as well. I kind of wish I would have gone with at least a skirt rather than wide-leg pants and a cream-colored blouse; this was totally not an outfit for a club. Mateo takes my hand as we make our way inside the building.

He speaks quietly, "Stay close to me, Melina, we're in mutual territory, and the last thing I want is for something bad to happen to you." My eyes widened at this information. Mutual territory? Between whom? Jackie couldn't have possibly known such a thing.

Music blares as the temperature is a few degrees warmer inside. The place looks nice; Mateo guides us to a private room near the dance floor, where extra security stands guard. A hostess in a black bodysuit and bunny ears immediately serves us drinks. We sit down, and he whispers in my ear, "An average person wouldn't notice this, but do you see all the different types of security guards in suits? They belong to different mafia families.

This club is common ground, which usually means we all have to keep the bullshit outside of these walls." He points with his glass nonchalantly through the thin curtains as he explains this location.

I suddenly feel like we're in a pit waiting for something terrible to happen; I take a deep breath setting my glass down.

"Don't worry, baby, it'll be okay. Come here," He suddenly pulls me into him, tapping my thigh for me to swing my leg over his lap to straddle him. He begins rubbing my ass with one hand as he finishes his drink with the other.

Being this close to his dick is making me a little unhinged, "You know it's hard not to want you inside me when your close to me like this." He smirks, "Is that so." He slightly presses himself up against me, "I could have you right here on this sofa baby, all you have to do is say the words." I look at his lips. My pussy pulses from his words and move to run my hands through his hair. God, he is so tempting.

We suddenly hear a familiar voice, "Melina! Come on, babe, let's go dance!" Jackie enters the room wearing a sexy tight skirt and rope top set. Surprisingly Troy is here too. "Hey Melina, good to see you," he says. I move out of Mateo's lap saying, "I was beginning to wonder where you were Jackie, and Troy, it's great seeing you too."

Troy immediately sees who's sitting behind me and says, "Good to see you, Mat." He moves to sit with Mateo and Jackie reaches for my hand. "Come on let's get drinks first!" she yells, pulling me out of the private room. I quickly look back at Mateo, who nods approvingly towards me.

We stop at the bar, and she orders two strawberry daiquiris. We down two glasses of sweetness, before Jackie and I head out to the middle of the dance floor and start letting loose. We dance around and soon begin laughing and get lost in the time together. I miss her more than I realize.

Soon the song changes to a slow pace, so we start slow dancing and grinding on each other; Jackie looks like she's already had a few too many drinks as her eyes are squinting, and we keep laughing every time she moves offbeat.

"I need another drink!" I try yelling over the loud music to her, and she agrees. We find our way back to the bar, plopping down on two stools, "Two screwdrivers, please!' Jackie says bubbly, and we're served our drinks in no time. We clink our glasses to sloppy cheers when someone suddenly comes up behind me, wrapping their hands around my waist and saying, "Hey baby, I saw that ass moving on the floor."

"Hey, get off of me!" I immediately scream as the unknown figure doesn't loosen his grip.

I start to claw at his hands from around me, but he must be too strong, or I must be too drunk. "She said to get off her!" Jackie tosses her drink onto him. He frowns wiping his face, "Stupid bitch!" he lunges at Jackie but quickly gets knocked to the ground. "Didn't you hear her!" In a flash, I see Mateo standing over him, yelling and repeatedly punching him in the face. I scream, "That's enough, Mateo!" but he doesn't stop swinging. Everything seems to be moving too fast.

People have already started to form a circle, and I panic as Mateo appears to be in a trance. "Stop it!" I yell again afraid to reach for him. Suddenly I can hear Troy bickering with Jackie while trying to grab me. "No!" I scream, protesting, "I'm not leaving!" Suddenly, two of Mateo's bodyguards drag me out.

17. I Met a Magician Named April

We stumble into one of the SUVs, and I quickly feel around for my phone while getting deja vu. I sigh when I feel it in my pocket. I look over at Jackie, who's on the verge of passing out. "Are you okay?" My head is spinning. I'm unsure who's driving and where, but my eyes are getting heavier by the second. She laughs, holding her head, "Yeah, I'm fine!" She lays back immediately, closing her eyes, so I try to focus on contacting Mateo. I ring his number. No answer. I try it again, and still no response.

"He's not going to answer you," Troy's voice startles me from the passenger seat. He seems calm, too calm, has he been sitting there this whole time? "We need to go back for him," I state.

"Orders are to get you girls to safety first."

I try his phone one more time, and he doesn't answer. I sigh in defeat, hoping he's okay.

After arriving, we sit in the living room. Jasper is already off, so I barely make it into the kitchen to get water and pain pills to feel better. I keep an eye on Jackie as Troy stands on watch with the other bodyguards. Intoxicated as I may be, I can't help but notice Troy is not as rattled by the situation, he's almost too calm.

Making my way back into the living room, where Jackie lies now sleeping on the couch, I drink the water and down the pills before walking over to Troy, "Jackie's passed out. Can you help me take her to one of the guest bedrooms?"

"Sure thing," He responds, moving to the couch.

Troy moves to lay her on the bed, and his cell phone slips out of his pocket; I move to pick it up to hand it to him and see a private message from Mateo. What? I frown as I hand it back to him, and he successfully lays Jackie in bed.

After closing the door, Troy immediately begins walking back to the living room, and I follow accusingly, "So he can message you but not respond to me?" I wait for a response while trying to keep up with him. Still, he says nothing, and my head starts to pound again, so I stop following him. All I can do right now is go to sleep and hope everything is okay in the morning.

Waking up, I can hear Mateo talking quietly on the phone, his voice low and tired, "It doesn't matter, I'll pay the damn fine; just send him my sincerest apologies." I sit up, and he turns to face me and hangs up the phone. Bruises and scabbing are visible on his knuckles while loose hairs dance messily over his tired eyes.

Wearing a long sleeve button-up and black slacks, he heads over to me, "How are you feeling?"

"I'm fine," I sigh as he slowly approaches the bed. I swing my legs to the edge, and he stops in front of me. "Are you okay?" I ask, pulling his hand up to examine his knuckles. I frown at the bruising, "Did you kill him?"

He doesn't respond, which gives me my answer. A man died because of me last night. I apologize, "I'm so sorry." He squats down in front of me and kisses my hands, "It's not your fault, baby girl." I look away; this is the lifestyle I will live if I really want to stay here. He turns my head to face his, "We're staying home today." I almost agree before remembering the event later today, "What about the charity event? Can we still go?"

He sighs, looking into my eyes only a moment before giving in, "If that's what you want, yes, we can still go." I ask the next question that pops into my mind, "Does Troy work for you?" Mateo stills, briefly taken aback. "Yes," he replies simply. "Does Jackie know? Are they still here?" I frown, upset; it's one thing for me to be caught up in this lifestyle, but my best friend? "They left earlier Melina. She doesn't know, and it's not our place to tell her," He responds as his phone rings again. He kisses my head before leaving the room to answer it.

I check my phone, which reveals it's Saturday morning. I quickly send Jackie a text checking in on her. I debate telling her, but I'm afraid of what kind of drama that'll cause for their relationship. So I leave it alone for now and head to the closet. My first thought is to put on yoga pants and a tank top, but then I decide to put on a short full body black lace gown, only wearing black panties with them; after all, we were going to be spending time together, might as well have fun. Jackie responds with a quick text:

I'm fine, just a little startled. Troy said he has business to attend to today, though I'm hoping we can spend time together. Alas, work never waits.

I text back, sympathizing with her, before I quietly leave the room walking into the kitchen. As usual, a couple of bodyguards are around, but I pay them no mind. I ask Jasper for a cup of coffee before heading into Mateo's office, thinking he'd be there. I try to be quiet as I enter; memories of that first-night flood my head, I smile to myself. I don't stay long as no one is in here.

I leave, passing by the laundry room. The doors open, so I can see Erica holding up Mateo's shirt from last night, only it is covered in blood. She shakes her head at it before noticing me. She immediately tosses it before giving me an apologetic smile. I awkwardly smile, feeling uneasy as I head back to the kitchen area.

I shake my head setting my cup on the edge of the dinner table, I don't know why it's so difficult for me to wrap my head around this new Mateo. I remember when he used to be afraid of becoming his father, and now, he *is* him—Head of The Crows.

Mateo snaps, startling me, "Everyone out!" I jump, turning around to face him as he dismisses the bodyguards from the dining room area. Only after they've left, he speaks to me, "My father always told me temptation comes in many forms." He takes me in, looking me up and down.

I almost forget what I'm wearing as I glance down at my body, "you like?" I laugh, reeling myself in from my thoughts. Mateo walks up to me, sliding his hands around my waist, and moves to whisper in my ear, "Like is an understatement. However, I'm starting to think you enjoy punishments for showing off what belongs to me." My body responds to him, and his possessiveness. I wrap my arms around his neck being seductive, "Oh yeah, and what will you do to me then?" I can feel his dick harden as he pulls me into him, "You have no idea the things I want to do to you, with you."

This excites me as I look at this beautiful man in front of me; I speak slowly, "Show me then." This lights a fire in his eyes, and he slides his hands onto my ass. He moves slightly to whisper in my ear, "Do you trust me?" His voice rings low and seductive, which makes my pussy pulse. "I trust you," I breathe as I feel his breath on the side of my face. He squeezes my ass and immediately pushes me up against the table.

My hands are still wrapped around his neck when his lips find mine. My heart rate quickens as he suddenly moves to pick me up and plop me onto it moving closer between my legs. "hold your wrist out," he commands. I move my arms in front of him, and he takes off his belt, wrapping it around my arms and locking in the buckle.

"Too tight?" he asks. I try moving my wrist around, and I can only move them in sync, but it doesn't hurt much, "No." He smiles and moves to bite my bottom lip; I moan as desire pools in my panties. He slides his hand up my black laced gown and balls it into a fist, "It's a shame how I'm about to ruin this pretty little gown of yours." He pulls downward, and my straps pop off, revealing my breast. He licks his lips, as the restriction of my wrist holds me in place, squeezing my breast together in the process.

He moves one hand in between my thighs; I manage low and sharp breaths as he rubs gently against my clit before tearing off my panties and discarding them. I mentally note how easily lace rips as he quickly cups my breasts and kisses them causing me to throw my head back in pleasure.

He uses the belt guiding me to lay back onto the table with my hands above my head, "You take my breath away Melina." Mateo starts trailing kisses down my neck, "Captivating everyone around you. Are you my little temptress baby girl? Here to ruin me and claim my soul?" I moan at his words and the contact of his lips. His kisses trail down my body while still holding my breast, stopping above my clitoris, he says, "Be a good girl and stay still for me."

Before I can respond, Mateo dives his head in between my thighs, my back arching in response and I moan, but as soon as I move, he pinches my nipple causing me too wince. He looks up at me, smirking, "Stay still." Then returns to licking my pussy; I move again, and he pinches them harder.

God, this is so mind fucking I could cry, "Mateo," I beg, but he ignores me, so I take soft breaths and fight the urge to move against his tongue. All I can do is moan at the pleasure as he picks up the pace. Reaching closer, my breath becomes harder to control, and tears brim my eyes. Mateo whispers sweet nothings as he licks and flicks. He suddenly sticks two fingers inside of me, fingering me roughly and soon causing an orgasm to wash over me.

I moan incoherently as he slowly rises to his feet, "Such a good girl, would you like a reward?" he coos looking over me, only pulling his slacks down enough to pull his cock out and rubs it against my pussy. "Mhm," I moan, wanting him. He continues to tease me, though, rubbing against me slowly, "Tell me your mine," his voice is low and intoxicating. "That's not fair, Mateo," I whine.

"I know," Mateo breathes, still rubbing his cock against me. "Tell me anyway," He says again suddenly shoving the tip in. I gasp, "I'm yours." He sinks deeper into me with my words, using his left hand to grip the belt around my wrist, and moving to kiss my neck. "All mine," he breathes into me as he begins rocking inside me.

I want to touch him, to pull him closer into me, but instead my arms are stuck above my head. His pace quickens and I'm pinned in place, forced to take his poundings. He praises me, "Such a good girl." I moan in response, while he moves to grip my waist and pounds harder. "Oh god," I whisper as the pleasure overwhelms me, "Mateo, I want to touch you."

He slows down as he pulls my arms up and undoes the belt. Immediately I sit up and wrap my arms around him while he grips my ass and speeds up again. "Fuck baby," he moans into me, his grip tightening as he reaches his climax, his poundings become more rigid and less controlled. I move forward to whisper in his ear, "Come for me, Mateo."

He growls in response as he continues thrusting into me. Mateo pulls out and strokes himself a few times and his moans are like a sweet melody as I feel the warmth from his cum spread over my stomach and onto my lap. I run my fingers through his hair as he rests his head on my shoulder, coming down from the high. A moment later, he moves to pull the ripped gown off over my head and uses it to clean me. Completely nude, I sit on the table while he's unbuttoning his shirt.

I don't think I'll ever get used to seeing him shirtless. "Here," he says, wrapping it around me as I put my arms in the sleeves. This feels nice, intimate. I watch his face as he buttons it up. "What are you thinking about?" I ask, feeling vulnerable. "You. Being here with me," He says, taking a deep breath. "Come on," He holds out his hand, and I take it sliding off the table.

I feel little as he guides us to his bedroom. He begins taking off his slacks, "Lay with me." The sleepiness in his voice gives me butterflies as He pulls the blankets back. The sun has yet to set, but I join him anyway. Settling in bed, he pulls me close and closes his eyes, "The stylist will be here around seven for you."

"Okay," I respond excitedly. Mateo slides his hand up my stomach and caresses my boobs; smiling, he says, "I love these." Without another word, I lay happily in his grip, and I can feel his breath slow at an even pace upon my neck. I feel oddly at peace here in his arms. Soon I too drift off to sleep.

"Melina, wake up, baby," Mateo calls softly, causing me to stir. "Hmm" I wake, and it takes a few blinks for my eyes to adjust to my surroundings; I can hear water running in the background. "I'm going to shower, we have thirty minutes before your stylist arrives," he says, entering the bathroom.

I sit up, still a little fuzzy from our nap, when I hear Mateo's phone ping with a message on the nightstand. I stare at it, unsure if I want to cross that boundary. It pings again, so I get up and head into the bathroom. Considering his occupation, I'm sure whatever it is, it won't be good.

The bathroom is pretty spacious, with a glass rainfall shower and a separate floor tub. I stop quietly a few feet from the shower door. There, he stands peacefully under the water with his eyes closed. "Mind if I join you?" I speak softly, taking off the shirt and opening the door. He turns around immediately, pulling me into him under the water, causing me to squeal. The water makes his hair look longer as it clings to his face. He smiles, "I was hoping you would."

I laugh, "Oh really," growing conscious of my naked body pressed against his. He kisses my neck as my curls begin to shrink from the water. "You are so beautiful, Melina," He looks into my eyes as the water runs down his face. Good grief, this man holds so much power over me, I'm not sure he knows just how much. "Let me wash you," I ask, and he loosens his grip around me just enough for me to reach for his body wash and washcloth. I'm not surprised to see my body wash next to his as he's brought almost everything of mine here.

He takes deep and slow breaths as I quickly lather the washcloth and start on his chest with one hand as the other follows. I know I just want to touch him. His thin patch of chest hairs follows my every motion as I wash him; all the while, he watches me intensely. I slowly meet his eyes as my hands travel to his cock. His breath falls as I wrap the cloth around him and begin stroking. I'm honestly not trying to start anything, but I can't help myself. Excitement rushes through me as I feel him growing in my hand.

He curses under his breath before stopping me, "Baby." He breathes, "As much as I regret stopping you, the stylist will be here any minute." Still staring into his eyes, I respond embarrassingly, "Okay, right." I move to rinse the washcloth, but he stops me again and smiles, "My turn."

He takes the washcloth from me, rinsing it, then lathering it up with my body wash, "turn around." I stare at him a moment before doing as he says, facing the wall I feel him start on my shoulders before slowly moving down my back and onto my ass.

Soon he presses himself into me, resting his head in the crease of my neck as his arms wrap around my waist; he begins washing my breasts, antagonizing slow gripping and fondling them. A small moan escapes me as he trails down to my vagina, his free hand still touching my breast. "Mateo," I call breathlessly, and I feel his dick jump at the sound of my voice. Maybe we should call off the stylist and just stay home. Mateo turns me around again, kissing me as the water falls onto us, rinsing off my body.

All too soon, he pulls back, reaching beside me to turn off the water. We hear a knock on the bedroom door, he sighs, "Time to get ready." Stepping out of the shower after Mateo, he bites his lips at the sight of my hardened nipples due to the cold air, "I'd like to bite those." He moves to wrap a towel around me before wrapping one around his waist.

"I'd like that too," I say seductively as we hear another knock at the door. He lets out a frustrated groan as we leave the bathroom, and he opens the bedroom door. The stylist barges in, saying, "Mat! It's such a pleasure to meet you, honey!" She looks a bit older but still has a spring in her step.

She stops right in front of me as a few people walk in behind her with rolling racks and big cases, "My name is April, darling. I am your stylist, makeup artist, and hairdresser. Hell, I'll even be your shoulder to cry on."

I smile at her nervously. She's Caucasian, Her blonde hair tide into a neat high bun. Her eyes are beautifully bright and round, her voice sends a wave of euphoria through me. I look over at Mateo, and he reassures me while heading into the closet to change,

"Don't worry baby girl, she is the best. She's been working for the family for a long time."

"Damn straight I am!" she says confidently. Her eyes follow him into the closet, "Though this will be my first time working with you, Mat." Looking at me she continues, "and you are my muse!" After her people have set up her supplies, she claps her hands, "Alright Mateo dear, a little privacy." She moves me to sit in the chair in front of the vanity mirror. Mateo reemerges, now wearing a pair of black slacks and carrying some clothing in his hand, "I don't appreciate being kicked out of my own bedroom." He walks over to me, planting a kiss on my head. "There's a first for everything, dear!" She enthusiastically shoos him away as I laugh.

***

I stare in awe at myself in the mirror. I've dressed up before, but this feels like a different person staring back at me; she's beautiful. April straightened my hair causing the length to be two inches longer, which I do not often do to prevent heat damage. She gave me a natural face beat with a long but thin eyelash set because she wants all the attention to be on my dress.

This beautiful dress she got from Jackie's newest collection. It's a silver floor-length bodycon dress with a design of white crystals over the entire dress, that shimmers in the light. The sleeves have strings of crystals hanging from the cuffs. It has a built-in corset, making it hug me in all the right places. The look is complete with matching earrings and a necklace. I feel so beautiful, like I belong on the red-carpet of a movie premier.

"Well?" April urges, standing by in awe.

"I-I'm speechless."

She smiles happily, "You and the rest of the crowd!" She claps her hands together complimenting herself, "April, you have done it again!" She sends a quick text, and people file in to start packing up her things.

"Thank you," I say, and she hands me her business card. "It was my pleasure, darling. Whenever you need me, give me a call." She leaves the room, and I move to grab my phone, snapping a picture to send to Jackie, thanking her for such a beautiful dress. She immediately responds;

Jackie: I'm so glad you like it, it looks beautiful on you, Melina

In the spur of a moment, I decide not to wear my panties in hopes of dazzling the evening. A few moments after I toss them to the side, Mateo knocks on the door, "Melina?"

I turn to face him, and he's leaning against the door frame, fully dressed in a black suit with His hair slick back in a low ponytail. "You clean up nicely," I say as heat rushes through me.

Mateo smiles looking me up and down before standing upright, "I hate that I have to share you with the world" He holds out his arm, "Shall we?"

I smile. Taking his arm, he guides me through the house and out the front door where a limo waits. As he helps me inside, we share a private laugh at the memory of our last limo encounter. When the driver finally takes off, I feel a wave of happiness as Mateo's fingers are laced with mine. "Mateo," I begin looking up at him.

"Yes," he says casually.

"I want this with you. I want to be yours," I speak honestly. His face rushes through emotions of shock to awe and desire all in the same second, "but under one condition. I want my freedoms; I want to come and go as I please. I don't want to be kept like some house pet. I want to work and visit family and-"

He cuts me off, "Okay."

"Okay?" I repeat him, unsure of what this means. He turns to me, placing his hand gently on the side of my face, "You can have whatever you want, baby; just allow me to keep you safe." His face is now so close to mine. "Okay," I lightly laugh, and he immediately moves to kiss me. His tongue slid along my bottom lip before biting it, causing me to moan. Heat spreads through me as our kiss intensifies, "Mateo." I pull back, warning him, "We can't;

I don't want to ruin my makeup or your clothes." but it's too late for that, desire lights in his eyes and in his pants.

"Pull up your dress and lay back," He commands, and I listen, immediately pulling up my dress which reveals my bare skin. "Oh, you naughty girl," He grins, desire lacing his voice. He moves down between my legs, leaving a trail of kisses, "Watch me."

We make it to the charity event successfully without ruining any of our clothes. As we walk up to the doors, Mateo holds me close, "This is an annual charity social event. Every year, the organization is different, and every year each family tries to outdo the other."

I listen intently. If this will be my life, I need to pay attention. "There are four major families that come to this event; Crows, Cruz, Nunez, and Riviera" He spits out the name of the last one. "When people hear those names, you know it's important." He continues, as our security surrounds us while we walk through the entrance. I'm expecting a luxurious restaurant or something, but this is like a live-action theater or an opera building.

Beautifully gold-carved archways line the halls. Red carpet covers the floors and walls; my first thought is how much vacuuming is done on a daily basis.

We make our way to our personal seating box on the second floor. A waiter stands by the entrance as two chairs sit at the edge of the box facing the stage with little tables attached to them. Mateo guides me to my seat first, before sitting next to me. I take a deep breath feeling nervous. There are three other seating boxes on the second floor full of people. Families, I assume. "I'll be right back, Baby," Mateo kisses my forehead before leaving two of our security guards here with me.

Everyone else is sitting at round tables at ground level that's facing the stage. I look at the box directly across from ours. Two men sit in conversation: they're discussing something over one of their phones. An elderly man walks in, they quickly straighten up. He slaps one of them beside the head as he passes him, and I laugh a little to myself. That must be their father.

They look up, immediately making eye contact with me, sending chills down my spine. I take a deep breath quickly, looking elsewhere. A man walks out on the stage, "Good evening, everyone, and welcome!" His voice sounds warm and inviting, "This year we like to honor a lifelong supporter. But first..."

"You okay, baby girl?" Mateo suddenly returns, sitting next to me. "Yes, I'm fine," I say, glancing back across the way. Both men now focus their attention on the stage. We turn our attention back to the stage as Mateo rests his hand on my thigh, The speaker yells proudly, "Jose Rivera the third!" The room erupts in applause as the spotlight moves to shine the box across from us. Mateo curses,

"Pieces of shit." I look at him, confused, as the older man stands gracefully, bowing before the audience.

Feeling the urge to go pee, I whisper, "I have to use the bathroom, I'll be right back." I begin to move, but Mateo stops me, "I'll go with you." Shaking my head, I say, "My freedom Mateo. I don't need an escort, I'll be quick." He hesitates a moment before allowing me to go. Besides, I think I saw a bathroom near the entrance when we walked in.

I make my way back to the main floor. It's quiet down here. I see the bathroom sign and quickly follow it. I walk into the girl's bathroom, and a woman is talking quietly on the phone. She pauses, looking at me, so I smile at her as I quickly choose a stall. I don't realize how bad I actually have to pee until I start doing a little dance while trying to lay a few seat covers on the toilet. Quickly lifting up my dress, I relieve myself. When I'm done, I flush and head toward the sink, realizing I'm now alone in the bathroom.

18. Fucking Crows

I take my time, letting the water heat up.

Finishing up, I dry my hands, using a napkin to hold the door handle as I open it. Frightened, I gasp as two muscular men are standing right outside the door. They reach for me, one wrapping his arms around my upper side, the other quickly grabbing my legs.

What the fuck? My mind short circuits. No, this is not actually happening. I thrash around and squirm as hard as possible.

There is literally no possible reason for Mateo to kidnap me again, so this, this was real. I have to keep fighting. I scream, scaring the one with his arms around my legs briefly, but his partner immediately covers my mouth. I can hear shuffling, and I panic as I realize we are moving.

They are actually carrying me. I can barely move my arms, but I try reaching above my head to scratch this man's face or something to get him to let me go, but then he bites my hand, causing me to scream and wince at the same time. This is happing all to fast as it takes a moment for my eyes to adjust to the sunlight.

"No!" I scream again. Everything's moving too quickly, and in a flash, they shove me into the trunk of a vehicle. "Hold her down!" One yells as the other reveals a needle. My eyes widen as they push me into the floor of the trunk, immobilizing me. I scream as the needle pierces my skin. "That should settle her down," one of them says. Nodding in agreement they close the trunk.

I turn to pound on it. "Mateo!" I cry as the tears begin to swell. Defeat bottles thick in my throat as I hear the vehicle start and my body goes numb. What's going to happen to me? I curl into a ball, despair washes over me as I close my eyes.

I don't remember how long the drive was, but I must have fallen asleep because I wake up in a dark place. Immediately I try to move but realize my arms and legs are strapped to the chair I'm sitting in. Suddenly a tiny led light flickers on in front of me, "You're much feistier than you look." A man emerges from the shadows of the wall in front of me, grinning.

The light is too dim to really see him, but I recognize his face. He's from the box across from ours at the charity event. "I bet you're not as innocent as you look either," My head immediately jerks to the right of him; another man speaks, revealing himself. I recognize him too. "Now, now, Marco. Be nice," The first man speaks again. His voice drips with sarcasm, "We don't want to damage the goods."

He moves closer to me, and I see he's still in the same suit, so I haven't been here that long. Marco smiles at me, "Of Course not, Brian, but what's a kidnapping without a little fun?" They both move to stand over me and if fear is what I felt before, What I feel now must be terror. Pure, stomach-churning terror. I can hear my heart beating in my ears and my hands feeling hot and sweaty. "What. What am I doing here?" I ask quietly, guarding their expressions, for fear I might say the wrong thing.

The one called Marco, begins to walk around me, "You are our money maker, darling." His voice gives me chills, and I realize I'm still in my dress as cool air flows between my thighs, just perfect. Marco's phone begins to ring, He makes eye contact with Brian, and they smile. "Ah, just in time! If you'll excuse me, I have an important call to take," Marco leaves the room as he waves a disposable phone. I watch him leave through a heavy black metal door.

"Melina, is it?" Brian sets down a beaten chair in front of me. "My brother's right, you know; you are tempting, but alas," He puts up his hands in a passive gesture, "I'm not going to touch you, but my brother." His sarcasm makes me want to slap him, "He lacks self-control." Panic rises in my chest as if fear isn't already present. "So, in your case, you better hope Mateo has a lot of money and decides fast," His voice feels like he's warning me of a simple mishap rather than threatening my life. Who the hell is this guy? "Who are you?" I ask.

"Oh, we'll get to know each other in due time, darling," Brian says, standing as Marco comes back into the room. "Someone wants to say hi, Melina," Marco waves the phone walking over to me, and places it on my ear. "Melina Baby?" My heart shatters at the sound of Mateo's voice. "Mateo," I begin, but Marco pulls the phone away.

"There," He watches me as he speaks, "You have your proof, you also have 48 hours to come up with the money, or we'll send her back in the same way Your father was sent." He hangs up the phone. I feel the warmth drain from my face, and my feet go numb, are they related to Natalie? If this is personal, I don't think I'm actually going to make it out of here alive. Marco turns to leave, "I'm going to get a beer. Want one?"

Brian responds shaking his head, "No, I'm good. I think I'll sit with her a little longer." He moves to sit back down again, staring at me, "Why are you so quiet? Quiet is boring. Tell me, What's your favorite color?" Is he out of his fucking mind? He waits, but I say nothing, focusing on my breathing. In a flash, it's like his mask falls as his hands are quick in a grip around my neck, "Don't be like that, don't make me force it out of you."

I choke out the first thing that pops into my head, "Silver." He removes his grip on my neck, "See. That wasn't hard at all. I mean, I could have guessed that, look at the beautiful dress you've got on." Just like that, his charade is back in place. Now I'm unsure who I should fear more. "Well, I'll let you get some rest. I'm sure you're tired. We'll chat a little later," He smiles. I watch as he leaves without another word.

Now that I am alone, I take a deep breath, trying to calm the tension in my chest. I look down as my thighs completely fill the white chair, I'm sitting in. Both my thighs press against the armrest where my hands are secure with rope. The chair feels cheap and plastic. Maybe I can break it.

I lean to my right, trying to untie the knots of the rope with my teeth. The texture of the rope gives me chills, but I won't let that distract me. I bite down on the same part a few times before it loosens, and I nearly gasp with relief. I quickly reach for my left arm undoing the knots quietly. Adrenaline kicks in as the rope falls to the floor, and I immediately stand.

The outsides of my thighs ache but I ignore it. My eyes turn to the metal door. I walk to it quietly as my heart pulses loudly in my ears. I breathe unevenly as I approach the door.

I first press my ear against it, the coolness giving me goosebumps. I don't hear anything, so I reach for the knob and slowly turn it. It's unlocked. I don't hesitate as I move to push it open and start running, but I immediately smash into the same men that took me from the bathroom.

I yell as both men aggressively push me back, making me lose my balance and fall backwards. I partially catch my fall, wincing at the pain in my wrist from the impact. I look up as Marco emerges from behind them, "It's always the first-night people try to escape. Boys put her on the chain by the wall and give her a little something to help her sleep."

My eyes widen, and before I can say anything, they both grab me, dragging me to the corner of the room behind the chair. There lays a dirty twin-size mattress, I didn't notice before.

One forces my face into it as I wince at the pain of another needle. In the same breath, the other clamps a single cold black iron cuff around my left wrist. After hearing the clamp of the cuff, my heart aches; how will I get out of here now? "See you in the morning," Marco waves as tears begin to fill my eyes and tiredness wash over me.

I wake in a rush as my reality floods my brain; sitting up, I feel the coolness of the cuff and the urge to pee. I look around, seeing that I'm alone with that dimly lit bulb being my only light source. I sigh. I wish I knew what time it is. I wonder if Mateo knows where to look.

I flex my wrist feeling a bearable soreness; the movement creates a light sound of the chain moving around on the floor. Soon I hear the door jiggle, and in walks Marco, "Good, you're awake! You damn near slept the whole day away."

He tosses a black grocery bag on the floor before pulling up the chair in front of me, causing me to scoot back up against the wall. "Melina, I have good news!" His voice sounds sincere, but his body language is mocking, "No one touched you last night, while you were unconscious, I mean." He pauses, smiling; the idea makes my stomach turn as he waits for a response I don't give.

He sits upright, relaxing, "Well, at least I thought that was good news considering you're still in that lovely dress of yours. Don't you want to take it off?" He moves to pull out a key, this clearly captures my attention, "I'll ask again. Would you like to change?"

I slowly nod my head, looking at the key. If he takes this cuff off, I'll have another chance. He smiles, "Good, now when I unlock your chain, don't try anything, or I'll be forced to sedate you again." He says as he grabs the bag with the change of clothes tossing them at my feet, "Do you understand?" I nod my head, but that's not enough for him. "I need a verbal response, Melina. I know you haven't lost your voice," He dangles the key in front of me like a shiny souvenir. I frown, this piece of shit really thinks he has power over me.

Then again, he does. I bite my tongue before speaking slowly, "I understand." He smiles, satisfied, squatting in front of me. He watches me as I watch him move the cuff on my wrist and inserts the key. When it clicks, he pulls it off, taking a step back. My heart beats with adrenaline. Marco smiles, "There." He waves a hand in the air, "Go ahead, change." I stand slowly. He isn't serious, like I'd give him the pleasure of undressing in front of him. I debate about running for the door now or waiting for another chance, but there might not be another chance. Which is the *better* chance?

I dart for the door, not sure if I'll ever see the outside ever again. I make it right in front of it before being tackled to the floor. I huff as the impact knocks the wind out of my chest. I can feel the weight of Marco on top of my back, so I try turning over. "Get off of me!" I yell, and he laughs, allowing me to face him before forcing my hands above my head. My breast lay in the way as I take deep breaths. "You have a lot of nerve for someone being held captive," He glances down at my breast as the feeling of him on top of me, unable to move, completely in his control, forces unwanted memories back into my mind.

My eyes begin to water, and he coos, "Awe don't worry, I'm not going to hurt you." Sarcasm laces his voice like venom. He starts sliding one of his hands down over my breast before sliding it down and under my dress. I close my eyes as I curse myself for not wearing underwear, for meeting Mateo and wanting to be with him. For wanting to be a part of his world even after all those years went by.

"Mateo doesn't know how lucky he is. Then again, maybe he does," He continues slowly snaking his hands towards my inner thighs, and the roughness of his fingers makes me shiver, "Please stop!" I cry out, my mind racing back to my childhood, to those dark nights. He ignores me as I feel his hand move over my vagina, and he cups it, "This is going to be so much fun." He's cut off by the sound of his phone ringing in his pocket.

He pauses for a moment before reaching into his pocket. I open my eyes as he removes his hand from under my dress. Still pining me down, He pulls out his phone, looking at the caller ID, and then quickly stands and answer, "Father!" His voice is loud and casual, no trace of his sinister intentions, "The girl? What girl?"

He laughs, lying on the phone and standing to move off of me, "Father, please, we have nothing to do with that!" I sit up quickly scooting away from him; his attention is no longer on me as he walks out of the room. Immediately tears begin to fall, and I cry uncontrollably into my arms.

After a while of sobbing, the energy to do so fades away from me. So I decide to change into the baggy clothes he left before either of them returns. I quietly explore the small room, trying to find something to use as self-defense, but there aren't many options.

I could use the chain but is it strong enough to knock one of them down, or I can try and break the chair, but would it be sharp enough. It is plastic, after all. Before I can decide, I hear the door again, and fear rises in my throat. Brian walks in.

He looks just as fearful as I do, which litters my mind in confusion. Fear has me stuck in place as he sits in front of me speaking in a broken voice, "I know you think we are monsters." I don't respond, still in defense mode.

"You know Mateo's a monster too, Melina. His family has done plenty of wrong. I mean come on he completely *massacred* the Cortez family," He looks away briefly, laughing, "Well, only after they kidnapped his father and sent him back in pieces."

I gasp in shock. In Pieces? Literally? That's not what Mateo told me. He killed them? All of them, even Natalie. It sounds like a horror movie. Brian continues talking, "Oh, you didn't know that did you? Yeah, well, not all by himself, but you know, an eye for an eye kind of thing. He saved the head of the Cortez for last. Everyone feared him and wanted nothing to do with him, but as time went by, he was able to get right back into the grace of the mafia and take the damn throne!"

He spits on the ground, "Fucking Crows." He finally looks up at me, "You're my chance to get some damn respect around here." He lightly hit his chest, "On the Riviera name!" He stands and takes a deep breath, "I'll kill you if I have to." He leaves without another word, leaving fear to pump through my blood.

I have to get out of here, or I'll die. I quietly walk over to the door, pausing momentarily, and pressing my ear on it. I don't hear anything, so I slowly reach for the knob. I lay my hand on it for a second before it swings open, causing me to step back and gasp. The two men I recognize now look beat up and bruised. It hasn't been 48 hours already, has it?

***

I fight and squirm with a burlap sack over my head and hands tied behind my back. I can only see the changes in lighting but not where I'm being taken. I put up a struggle with the little strength I had. Until I am put in the back seat of a vehicle. I can hear my heartbeat in my ears as I sit, catching my breath. This is it, isn't it? I hear one of the front doors open and close before hearing the engine roar to life. I quickly lay on my side to try and unravel the duct tape around my wrist.

"Miss Sky, with all due respect, please stop moving and try to enjoy the ride," An old brittle voice begins, "You aren't going to die, not today at least."

Relief and confusion flood my mind simultaneously. "Who are you?" I ask, but I get no response. I lay debating whether to trust the older man or not. I sit up and ask, "Can I at least get the tape off?"

"Not until we get where we're going, Miss Sky."

I sigh, sitting back, forced to endure this ride. If this isn't a joke, and I'm really not going to die, then where the hell are they taking me? I try to turn my brain off as I'm only asking questions, I won't get answers to. A while into the ride, my body relaxes, and I can feel the soreness on my wrist and in my chest. The car stops a few times before going at a steady speed.

After a while, I hear the change of the wheels from driving on the pavement to the dirt before coming to a slow stop. The old man speaks again, "Miss Sky, I do deeply apologize for any harm my sons might have caused you." He doesn't wait for my response before I hear two doors open and close. I wait to be grabbed again, but I am not, so I listen.

I hear his voice through the car, it's low and almost sounds fearful, "I want to apologize once more, I had no idea my idiot sons would do something like this. I assure you they will be punished for their behavior." I hear footsteps getting closer before I hear the door on my right side open. I don't move because I'm afraid of what will happen. I feel a hand wrap slowly around my arm as the sack is removed from my head. My eyes begin to water at the man in front of me.

"Melina," Mateo calls and I fight the urge to burst into sobs. "Mateo," I breathe out. He pulls out a pocket knife to cut off the duck tape, then quickly guides me to another SUV as a silent standoff of men surrounds us. He ushers me in and begins to pull out something from his pants, but I grab his arm, "Mateo, stop!" He looks at me, eyes blazing and his hand just above his gun.

"Please don't do this. He let me go," I beg, looking into his eyes. He pulls my head to his and whispers, "Someone has to pay for this."

"Please Mateo," I whisper, holding onto him. His eyes still blaze with rage, but he climbs into the car with me. "Let's go," He tells the driver, "Before I change my mind." He shuts the door and pulls me into him, "I am so sorry baby girl." He begins softly kissing my head as I relax into him. I feel exhausted as he holds me. Not wanting to think of anything, I close my eyes to rest.

19. Rage and Revenge

"Melina, Baby, wake up."

I feel a nudge before I jolt up. It's dark out, and we're parked in front of the house. Mateo holds his hand out and helps me out of the car. He doesn't let go of me as we walk into the house. "How are you feeling?" He asks, and I notice there are only a few security guards near us. He examines me as I respond, "I'm fine." I move my wrist taking a deep breath, "Sore."

He looks me in my eyes, "Did they hurt you?" Carefully thinking of my response, knowing what he's capable of, I say, "No, not really. I'd like to shower." He looks me in my eyes, searching, clearly unsatisfied with my response. "Of Course," He guides me into his bedroom, and I think of the last moment I was here, in that dress. Unwillingly I remember Marco's hand rubbing against my thigh, and it causes me to shiver.

"What's wrong?" Mateo asks, noticing. He turns me to face him, and I sigh, looking into his searching eyes. I can't bear telling Mateo that Marco had touched me. I mean, He didn't hurt me, right? So maybe this I can survive, even if I have to keep it to myself. If I tell Mateo that he felt up on me, he'll kill all of them—even their father.

"It's nothing; I'll be okay," I say softly before turning toward the bathroom. Mateo follows close behind me. I see fresh clothes and a towel sitting on the countertop as I move to turn the water on. I can feel him still watching me, so I speak over my shoulder, "Mateo, can I have a moment to myself, please." He stand there, deciding, before walking up behind me and kissing the top of my head, "I'll be right outside the door."

When he shuts the door, I take a deep breath feeling the soreness in my chest and turn around to face the mirror. I look dirty, my hair is a frizzy mess, my curls are coming back in certain areas, my hair desperately needs a wash. I slowly undress, taking off the baggy clothes and seeing my naked body underneath, unchanged yet affected. The makeup on my face is smeared and dried up. I look like a wreck.

I get into the shower and quietly try to wash away the memories of everything that's happened to me since walking out of that bathroom. I don't know how long I was held captive, but it feels like it's been days since I've been here; I feel odd, out of place. After washing myself twice and washing my hair. I rinse off and grab the black towel from the counter, taking my time to dry off. I check the tag of the nightgown, and of course, it is my brand. I take a deep breath before slipping it on.

It's well into the night as my stomach rumbles. I open the door feeling clean. Mateo is silently pacing the room. He stops when he sees me. "I'm hungry," I say. He walks over to me, "I hoped so." At first, I didn't notice, but he has a little table and two chairs set up by the window, and next to them stands a food cart on wheels.

He continues, "I had Jasper fix up something light." He holds out his hand for me, and I hesitate before walking over to the table myself, he follows behind me. We sit, and he lifts the lid of my dish, revealing a BLT and French fries. I smile at the familiar dish before picking it up and taking a bite.

Mateo continues to watch me, only picking at his fries. After a few minutes, he breaks the silence, "I thought I lost you, Melina." He sits back, running his hands over his face and then through his hair, "I had no idea who took you, I was prepared to kill anyone for you Melina, there is not a soul I would have spared until I found you. Then I got that call." He stops, taking a deep breath, and I can't help but look at him through a different lens.

I know this is his lifestyle. I know this is who he is, but it's gruesome to hear, "I don't want to talk about it, Mateo." I wipe my face with a napkin before standing, "I am here now, okay, and I'm tired." He takes a deep breath recomposing himself and stands as I climb into the bed. He starts to head for the door, but I call to him, "Please don't leave me alone." He smiles sadly, "I wasn't leaving you, baby girl, just grabbing a water and my laptop. I'll be right back." I breathe in as he continues out the door.

As he said, he returns quickly with his laptop and two water bottles. He changes into a pair of sweats before kissing my head goodnight. He sits upright beside me in bed, placing his laptop on his lap. I scoot close to him but lay facing the window. I close my eyes briefly, but this doesn't feel right, "Mateo?" I call out loudly. "Yes," he responds. I don't respond, not even sure what I want right now. He sets his laptop on the end table and turns to me, "What can I do for you, baby girl? How can I help?"

"Just. Just hold me, please," I ask, and that's all it takes for him to take his shirt off and slide under the blankets next to me. He pulls me close, and I melt into him. "I don't want to go to any more events," I speak quietly. This makes him nuzzle his head into the crease of my neck. He whispers and kisses me, "I'm so sorry, baby." It doesn't take long before I feel how exhausted I really am and fall asleep.

I was sure my nightmares would come back but I wake to the sound of Mateo on the phone. I sit up, the morning sun shining through the window. "I don't care how, make it happen, we'll be there in-" He stops talking mid-sentence as he makes eye contact with me. "Make it happen," is all he says as he hangs up the phone. He asks, "How are you feeling?"

I yawn, my voice a bit raspy, "Honestly, I don't know right now." My mind flashes back to the image of Brian calling Mateo a monster. "Mateo," I begin and he moves to kneel in front of me. I continue, "You were gone for three years, Mateo. Three years and then you show up and say you want me. They said you *massacred* Natalie's entire family? That you're Father…" I trail off as I see I've taken him by surprise. I continue, "So, what happened and don't you dare lie to me or I promise you will never see me again."

Mateo is quiet. I think he's lost in his mind as his face hardens. He looks away from me as he begins, "Somewhere between saying goodbye to you and sedating your grandfather. Natalie's father called me, wanting to discuss the situation, he believed this was all a misunderstanding. I told my dad that it was bullshit."

He pauses for a moment looking back at me, "He should know the rules, the game, but he insisted. So I went to meet with her father and things went south, it was a trap. As soon as I stepped foot in their territory I was fucked, but I made it out." He takes a deep breath running his head through his hair at the memory.

He continues, "I went to the hospital when my guys told me about the negative reaction your grandfather had. That's when I had you brought there. The day I left you in the hospital, I wasn't planning to. After you went into the room, Adam informed me my father heard about the set up and went after me."

Mateo shakes his head, "He wasn't so lucky. I spent days planning to rescue him, and weeks sending men to their death with every failed attempt, all while trying to keep tabs on you. The first day I received a piece of him."

He pauses again, his face turning pale at the memory, "Was the day after your graduation. The day Natalie and I were supposed to be-wed. I waited thirty days to get every piece of him back. So, we could cremate what was let of him and then," Mateo smiles darkly, no longer present in the room and it gives me chills.

His voice darkens, "Rage and Revenge were my best friends for the next eight month. I wanted all of them gone, I wanted them to pay, but most of all I didn't want them to get the chance to ever come after you. I sent a bullet through Natalie's head, then one in her brother chest, but their father, I took my time with him." The darkness in his eyes as he speaks tells me every single word is true, "Then I lost myself, and when Sofia began to notice. I knew I needed help. I knew what I'd become, everyone did, except for you."

His face softens, "The day you moved into your apartment, I wanted to be there, but I knew I wasn't safe for you. So, I started speaking with a therapist, a few of them, actually. They can't erase the memories or nightmares, but they helped me deal with them until I felt sure enough I could have you again." He finishes leaving the air for me to speak.

I wish I had something to say but I can't say anything I'm utterly shocked and horrified, by this man. So many emotions wave through me as I think about how different these past three years have been for us. I can't help but stare at him in a different light, a darker one.

I take a deep breath, whispering, "You really are a monster." I cover my mouth unsure if I meant to say those words. Gory images flash behind my eyes into my mind. Mateo reaches for me and I jerk away from him. "Please don't," I say, I just need a little space. He takes a step away and my heart breaks a little from the look on his face. I speak quietly suddenly fearing him, "I-I want to go home, right now."

He stands as waves of pain cover his features, "I'll have a car ready."

The car drops me off in front of my apartment and I'm thankful Mateo let me leave alone. I just need time to process everything. It's clear to me now more than ever, His life will always be dangerous. I walk inside my apartment with suitcase and mostly everything is where I left it. I slump on my couch and call Jackie. "Hey love what's up?" she answers. "I need to talk to you, is it a good time?"

I ask. "Yeah, it's fine Tristen won't wake up for another hour or so. Is everything okay?" Concern laces her voice. I move to sit on my couch, "Yeah, I just. I came back to my apartment." "Did Mateo do something wrong?" she asks. "Yes and no." I sigh, I rather spare her the details. "Okay, let me ask you this; did he hurt you?

"No," I respond. I mean I was kidnapped because of him, but he didn't hurt me.

"Did he lie to you?"

"No," I sigh, almost wishing he did. *Almost.* "Then why did you leave?" She questions simply. "I don't know," I reply frustrated. She tsks, "Wrong answer."

"He's done some really bad things Jackie," I rub my face. "Are you trying to convince yourself to leave him?" She questions and I don't respond. I mean any other man would have been sent to prison or the chair for what he's confessed to me, but he isn't just another man. He's the son of the Mafia. Normal rules don't apply. Jackie speaks again after not getting a response, "Do you want to leave him?"

I stand, "I should." I hear a door creek on her end of the phone and she starts to whisper, "That doesn't answer the question, Melina. Which tells me you have your answer. I have to go, Tristen's waking up and Troy wants to talk this morning. Love you." and with that she hangs up the phone.

20. Trust and Distractions

The next day I decide I should give my job a call, if it still even my job, "I understand that, but it was an emergency, it was completely out of my hands." I try to sound polite as I pace my living room floor. "But sir-" I try to say but he cuts me off. I sigh, "Yes sir, I understand."

Feeling defeated I hang up the phone. Slumping down onto my couch I feel my eyes water. I worked so hard for that position and now, they want to talk with corporate. The microwave beeps with the muffin I forgot is in there.

Miserably I stand to get it. I grab a napkin before reaching to grab the hot pastry. I blow on it briefly to cool it off, before biting into a warm lemony treat. Suddenly there's a knock at my door.

I finish chewing, wondering briefly who It could be, but deep down I know exactly who's on the other side of my door. The knock comes again, and I set the muffin down hurrying over, taking a deep breath before swinging the door open.

Sad brown eyes stare down at me, sinking into me, "Melina." I sigh and I don't ponder if it's of annoyance or relief, "What do you want Mateo?" He half heartly smiles at me, "Come with me?" I fold my arms across my chest, "Mateo I can't. I might need to figure out a new job."

His voice is low and begging, "Melina Please, I know what you may think of me, but I still want to be here for you." He holds out his hand, "Please baby girl, come with me."

Within the next hour, I follow Mateo dressed in a simple tan dress as we board a private plane. I've only been on a plane once, and it was not fun. It's so weird being out in the world, about to go God knows where, as if I haven't almost died.

The little plane is surprisingly spacious, with four cushion chairs and a small couch in the front. However, Mateo guides us to the back of the plane, which is separated by a small door. "Tell me when we take off," Mateo says to one of the Bodyguards as he closes the door. There is a small bed to the left, a set of chairs, and a table to the right. How often do you fly to have a bed in a plane? I decide to sit in the chair and Mateo sits in the other.

"How are you feeling?" Mateo asks, sitting across from me. "I'm okay," I say, rolling my eyes, feeling like I've said it a trillion times. I quickly change the subject, "So, how long is our flight?" I ask, crossing my legs. "Not that long," he responds, still eyeing me.

"Not that long," I repeat him sighing. "Are you going to tell me where we're going?" I ask, deciding to move to the bed and lay down.

I don't know how long this will take, and he clearly doesn't plan on telling me so I might as well get comfortable. "No, but I'll give you a hint," he smiles at me, taking out his phone. "It'll be warm," he suddenly snaps a picture of me, causing me to frown in confusion.

I ask, "Why'd you just take a picture of me?" He looks at it briefly before putting it away, "While you were gone." He speaks slowly, guarding my expression, "All I could think about were the worst possibilities. When I heard your voice over the phone, how scared you sounded, I thought for a split second that I'd never see you again. I couldn't bear it, and it made me realize I don't have a single photo of you. Well, one with your consent, that is." He moves to sit beside me on the bed, leaning down to kiss my forehead, "I can't lose you, Melina, you are everything to me." I lay looking up at him, his words seeping deep into my pores, directly to my bloodstream and to my heart.

"I thought I was going to die," I speak softly, looking into his eyes. I can see the pain behind them reacting to my words, "and I hated you for it." My eyes begin to water as I choose not to finish. Suddenly, there's a quiet knock at the door, "Refreshments?" a soft voice hums from the other side of the door. I take a deep breath, "Yes, please." I sit up taking advantage of the interruption to discontinue the topic. Mateo looks as if he wants to speak, but instead, he stands clearing his throat and moves to open the cabin door.

***

After an hour and twenty minutes of a quiet flight, we land at a private airport. We ride in comfortable silence in the back of an SUV. When the car comes to a stop, we get out, and I stand immediately facing a beautiful, luxurious lake house. I look over my shoulder and see a thick green forest going back as far as the eye can see, "Where are we?" I ask, turning to look back at the house, amazed.

He wraps his arms around my waist, following my gaze to the front door, "This was my mother's safe space; she'd always come out here when she and my father were in a spat. Sometimes, she'd bring Sofia and I with her, when it got ugly." I look up at him with soft eyes trying to picture a little Mateo. "Come on, let's go inside," He says as I follow him, while our luggage is brought inside.

The house is furnished with luxurious wooden fixtures and a fireplace. The sun shines through the back window lighting up the dining area. This place feels so personable and cozy. "The bedroom is at the end of the hall, and there's a hot tub in the back," he says as the last of our things are brought in, "but we're not staying just yet, come on."

We soon find ourselves standing on fairgrounds not far from the lake house. Children are running around everywhere, and laughter fills the air. I can feel the warm sun against my skin as Mateo turns to me.

"Do you trust me?" he asks, holding out his hand. I take a deep breath placing my hand in his, "I trust you." A small smile plays on his lips as he begins wrapping a blue paper wristband around my right hand and then his. I try relaxing being out in public, especially since I've noticed he upped the security.

We stop in front of a ring toss game, watching a few children laugh and cry, trying to toss red rings onto the neck of the glass bottles. "Want to try?" Mateo asks as I glance at our four body-guards who scare some of the smaller children. "Sure," I say, and Mateo moves to get a little basket full of red rings. We sit on two stools, and he holds the basket up to me. "Oh gosh," I say, already knowing I won't be good at this. I pick one up, and he smiles at me, "Relax, it can't be that hard."

I roll my eyes and toss it toward the closest bottle near us. It hits the side of it, making a slight clinking noise before disappearing to the bottom. I pout, "Of Course, I miss." I pick up another and hand it to Mateo, "You're turn." He smiles at me as he looks around briefly before tossing one and landing it around the neck of one of the bottles. He smirks, "Told you it's not hard." I roll my eyes, smiling at him, "Yeah, well, that was a lucky shot."

"Maybe," he picks up another ring and tosses it, making it around another glass. I look at him in disbelief, and he laughs. I pick up a small handful and toss them back-to-back, missing all of them. This makes him laugh harder, "Maybe ring toss isn't your strong suit." He stands and gives the basket of remaining rings to a few kids playing beside us, "Lets find something else."

We walk over to a brightly colored booth. "Step right up! Do you want to win the pretty lady a prize? Pop ten balloon cats in under a minute and win our mystery prize!" The man in the booth advertises the game, and Mateo places his hand on my hip and pulls me close to him. I smile teasing Mateo with the mans words, "Come on, don't you want to win the pretty lady a prize?" He huffs but steps up to the rifle like, dart gun.

The man begins stating the rules enthusiastically, "Pop all 10 balloon cats before the timer runs out! Make sure you stay behind the dotted line, any cheating, and you're disqualified!" Mateo looks at him un-entertained until he finishes talking. As soon as the timer begins, a whimsical sound plays as the balloon cats start sliding at an unrealistically fast pace, moving left, right, and occasionally up and down.

Mateo begins shooting with ease, and I flinch at the popping sounds, quickly covering my ears. I watch in awe as he moves with perfect aim; he easily pops all ten with 10 seconds remaining on the clock. He sets the rifle down, and I clap childishly for him and smirk, "That was fun!"

He turns towards me as the man hands me a small plastic-wrapped prize, "congratulations, miss." There's no trace of enthusiasm he previously had. "Thank you," I say, ignoring his demeanor. The sun is setting, and I notice a mirror maze across the way. "Can we go in there?" I ask excitedly as I hand Mateo my prize. "Don't you want to see what you got?" He asks as I grab his hand.

"I'll look at it later. Come on!" I say as he hands the prize to one of the bodyguards, who follows us to the mirror maze. "Are you sure?" Mateo asks. "Yes, I'll be fine, just stay close to me," I laugh a little trying to reassure him. We quickly enter, and Mateo allows me to lead. My anxiety rises a little as it immediately goes dark, with single ceiling lights dimly lighting the paths. Mateo holds my hand as I use the other to feel for the mirrors; I walk slowly as you can no longer hear the noise from outside.

I push on a glass, and it opens up a separate path, "left or right," I ask out loud. Mateo responds, "Wherever you go, I'll follow." I smile as I choose left while still holding his hand; I immediately bump into a glass wall. "Ouch," I say, dropping his hand to rub my forehead. "Are you okay?" He asks, turning me around to face him.

The concern on his face makes me laugh, "Mateo, I'm fine." His eyes look like his mind is racing a mile a minute, and my blood rushes through my body and to my core as I realize how close we are in such a small place. "Why are you looking at me like that?" I ask quietly. He looks at me, then my lips, "do you remember your safe word?" he asks in a low voice.

"Yes," I say breathlessly, and he slowly wraps his arms around me as I lay my arms around his neck. I stare into his eyes as he inches closer to my face, closing my eyes only when our lips connect. He kisses me oh so gently, and I realize how much I miss this feeling of contentment, of safety. Being in his arms creates a personal bubble of peace. Soon our kisses intensify, and I bite his bottom lips, which causes him to moan lightly.

This ignites him, and his hands slide down my back to grip my ass. He moves, pushing me up against the glass behind me as I wrap my hands around his face, quickly moving to kiss him deeper.

I feel him move his right hand around toward the front of my dress. Lost in our kiss, his hand finds its way up my dress as he begins kissing my neck.

I feel his warm hand rub against the left side of my stomach before moving slowly to my inner thighs, and suddenly, I flash back to Marco's rough hands, and I physically shiver; my mouth fills with a vile taste, but Mateo doesn't notice. I grab his hand to stop him. "Roses!" I yell, feeling disgusted and cowardly.

He immediately removes all contact, taking a step back and giving me a moment to breathe. I look away, trying to calm my nerves. He waits patiently as I wipe away the tears threatening to escape. "I'm sorry," I say stupidly. Keeping his distance, he says, "You have nothing to be sorry for Melina." When I finally look back at him, his face is filled with sorrow, and his hands sit stuffed in his pockets. I ask, "Can we go, please. I'd like to rest." He nods, allowing me to lead again.

The sun is almost gone as we emerge from the maze. Nothing around us has changed, but the atmosphere now feels so cold. We walk silently back to the vehicle, and Mateo makes a point to keep his distance.

I sit in the back of the car, expecting him to join me, but he doesn't; he sits upfront with the driver. The ride is quiet as I recount the experience in the mirror maze, sighing. I lay my head against the window as the driver starts the car.

21. Forever Yours

We've been at the Lakehouse for a full two weeks now. After calling Jackie and venting, she's been checking in on me and insisting I come to visit, but I don't want to, not yet at least.

Since the incident at the fair, Mateo has made it a point to keep me busy with all kinds of activities like hiking and sightseeing. We even went on a train ride touring some of the oldest trees.

Don't get me wrong, I've been enjoying myself, but Mateo's been so distant. We're doing all these things together, spending time together, but intimately distance. I've since tried initiating sex on three occasions, but he always has some excuse, and quite frankly, if this doesn't change, I might go crazy.

It's well into the night as I sit on the phone with Jackie while baking some comfort brownies. Mateo is sitting shirtless near the fireplace attending to his work. "I swear, Jackie, I'm going to hang him," I whisper while cracking two eggs into the bowl. "Oh, Melina, just try talking to him," she says as if I haven't tried. "Yeah, maybe if we had the time," I lay my phone between my ear and shoulder as I pour half a cup of water into the bowl.

"Make the time, Melina. Come on; we're not a bunch of teenagers. I have to go. Keep me informed," she says. I look at him over my shoulder, and he hasn't moved, "Okay, I'll talk to you later." I hang up the phone and begin mixing all the ingredients together.

The oven beeps, letting me know it's hot enough to put the brownies in. I quickly pour the mix into a rectangular pan and place it in the oven. I set a twenty-five-minute timer on the oven before washing my hands and walking over to Mateo. He looks up at me and smiles, "Hey baby girl, we have another tour tomorrow morning-"

"No," I cut him off. "No more tours or outings, no more dis-tractions," I say, sitting down next to him. He closes his laptop, "Are you okay?" Concern laces his voice, and it drives me mad. I sigh, "Yes, I am okay, I am fine. I would like to stay here tomorrow, maybe we can do something simple like watch a movie together or play a board game." My eyes wander down his body, making me hot and bothered, "Maybe if you're up for it, we can see where the night takes us." I move closer to him, moving his laptop out of his lap. "Mateo," I say moving to straddle him, he rests his head on the back of the couch, looking up at me.

I can see the fire behind his eyes, and I can certainly feel his bulge. "I want you," I whisper against his neck before kissing his skin. He wraps his hands around my waist, "Melina," He begins. His dick pulses underneath me, "I have work I need to attend to." He lightly taps my ass, asking me to get up.

I blatantly stare at him. Bruised by the rejection I hurry off of him, "I'm getting in the shower." I storm into the bathroom, being sure to slam the door behind me.

I turn on the shower head, and the cool water welcomes my frustration. I wait for the water to heat up before I move to wash my body. While taking a deep breath, the heat calms my nerves.

A few minutes pass as I recount all that's happened between us. I hear the door open and close. "Melina," Mateo calls my name, but I refuse to acknowledge him, and he sighs.

I hear him undressing, and in a few seconds, he joins me. "Glad to see your attitude has returned," he jokes casually, and I don't respond, keeping my eyes on the stream of water pooling in my hands. "Melina," He calls me in such a stern yet broken voice. So I finally turn around to face him, the water now hitting my back. He continues, "That day on the plane, you said that you hated me." He pauses, searching for his words.

Is that what's on his mind? "I don't hate *you*, Mateo," I begin. "I said that because this life with you is not simple or easy, and it most certainly will never be normal. That's a lot to commit to, and then the fear of actually dying," I speak truthfully still terrified of the thought.

He asks, "Is that what triggered you in the mirror maze?"

I nod, "That's a part of it, but that's not why I said I hate you." I turn around to face the water again. "Mateo, the moment I saw your face, I missed you so much. When you took that stupid sack of my head, I knew I'd endure anything for you if it meant I'd be with you for the rest of my life, by your side. I'd give anything for you, Mateo. That's why I said I hated you," I say opening my heart, not daring to look back at him.

He slowly turns me around to face him and lifts my chin, making me look into his eyes, "I meant what I said in the maze. Where you go, I'll always follow you; you mean everything and more to me, Melina." He moves to hold my face in his hands as he stares into my soul, "I want you, baby girl. I'll always want you, even If you think I am a monster, this monster will always love you."

My heart flutters, and I feel that warm calm in my chest, "I love you too, Mateo." I continue, realizing what this feeling is, "and I don't think you're a monster Mateo. I'm sorry I called you that. Like you said, tragedies change people."

Looking up at him, I see the light in his eyes reflect this same joy as mine. He leans down, his face inches away from mine, "I love you, so much baby girl." Our lips connect, and I feel like a moth to a flame as I pull him closer to me. The heat of the shower fogs up the bathroom, making the space between us feel like a warm bubble. "I want you inside me," I beg, whispering into his lips.

He pulls back briefly, "Are you sure, baby?" Looking into his eyes, I want him more than I want to breathe. "Yes," I say eagerly. He watches me as I move to kneel on the shower floor.

I wrap my hands around his cock and begin stroking him. His head falls back as he moans, "fuck baby." His voice sends a wave of electricity coursing through me. I move, sliding my lips over the tip of his cock before taking him in my mouth, making him moan more. He looks down at me, "You look so beautiful with my cock in your mouth." He places his right hand on my head and guides me up and down his cock, "Such a good little girl."

He grabs my head with both hands and begins to face fuck me. I gag, trying to breathe as he rocks my head back and forth, enjoying every stroke. He pulls out abruptly. "Stand up," He says, and I move, doing as I'm told. "I want to be in that pretty pussy of yours," He quickly turns me around, pushing me against the cool wall. Within seconds, he slides into me, smacking my ass at the same time, causing me to let out a loud moan.

He begins stroking slowly, "This is where I belong." He spanks me again, "Deep inside of you." His words find a place deep in my soul. "Mmhm," I moan in response. The feeling of his cock sliding in and out of me makes my pussy throb, "Yes, Mateo. Deep inside me."

He picks up the pace wrapping his arms around my waist, then begins to pound me with long and hard strokes, "Yes, baby, that's it." My voice grows louder as pleasure pools in the pit of my stomach, "Oh yes, fuck yes!" The water pouring over us makes the sound of our skin clapping louder and more disoriented.

"That's a good girl," He coos, smacking my ass again. He slides his right hand around to my clit and rubs it. "Tell me your mine, baby." My body reacts to his voice and his touch as that familiar high builds inside of me. "I'm yours," I moan wholeheartedly, lost in the pleasure of the warmth of the water and the feel of my orgasm reaching its so close.

He slows his paces to an agonizing deep stroke and puts his left hand around my neck, pulling me into him as he's still rubbing my clit, "Say it again, baby. Whose dick are you about to come on, huh? Who did you beg to be deep inside you? Tell me, baby; I want to hear you say it. His words fill my head like puffy clouds of ecstasy, "Yours, Mateo." I moan, "Forever yours." I feel his dick pulse inside of me, happy with my response, "Yes, baby girl. You're mine forever."

A few more strokes and an orgasm washes over my body as he holds me in place. He allows my body to calm before pulling out of me and turning off the water. Suddenly we hear the oven beeping, letting us know the brownies are ready. I look up at him and laugh, "Oh my gosh, I completely forgot the brownies were baking."

He taps my ass, "Well, go and get them." We get out of the shower, and I wrap a towel around me. When I open the door, the smell of fresh brownies fill my nose, and the cool air makes my nipples hard. I rush into the kitchen, dripping a trail of water behind me as I quickly turn off the stove and set the pan on the counter. That could have gone really bad. I mentally beat myself up before heading to the bedroom.

I enter the room, and Mateo is waiting with a towel wrapped around his waist. "I'm not done with you yet," he says, and I move to the bed, dropping my towel. He commands, "Lay down baby on your back; I want to see that beautiful face of yours." Of course, I listen, ignoring how my wet body feels against the blankets.

He tosses his towel as he crawls up in between my legs and rubs his cock against me before slowly stuffing it in me. "So wet, baby girl," he says as the wetness from my orgasm creates extra lube. He leans down to kiss me, and he begins stroking slowly. I moan into his lips, and I get lost in the feeling. He gradually speeds up his rhythm, pounding me while laying sweet kisses on my neck, and it feels so freaking good. "Yes Mateo, please," I say as my fingers glide through his hair. "Please cum inside me." I beg desperate to feel him fill me. He pants as our movement creates a bubble of warmth around us, "You want it inside you, baby?"

"Yes, please," I beg again, and he sits up, gripping my hips and pulling me closer to him. Immediately he starts pounding into me relentlessly, "I love this beautiful body of yours." I cry out in moans as his rhythm is intense and persistent. He continues, "I love you, Baby girl." I can feel his pace slow as he thrusts into me a few more times before I feel the warmth of his cum filling inside. I gasp as he groans while lightly pushing it deep inside of me. He doesn't pull out as he takes a moment to come down from his high.

When both of our breathing calms, he slowly pulls out, and my body's instant reaction is to push.

He smiles down at the sight of his cum dripping out of me, "I think this is my favorite sight." He moves, kissing my forehead before getting up to get a towel. I sit up, trying to look at it myself, but I can't see much. He returns with a towel, a glass of water, and a small pill. I say, "Next time, we're doing it in front of a mirror." He smirks as I push one more time trying to make sure I got it all out, before reaching down with the towel to clean it up.

After he sits in bed next to me and hands me the water and pill, "If we're going to be doing that often, we should talk about birth control." I consume the pill and quickly take a sip of water before responding, "What if I like playing Russian roulette?" He laughs as I hand the glass back to him, "Is that right?" He sounds amused as he sets the glass down, and I stand. "Where are you going?" he questions, getting comfortable.

"To make sure I got it all out," I say as I begin digging into one of the drawers to pull out a random shirt to throw on before heading back into the bathroom.

When I return to the room, Mateo is lying under the blankets. I quietly join him in bed, and he pulls me into him, "I don't want to lose you Melina, ever again." he speaks quietly with his eyes closed, sealing my fate with every breath. Kissing the top of my head, he wishes me goodnight, and I listen to the pattern of his breathing before drifting off to sleep.

***

I awake to Mateo still wrapped around me and the strongest urge to pee. I try to move quietly from under his arms, but he stirs, pulling me closer into him. "Stay," he says sleepily.

I quietly laugh, "I would, but I have to pee." He groans dramatically before releasing me from his arms, and I laugh at him, "I'll be back." I leave the room, and just as I open the bathroom door, his phone rings from the living room, I yell, "Your phone's ringing." I continue into the bathroom.

I hear him come out of the bedroom as I sit on the toilet. He answers grouchily, "This better be good news." I wipe and flush as I'm not intentionally trying to eavesdrop. He continues, "He wants to negotiate?" He sarcastically laughs as I quietly move to wash my hands, "Negotiation left the table when they kidnapped her! They *will* answer for this!" I hear him hang up the phone, and I quietly turn the water off before slowly emerging from the bathroom.

He's standing in a pair of sweats, frustration clear across his face. "Was that about me?" I question knowingly. Mateo doesn't respond as he sits down on the couch and sighs. I continue moving to sit beside from him, "You told me you'd let them be." He scoffs, "They kidnapped you. They are lucky I spared their father because of you."

"What can I do to make this go away?" I question; I don't want people to die because of me. He sees a notification on his phone before responding, "There are rules, Melina, and there are consequences."

I don't respond, having a hard time *not* having a say in this. He sighs pulling me into his lap, "Baby, I've done horrible things, monstrous things, but I'd do it all again for you. I am a monster, but I am *your* Monster, and as long as you'll have me, I will protect you."

I'll have to come to terms with this since my heart has already spoken for my mind. "Okay," I say, leaving the conversation as is. He receives another notification on his phone. He takes a deep breath, "I hate to ruin the fun, but we need to go back home."

"Okay, I'll go pack our things," As I say this, my phone rings on the coffee table, and Mateo watches me stand to answer it. "Hello," I say, unsure of who it is.

"Is this Melina Sky?"

"This is her," I reply.

"This is the head of your regional department at the art gallery; I do want to apologize, as I know you're on vacation." The man pauses as I look over at Mateo, wondering if he has something to do with this. I smirk to myself, thinking back to when Mateo was ranting about my old life being dead.

"When you return, we've promoted your position to general manager, the vacancy came rather quickly, and you're most qualified since you're already the AGM. Anyway, when you get back, they'll be paperwork on your desk in detail about your new position," he finishes.

"Seriously? oh my god, thank you!" I say in disbelief. "Congratulations, and enjoy your vacation," He doesn't give me another chance to respond as he hangs up. I stare at Mateo, dumbfounded but happy, "Oh my god!" I won't bother repeating every word as I'm pretty sure Mateo knows exactly what that call was, "I thought I lost my job...but I got promoted!" Mateo smiles at me, "That's wonderful baby girl."

Within an hour, we are back on his private plane. I lay on the bed and press send on a text to Jackie, letting her know what we were doing. I look over at Mateo, who is mindlessly typing away on his laptop. I watch him for a few minutes before he moves to kiss my forehead, "I need to make a call. I'll be right back." He leaves the back room, and I get a notification of Jackie's response:

Jackie: Call me when you land; I have bad news.

My heart sinks at the response, not knowing what could be wrong. I try calling her, but my air signal is not so great. My mind races as I have to wait until we land. My brain runs a mile a minute thinking of all the horrible things that could happen.

Mateo's been watching me fiddle the entire time. Why would she drop something like that, then expect me to be able to wait to hear about it? When the plane finally lands, I almost trip over my feet, trying to reach an area with a better signal.

I finally call her, and she answers in two rings, "What's wrong? What happened?" The wait caused my anxiety to build to an all-time high as I nearly yell through the phone. "I'm sorry Melina, your grandmother has passed away. One of the neighbors called a wellness check on her because she hadn't gone outside in four days. They found her body."

After hearing those words, my hand unconsciously moves to my necklace, and my anxiety withers away. I take a deep breath, "Okay. When do I need to be there?" I haven't spoken to her since my grandfather's funeral. So many words are left unspoken, but I'm not upset, and I don't feel sad. Jackie tells me all the details and text me the information before I hang up the phone.

I turn to the car, where Mateo patiently waits inside to take us home. I get in and shut the door, but before I can say anything, he shuts me down, "Absolutely not; we are not going." My eyes bulge with surprise, what the hell? "Excuse me?" I give him a chance to rephrase himself. He doubles down saying, "No, Melina, you are not returning to your hometown." I stare at him in disbelief, "My grandmother passed away, and you're telling me I don't have a right to be there?"

He runs his hands through his hair, "It's not safe, Melina; that town has been an unclaimed territory for the past two years now, it's Dangerous." I yell, upset, "Everywhere is dangerous, Mateo! You cannot keep me from my hometown. My dad still lives there!" He looks back at me frustrated, "Fine." He pauses for a moment, "You have two options, we go to your grandmother's funeral, and we'll bring six bodyguards, plus a surveillance team and two armed men on-site, or we don't go."

No way in hell was I going to cause such a distraction by simply being there, "Mateo, that's not fair. I want to be there with my family."

He doesn't budge, "And you can be, under those circumstances. So pick one."

"No, you don't get to swing your dick around; this is my grandmother's funeral. We go with two bodyguards, no surveillance team, and no armed men."

He laughs, running his hands through his hair, "Nope, four bodyguards, surveillance, I'll be armed, and we'll visit privately after the funeral is over."

I cross my arms briefly, thinking it over before giving in, "Fine, we'll go after."

22. Family and Monsters

Today is strange.

We returned to my hometown last night and booked a hotel room for a few days. We were going to the same place my grandfather's funeral was held. The service ended 10 minutes ago, so hopefully, it's cleared out by the time we arrive. I really don't want Mateo to cause a scene. I messaged Jackie ahead of time so she knows we're coming, and hopefully, Dad is there too.

The car ride is silent as Mateo is on edge. Mateo only lets me out of the car once the security clears the property. I wonder if this will ever feel normal to me. I wait impatiently as they speak over their mics; they're all dressed in black and white suits as they take their positions. Only when Mateo hears "Clear Boss" does he allow me to get out of the car. It feels so weird being back here, it's like nothing has changed at all.

Mateo opens my door, and I place my hand in his as we enter the building. Jackie welcomes us inside with red, teary eyes, "I'm glad you're here, Melina, I miss you." We embrace in a hug. "I miss you too," I say as we release each other, and she leads us to the front, where a cream-colored casket sits. My body begins to race as we approach. Jackie leaves me standing there with Mateo. Then Mateo squeezes my hand, "I'll be right behind you, okay." He leaves my side. It's just me and her now.

I finally look down into the casket; my grandmother's face looks so off and pale. I don't remember my grandmother wearing make-up a day in her life, but here she lays with light foundation and even blush on her face. My heart aches at the memories washing over me. So much love and hate is still unsettled inside me.

I hate my grandfather with every fiber in me but my grandmother. She was there for me, even if she was in the wrong. She was still a safe space for me. The tears begin to fall as I realize I'll never get the chance to forgive her or rebuild our relationship. I'll never know why she didn't try to stop it, "I'm sorry I couldn't forgive you sooner," I whisper.

I touch the necklace around my neck as I move to kiss her forehead, "Fly high and hug Mom for me." Mateo moves to my side as Jackie walks back up to me, I take a deep breath, wiping the tears away.

"Are you Ready?" Mateo asks. "Yes," I say, wiping my eyes some more.

"Before you go," Jackie begins, "You need to stop by the lawyer's office to sign some papers, I believe. I'll text you the address."

I nod, "Okay."

Jackie continues, "Will you be stopping by Michaels's house? You know Tristen and Grace are excited to see you." I hug her reassuringly, "Yes, we'll come by." Going to my dad's house is going to be a whole other situation as he doesn't know Mateo and I are together again. We return to the car, and Mateo lets me lay my head in his lap.

When arriving at the lawyer's office, Mateo insisted our security come up with us, which is annoying, but I don't argue about it. "Welcome," a woman dressed in a tan blazer set says joyfully, "All of the previously mentioned things are in the box, including the deed to the house, I just need a signature from you, and you're all good to go." She hands me a pen.

I weakly smile at her before signing the paper. I look over at Mateo, who's patiently sitting beside me, "I want to sell the house." I don't want any reminders of what happened there. Someone else can have it and create new memories.

I reach for the small box, and we quietly leave the building. While we walk back to the car, I debate whether I should wait until we're back home to look through it or if I should see what's inside now. "Are you okay?" Mateo asks, placing his hand around my waist as we approach the vehicle. "I'm okay, just lost in thought," I respond as he opens the backseat door for me.

I set the box inside first before getting in and sliding over then he gets in and sits beside me. "If you'd like, we can go back to the hotel and rest." He places a hand on my thigh reassuringly. I smile at him, "No, it's okay, really." He gently squeezes my thigh before directing the driver. I look over at the box as Mateo pulls out his phone; I decide to open it.

There's not much inside, but I pull out a small, sealed envelope. As I open it, I think it's another letter, but instead, I pull out a dozen old photos. As I look through them, I immediately realize these are pictures of my mother the day she gave birth to me, still in the hospital. I smile to myself as she genuinely looks happy, holding me. Warmth spreads throughout my heart as I set the pictures back in the envelope.

"Melina," Mateo calls me, "We're here." I look around, confused to see we're park in front of what looks like a garden instead of my dad's house. I get out of the car before Mateo can come around to my side. I walk to the front of the car, ready to bombard Mateo with questions, but I'm taken aback at the beautiful view of the land, "My god, Mateo." A colorful garden lays in front of me, with beautiful red roses, white lilies, and yellow tulips, "Wow, this is so beautiful."

I turn around to find Mateo silently kneeling before me, and my heart drops. He doesn't say anything at first as he pulls out a small black box, "I'll confess my love for you a thousand times and more. You're the beauty in my sad chaotic world, and I know this life isn't the safest, but I vow to protect you with my every last breath. I vow my life to yours. Will you give me the honor of making you my wife? Will you marry me, Melina?"

I'm speechless, breathless. So much has happened, but I know in my heart I wouldn't change a thing, "Yes Mateo. Yes, I'll marry you." I move to him, full with overwhelming happiness and joy as he stands smiling.

He slowly puts a beautiful yet simple diamond ring on my finger, and I stare at it in awe. "It was my mother's," he states. I smile, "Well, it's an honor. I'll cherish it forever." I move to kiss him, and he wraps his arms around my waist. "I love you, Melina," He speaks softly, and I repeat those exact words as I melt into him. He wants to be mine forever, and forever I'll be his.

"Now, can we go home? I want to get you out of this town."

I smirk, taking a step back to look up at him, "Don't tell me you're trying to get out of facing my dad." He rolls his eyes sarcastically, ", Yup, you caught me red-handed, now into the car you go."

I don't move just yet, "We're going to my dad's house before we leave Mateo."

"Fine, the quicker we get there, the faster we can leave this place," He opens the door for me, and I finally move to get in.

The drive to my dad's house is peaceful, and I feel high on happiness, though my thoughts are running a mile a minute. I have to tell my dad not only are we back together, but we are engaged. I move to take off the ring and place it in my bag. The driver parks the car, and we quickly head to the door.

I knock lightly, and we wait. "Your ring? You're not going to wear it?" Mateo says. Of course, he notices. "I will, just not yet. I don't want to make today about me," I respond, and the door opens. The smell of Peach Cobbler floods my nose. "You made it!" Jackie opens the door and immediately pulls me into a hug. After pulling back, she says Hi to Mateo and welcomes us inside.

There's a piano melody playing lightly through speakers, coming from the kitchen. "Where's Dad, and is Elijah here?" I ask just as my Legs are bumped into. I look down to see Tristen wrap his arms around my legs. "Hi, Auntie Melina!" Tristen says childishly with a grin on his face. "Hey Tristian," I smile at him, "You almost knocked me over, kiddo!" He lets my legs go, and I bend over to hug him properly. He immediately turns to Mateo, who's still standing beside me, "Hey, I remember you." Mateo smiles down at him, "Hey, kid."

"Come on, everyone's at the table," Jackie tells us, and we follow her into the dining room. As we walk in, the room ruptures in happiness, "You made it!" Elijah says happily. We all greet each other, and I look over at my dad, who's holding Grace, "Honey, can you take her please." He hands her to Hope, and I can tell he's not looking at me; he's got his eyes set on Mateo. If I was nervous before then I must be terrified now.

"Hey dad!" I say as he makes his way towards us. Mateo speaks, "Hello, Michael."

"Hi. Mat," my dad says sternly. He finally looks over at me, "Can I talk with you for a minute," Mateo speaks before I can, "Actually, if you don't mind, I'd like to talk with you Michael." I don't notice immediately, but everyone else stops talking and is listening in on our conversation.

My dad stares momentarily before agreeing, and they leave into the backyard. When the door closes, I take a deep breath and turn to everyone. "So what's for dinner?" I say, taking a seat by Dad's chair, grabbing two plates, and piling them with food. Everyone takes this as a chance to talk about something else other than the apparent tension in the room. Hope passes me a basket of bread rolls while still holding Grace. "You look good, Melina; how's the art gallery going?"

I make a silly face at Grace which causes her to laugh before responding to Hope, "My job is good; I got a promotion." Everyone responds with congrats at the table as I portion mashed potatoes and gravy, green beans, and fried chicken onto the two plates. "Yeah, it came as a surprise, really."

"Well, I'm sure you deserve it," Hope responds. I smile at her and begin eating my food. Soon, my dad and Mateo walks back inside, and my heart rate speeds up. I take a sip of water to try and mask it. They walk back over, now smiling. My dad even has his hand on Mateo's shoulder. I frown in confusion. Mateo and Michael join the table, and I stare at Mateo, waiting for an explanation.

He laughs, "You know staring is rude." He moves to pick up his fork, "Thanks for the plate, baby." Now I'm staring at him in disbelief, "You're not going to tell me what happened out there?" He laughs again, "Relax, Melina, I just talked with him, and as long as he knows I'll lay my life down to protect yours, he's good."

"Hmm," I respond, still unconvinced, but I leave it at that and resume eating and chatting with everyone. This is nice, I think to myself, as Elijah explains a trip he took a year ago to meet some girl that turned out to be a scam. Laughing, I place my hand on

Mateo's and take a breath of relief; I didn't realize how much I'd enjoy being around all the people I love.

After dinner, I notice Mateo and Troy step out front, but I don't comment on it. "We should move back to town, together," Jackie says as we sit on the living room couch. I smile, "Oh, Jackie, Your job literally takes you all over the world, do you really want to settle for our broken little town?" She sighs an agreeable no before I continue, "See. I promise to visit more, but truly I am happy where I am."

"I know," she pouts, "I just miss hanging out with you all the time." I laugh, and she continues, "But seriously, are you happy?" She moves to face me.

"Yes, I really, really am," I can't help but laugh again, thinking how just a few years ago, I could never imagine this much happiness in my life. "Good," she responds. "Are you happy, Jackie? I know you guys have Tristen and are engaged, but are you happy?" I ask, hoping she really hears me.

She smiles, "I am. Troy got this really good paying job in business." She smiles, relaxing, "It was sudden but I'm just glad it pays well, it's nice not being the only breadwinner of the house. Plus we might be able to have our wedding a lot sooner now." I smile, "That's really good Jackie. Yay weddings!" I clap in excitement before taking a deep breath. I don't think she knows the details of his work and as much as I want to tell her the depths, I don't want to ruin this moment, "I love you so much Jackie." We hug as Troy and Mateo walk back inside, both of their faces have seriousness written all over them.

I stand to meet Mateo halfway, "What's wrong?"

"I want to take you home now, baby girl," Mateo speaks, ignoring my question. "What happened? Is everything okay?" I try asking again. "Everything will be," He responds, leaving me confused, "Come on, let's say our goodbyes."

When we're alone in the SUV, Mateo asks, "I have an important question to ask you." This makes my heart rate pick up, "Yes?" He turns to look at me, "I have the men who kidnapped you sitting in a room, ready to pay for their actions with their lives." My eyes nearly pop out of my head; I hold my breath as he continues, "But they're lucky today because I'm in a good mood. So, I'll give you the choice. What do you want me to do with them?"

I exhale in shock, "You're asking me?" He doesn't repeat himself as he waits for my response. I don't want him to kill them, but I don't want them to hurt anyone else. I can't image if it was Jackie or anyone else that I love to be in the situation I was in, especially since Troy works for Mateo now. "Do whatever you have to do to protect our family, Mateo," I say, accepting the choice. After all, you can't change a monster. He nods, and I wait for him to pick up his phone, but he doesn't, so I ask, "Aren't you going to call someone?" He smirks, looking over at me, "The chaos can wait."

313

Epilogue

Three years later

I sit in the bathroom staring at two beautiful blue lines on the morning of my birthday. I am pregnant? I almost don't believe it, as I'm tempted to pee on another test, but I've already used 2 of them, and they all say the same thing.

"I'm pregnant!" I say out loud, trying to imagine a little Crow baby really growing inside of me. "Melina?" Mateo calls for me, and I hurry to open the door. I walk into the hall, passing a few of our wedding photos.

He's sitting at the dining table drinking his morning coffee, and I'm thankful Jasper isn't anywhere near, so I can share this private moment with him, "Do you know what baby crows sound like?" I ask casually as I walk over to him.

He looks up, confused, and repeats the question. I continue, "Yeah, you know, the small ones with tiny feet and little hands." I stop right in front of him as he stands, realization hitting his face, "Tiny hands?" He asks excitedly, "Are we having a baby?"

I nod my head in excitement, "Yes, Mateo, we're having a baby!"

"Oh baby girl!" he pulls me into a kiss and laughs, "We're going to have Crow babies."

"One baby Crow," I laugh, correcting him, "at least for now." Our love fills the atmosphere, "I love you so much, Mrs. Crow."

"I love you too, Mateo."

ACKNOWLEDGMENTS

The following people I'd like to thank are my love, Alex. My little sister, Lily, and my Parents. Without their support and motivation, this story would not have seen the light of day.

As well as my beta readers for hanging in there with the deadline and giving me vital and tremendous support.

Lastly, You the reader, thank you for giving Beautiful Chaos a chance and helping my dreams come true!

ABOUT THE AUTHOR

Amber Rodriguez is a spicy romance author who lives in a small town in California. She's a likes hot coffee, slow mornings, and all things nature and cottage core inspired. Spicy romance books have her heart, and she writes poetry on the side.

If you'd like to connect with her, you can find her on;

Website: www.amrbooks.com

On Instagram @booksbyamber118

On TikTok @booksbyamber118

On Facebook @Author Amber Rodriguez